"There is something you must do for me."

"Me?" He looked at her, his dark eyes shining in the firelight. "Your father was my friend. I'll do what I can, but I'm leaving town tomorrow and don't plan on ever coming back."

As if of their own accord, his eyes washed over her body. He looked away abruptly, embarrassed, it seemed.

She pulled the buckskin tighter, conscious of her wet dress clinging to her, outlining her hips and legs. "That's exactly why it must be you, Mr. Crockett. You and no other."

He turned toward her, then, and narrowed his eyes. They were black again. Black as a Dublin night in Liffey Quay. "What exactly is it you want, Miss Dennington?"

She'd likely burn in hell for what she was about to propose, but she mustered her courage and did it anyway.

"I want you to marry me."

Praise for Debra Lee Brown's previous titles

Ice Maiden

"*Ice Maiden* is an enticing tale
that will warm your heart."
—*Romantic Times Magazine*

The Virgin Spring

"Debra Lee Brown makes her mark with
The Virgin Spring, which should be read
by all lovers of Scottish romances."
—*Affaire de Coeur*

"Debra Lee Brown pens an enjoyable tale
of intrigue and adventure."
—*Romantic Times Magazine*

"A remarkable story. The fast pace, filled with treachery,
mystery, and passion, left me breathless."
—*Rendezvous*

GOLD RUSH BRIDE

DEBRA LEE BROWN

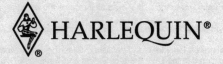

HARLEQUIN®

TORONTO • NEW YORK • LONDON
AMSTERDAM • PARIS • SYDNEY • HAMBURG
STOCKHOLM • ATHENS • TOKYO • MILAN • MADRID
PRAGUE • WARSAW • BUDAPEST • AUCKLAND

ISBN 0-373-29194-9

GOLD RUSH BRIDE

Copyright © 2002 by Debra Lee Brown

This edition published by arrangement with Harlequin Books S.A.

® and TM are trademarks of the publisher. Trademarks indicated with ® are registered in the United States Patent and Trademark Office, the Canadian Trade Marks Office and in other countries.

Visit us at www.eHarlequin.com

Printed in U.S.A.

Available from Harlequin Historicals and
DEBRA LEE BROWN

The Virgin Spring #506
Ice Maiden #549
The Mackintosh Bride #576
Gold Rush Bride #594

Please address questions and book requests to:
Harlequin Reader Service
U.S.: 3010 Walden Ave., P.O. Box 1325, Buffalo, NY 14269
Canadian: P.O. Box 609, Fort Erie, Ont. L2A 5X3

To my mother, Marilyn Berger
And my father, Lee Hargus

With love

Chapter One

Tinderbox, California, 1849

Kate Dennington arrived too late.

Months aboard ship, a fortnight tromping across the steaming jungles of Panama. Riverboats, mule trains and enough miles on her feet to wear holes in her shoes.

And all of it for nothing.

She ground her teeth behind pursed lips and met the solicitor's sympathetic gaze. "When did my father die?"

"Tuesday." Mr. Vickery looked past her out the window to the graveyard across the road. A fresh mound of earth stared back at them.

Tuesday. She swiped at her eyes, but her hand came away dry, as always. *No tears, girl. Bear up.* She could hear her mother speak it in the Irish, even now, so many years after her death. Denningtons didn't cry. Not ever.

"W-what day is today?"

She'd arrived in San Francisco nearly a week ago, ill from the rough steamship journey up the coast, and with barely enough funds left to make her way to the frontier mining town where her father, Liam Dennington, had hoped to make his fortune.

"Sunday." The honeyed voice belonged to a well-dressed gentleman who pushed his way through the throng of miners and tradesmen who'd gathered in Dennington's Grocery and Dry Goods the moment Kate had arrived.

Vickery stepped aside, as if in deference to him. "Um, this is Mr. Landerfelt—from Virginia. Eldridge Landerfelt. Head of the town council and proprietor of Landerfelt's Mercantile and Mining Supply."

Kate had seen it amidst the hodgepodge of tents, shanties and cabins that served as the center of mining trade for the densely forested area. Both the gentleman and his enterprise seemed far too rich for a town the likes of Tinderbox.

"Eldridge, this is Miss Den—"

"I know who she is," Landerfelt drawled. He looked her over, as if he were sizing her up.

Kate arched a brow and looked back. His haughty stance reminded her of an upstart prizefighter she'd once seen in a makeshift boxing ring in a warehouse in Dublin, near the tenement she and her brothers called home.

She had known there would be trouble the moment she'd decided to answer her father's summons herself. When Liam Dennington had taken ill, he'd sent for Kate's younger brother, Michael. But the letter was six months getting to Ireland, and by then Michael was newly wed with a babe on the way.

She'd had no choice but to come herself. The twins, Patrick and Francis, at age twelve were too young, and Sean at fifteen too reckless. So she'd left the boys in the care of Michael and his bride, boarded the clipper to America and hadn't looked back. The money for the passage she'd borrowed from disapproving relatives in County Kildare. What a waste.

Landerfelt frowned. "The question is, does Miss Dennington know the law?"

"What law?" She hadn't been listening.

"Yes, well I was just getting to that." Vickery handed her a creased parchment, its edges smudged with inky fingerprints. "Your father's will. I wrote it for him not two days before he passed. He signed it at the bottom—just there."

Kate swept her gaze across the spidery lettering. It might as well have been Greek. There'd been little time for reading growing up. She did recognize her father's flamboyant signature, though it seemed not as bold as she remembered it. "Aye, that's his hand."

"He leaves it all to Michael, your brother." Vickery shrugged. "That's who he was expecting, you see, who we were all expecting."

Landerfelt stepped closer, and Kate fought a natural instinct to back away. "But Mike Dennington's not who's come, and that changes everything."

"Mr. Landerfelt's right," Vickery said. "The land, the store, the horse and the mule—it's all in the will. By law it passes to the next of kin, should the primary beneficiary be…well, in this case, wholly unavailable."

"So it's all mine, then? The storefront, the goods, everything?" Kate scanned the rough-hewn timbers of the two-room cabin her father had built on land he'd won in a poker game. It certainly wasn't much. A fortune, indeed. What on earth had he been thinking? She offered up a silent prayer for his foolish but well-meaning soul.

"Yours until tomorrow." Landerfelt pulled a cigar stub out of his breast pocket and lit it.

Kate wrinkled her nose at the stench. "What do you mean, tomorrow?"

"You're the lawyer," Landerfelt said to Vickery. "Explain it to her."

"Um, yes, well…" Vickery pulled a sheaf of papers out of his portfolio and promptly dropped them. They scattered across the floor. "Oh, sorry. I'll just be a moment."

Landerfelt rolled his eyes. "It's the law, like I said. The property passes to you, and your father's business, too. But you can't keep it. Not in this town."

"What do you mean I can't keep it? Mr. Vickery said that—"

"Single women, especially *immigrants,* don't own property. Not in Tinderbox." Landerfelt flashed a nasty look at a Chinese girl peering through the store's front window. "And they don't own businesses, neither. It's better for the town."

"Oh, is it now?" Better for a certain competing store owner, Kate suspected. Landerfelt's and Dennington's were the only two supply stores she'd seen since leaving Sacramento City.

"It's a fairly new law." Vickery offered her the disorganized sheaf of papers he'd retrieved from the floor. Kate just stared at them. "Enacted by the town council just a few days ago, in fact." He flashed a look at Landerfelt, who stood there gloating.

"But my father's business, the store… I'll need to run it to—" The gravity of her situation dawned.

She would have to make not only a living in this godforsaken place, but enough to pay her passage home and still make good the small fortune she'd borrowed from her mother's sister.

They had all assumed her father would pay them back.

His letter...the wealth he described... Kate's gaze was drawn to the sparsely stocked shelves of the store and a battered old cash box that stood empty on the counter.

She would have to make the money. There was no other way. If she didn't, her aunt would make certain Michael wouldn't see a penny of his hard-earned wages. And him with a wife and babe to feed, not to mention the other lads.

"Not all trade is forbidden." Landerfelt cocked a blond brow at her. "Certain types of enterprises are allowed."

"You mean I can't run my father's store, but I might be allowed some other commerce?" She'd never heard of any law so ridiculous. No matter. Whatever she had to do to raise the funds, she'd do it, and go back to Ireland as soon as she might.

Landerfelt grinned. "Hell, yes. A certain kind of *commerce,* as you put it, would be damned welcome in Tinderbox." He raked his eyes over her body. They lingered for a moment on her bosom. "If you get my drift."

She was suddenly aware of all the eyes on her, of the hungry-looking faces of the miners crowded into the store. She had the distinct impression that food was not what they craved. She got Landerfelt's *drift* all right.

Her blood boiled.

"I'm sure I don't know what you mean, Mr. Landerfelt."

He chuckled—a slow, almost syrupy laugh in keeping with his Virginian drawl.

"Till tomorrow, is it? To dispose of the cabin and the land? I assume I may keep the horse and the mule?" She'd sell them, in fact, along with everything else that wasn't nailed down, to raise the funds to pay the debt and buy her passage home. With her father gone, there was no reason to stay.

"Five o'clock." Landerfelt reached into a pocket and withdrew a finely tooled money pouch. "Unless, of course, you'd like to sell it all—lock, stock and barrel—right now."

"To you?"

"That's right." He reached for her hand and she stiffened. The charming smile that oozed across his face made her want to slap him. All the same, she allowed him to spill the contents of the pouch into her open palm. A half-dozen ten-dollar gold pieces winked up at her.

"Oh dear." Vickery's eyes widened.

She did the calculations in her head, allowing for the unbelievable inflation that had occurred overnight, since word had spread that the streets of California were paved in gold. She couldn't read, but she was keen with figures. Years of stretching pennies to feed her wayward father and four brothers had perfected her skill for transactions.

"You're crazy, Landerfelt."

Her sentiments exactly. Why the horse alone had to be worth that much.

Through the crowd, Kate's gaze lit on the rough-looking frontiersman who'd spoken. She'd not noticed him earlier, and wondered when he'd come in. He lounged against a timber near the store's entrance, arms folded across his chest as if he owned the place.

Kate felt her face flush hot as the man's cool gaze washed over her. He wasn't dressed like the others in flannel shirts and wool trousers. Fur and buckskin clothed him from head to toe, but not any kind of fur Kate had ever seen. Lord, he was a sight! Wild black hair that was unfashionably long, and even blacker eyes.

She forced her gaze back to the coins in her hand. Landerfelt's offer would barely pay for her return to San Francisco and a room for the night, let alone her debt and the clipper passage home. No, she'd need better than a thousand dollars. More perhaps. With prices what they were, she could only guess.

She watched as the frontiersman pushed his way through the throng and stood looming behind Eldridge Landerfelt. He flashed his dark eyes at her, and she felt a bit of a rush inside. He was taller than she'd first thought, and had a dangerous look about him. A wicked-looking scar cut across his left cheek. She wondered how he'd got it. A knife fight, perhaps, or a run-in with a bear? In this wild place there was no telling.

He stared at her as if he knew exactly what she was thinking. She felt suddenly overwarm in the close quarters.

"It's not enough and you know it," he said.

Landerfelt faced him. "No? Then why don't you give the little lady some of *your* money, Crockett. If you have any left, that is."

A couple of miners snickered as a whispered buzz spread amongst them. Kate watched the cords on the frontiersman's neck grow taut. His eyes grew even blacker, if that were possible, and his face was as hard as County Wicklow's limestone cliffs.

"That's my price," Landerfelt said to her. He tapped his cigar ash on the counter next to them. "Take it or leave it."

Kate glanced at the coins in her hand and at Landerfelt's triumphant smirk. Aye, she was a woman alone in a foreign land, but no one played Kate Dennington for a fool. She knew nothing of prices or the value of land, but she was certain she could do better than the merchant's paltry offering.

"Keep your coin," she said, and slapped the golden eagles onto the counter.

Landerfelt's jaw dropped, and he nearly lost his cigar.
"Ha!" The frontiersman, Crockett, smiled at her.

She noticed his teeth; they were white and straight. This
close up, aside from his sun-bronzed skin and that wicked
scar, he didn't really look like the other transient men
she'd seen on the last leg of her journey from Sutter's
Fort to Tinderbox. And she'd seen plenty. Hundreds of
them, immigrants mostly, all flocking to the goldfields.

Crockett's voice, his demeanor, they were...refined, almost. She couldn't quite put her finger on what it was that
made him different, but would stake her last farthing he
wasn't born to this life.

All at once the store erupted into a cacophony of shouts
and tussles. The miners crowded forward, nearly pinning
Kate to the counter behind her. What on earth—?

"How 'bout sellin' me that last jar a peaches?" A squat
miner with doughy cheeks pointed at the shelf behind the
counter.

"I'll take all them tin pans ya've got left," another
cried out.

A dozen others called out their orders for goods. Kate's
head spun. What was she to do? Landerfelt and Vickery
were all but pushed aside as the miners crowded closer.
She looked to her father's solicitor for help. Vickery
merely shrugged, and fought to keep from losing his spectacles and his overstuffed portfolio in the ruckus.

One thing was clear to her. It was still her store, until
five o'clock tomorrow afternoon. Aye, she'd sell off the
remaining goods and... She didn't bother finishing the
thought. In a flash she was behind the counter, reaching
for that last jar of peaches.

"How much?" the miner said.

"How...much?" Lord, she had no idea. She'd only
been in California a handful of days. The currency and

coin were strange to her to begin with, and the prices of things seemed to increase by the hour.

The miner plunked a small leather bag onto the counter, and gestured to an odd-looking set of scales Kate had noticed when she'd first arrived. "I'll take that sack of flour, too." He opened the leather bag and sprinkled some glittering dust onto the scales. "How's that?"

"How's...what?" Apparently this ritual was supposed to mean something to her. Kate looked hard at the glittering pile and with a start realized what it was. "Oh. The gold, you mean?"

Of course! The man meant to pay her in gold dust. But how much should she charge? And how was she to value what he offered? Her hands grew sweaty and, without thinking, she wiped them on the skirt of her one good dress.

In a panic she looked up, directly into the black eyes of the only man in the room who'd had the nerve to question the dealings of her father's competitor. The frontiersman, Crockett. She wondered why he'd come to her defense at all. What was she to him?

"Stand aside, miss."

Before she could protest, he was across the counter, his hand on the scales. From a drawer hidden beneath the counter, he pulled a beat-up wooden box. Inside was a collection of a dozen or so metal cylinders, increasing in size from one tinier than her little fingertip, to one nearly as big as her palm. They looked heavy—brass, perhaps.

She watched, fascinated, as Crockett tried a couple of the smallest ones on the scale. She marveled at how quickly he got the side with the brass cylinder to balance perfectly with the side on which the miner had piled his gold.

"More," Crockett said.

The dough-cheeked miner carefully tapped more dust out of his bag onto the scale.

"Enough." Crockett pushed the peaches across the counter and gestured to the enormous bag of flour sitting next to him on the floor. "Three dollars for the peaches, and ten for the flour."

"Thirteen dollars?" Kate was stunned. She calculated the exchange rate in her head. Why, that amount of money would have fed her and her brothers for a month!

"That's right." The edge of Crockett's mouth twitched in a half grimace. "But don't get excited. Dennington likely paid five in Sacramento City for the flour alone, and another five for delivery. God knows what he paid for those peaches."

Kate realized Crockett was studying her. And he was standing far too close. Close enough for the fur trim of his jacket to brush her hand. She tried to step back but was hemmed in by more miners, clamoring to buy what remained of the store's goods.

"But, the prices...how did you know what to—"

"Mei Li!" Crockett waved at the Chinese girl Kate had seen earlier standing in the doorway of the store.

The sprite ducked into the crowd, and Kate didn't see her again until her head popped up on the other side of the counter. She wore a dazzling smile, and garments the likes of which Kate had never seen. "You wish me help?"

"Yes." Crockett yanked a list out from under the counter and handed it to the girl. A price list, Kate surmised, though she couldn't read it.

Both the girl and Crockett seemed to know more than Kate would have suspected about the operation of her father's store. She'd remember to ask Mr. Vickery about it later.

"Miss Dennington could use some help." Crockett looked at her again with those probing eyes.

She nodded, still wondering at the frontiersman's motives but grateful for the assistance he'd provided her. In seconds, the Chinese girl filled the order of another miner and waved forward the next in line.

Landerfelt scowled from the corner where he and Mr. Vickery had been shoved. He cast the stub of his cigar to the floor and pushed his way out of the crowd onto the muddy wagon trail the locals called Main Street.

Crockett's smile faded. His dark gaze followed Landerfelt out the door. Before Kate could thank him for his kindness, he pushed his way after him and was gone.

"Who on earth was that man?"

"That Will Crockett," Mei Li said, and proceeded with the next transaction.

Kate watched him out the window. He stood rigid, hands fisted at his sides, outside Landerfelt's storefront, as if he were waiting for something, for Landerfelt, perhaps. She'd felt the tension between them. "A frontiersman, is he?"

"Fur trader. Trapper."

Kate could well believe it from his garments. Still, there was an air about him that smacked of drawing rooms and Sunday teas. Not that she knew anything about such things. The two-room tenement in Dublin she'd shared with her father and four brothers was a far cry from such a life.

"He lives here in Tinderbox?"

"No. Will Crockett go north. To Alaska. For beaver. Fox. Good fur there. His boat leave few days."

"Really?" Perhaps he was a true frontiersman, after all.

"You keep store, yes?"

"W-what?" She hadn't been listening. Her gaze was still fixed on Will Crockett. "Oh, the store. No, how can I? Mr. Vickery said it was the law. Single women can't own a business." Well, not any decent business, she recalled with a shudder. "No, I'll have to sell it all. I'll need the money to get home."

And to make certain Michael and Sean didn't end up in debtors' prison. She wouldn't put it past her mother's sister. The only reason Kate was able to convince her to lend the money at all was the promise of weighty interest from the fortune her father was supposed to have made in California.

"No, you no sell," Mei Li said. "No one buy for good price. They want gold, not store. You get cheated."

The girl was right, and Landerfelt's ridiculous offer was proof. Kate scanned the faces of the miners fighting over the few items remaining in the store. She read desperation in their grim expressions, gold lust in their eyes.

"You work store for money. Mei Li help."

Kate shook her head. "No, it's impossible. Mr. Vickery said—"

"I know, I know. No single women. No *immigrants*." Mei Li rattled off something unintelligible under her breath—a Chinese curse, if Kate had to guess.

"Then the only answer is—"

"Easy answer." Mei Li looked up from her work at the scales and smiled. "You marry."

"What?" She nearly dropped the last pound of butter in Dennington's Grocery and Dry Goods on the floor.

"Will Crockett good choice. He like you, too. I see it in eyes."

Kate plopped onto the stool behind her and pushed her unruly auburn hair out of her face. The clamor of the miners faded as her gaze traveled out the window, snaked across the street and lit on the formidable figure clothed in buckskin and fur. The sky grew dark around him, and he seemed not to notice the light drizzle as he stared into the window of Landerfelt's Mercantile and Mining Supply.

Will Crockett, indeed. Sweet Jesus, what an idea.

Chapter Two

It was a hell of an idea.

But one that Will would never consider, not even to get back at Landerfelt. The notion of marrying Dennington's daughter sheerly for profit reminded him too much of how he had ended up out West to begin with.

He gazed at the out-of-place miniature propped against a pickax in the window of Landerfelt's store and pushed the newly hatched thought out of his mind.

Mary Kate Dennington's clear blue eyes stared back at him.

And all this time he'd thought the image was of Dennington's wife. ''Well, what do you know.'' He'd seen the Irish merchant pull the keepsake out of his pocket and study it countless times over the past few months. ''That's my Mary Kate,'' he'd say.

Will studied the image. The artist who'd painted it was good. He'd captured that…what exactly was it about Kate Dennington that drew him in? She wasn't pretty, at least not in that coquettish sort of way he'd been raised to admire. Yet there was a strength about her, a wholesome sort of courage in the way she'd stood up to Landerfelt that was damned attractive. Not that it mattered.

The point was, Dennington had been a decent man. One of the few men in Tinderbox Will had respected. The least he could do before he left town was see to it Eldridge Landerfelt didn't swindle his daughter out of what was rightfully hers.

Landerfelt had done enough swindling for one week. Will stuffed a hand into the empty pocket where the bankroll he'd been building for months had been stashed. That cash was to buy his passage on the steamer leaving San Francisco for Sitka in three days' time, and to set himself up in the fur trade once he arrived. Thanks to Landerfelt's latest power play, it was gone. Along with his horse and his best rifle. All he had left to his name were the clothes on his back.

He closed his eyes and tipped his face into the rain. When he opened them again there was Landerfelt, standing behind the counter grinning at him. Their gazes locked through the distorted glass of the storefront.

How in hell had he gotten that miniature?

Dennington had always kept it on him. He'd been sick with fever on and off for nearly a year. Will had made it a point to look in on him whenever he was in town. Surprisingly, over the last month the Irishman's health had improved. So much so that Doc Mendenhall had predicted a complete recovery. But on Tuesday morning Liam Dennington was found dead in his bed. Just like that. And the miniature scribed with his daughter's likeness was for sale in Landerfelt's store.

"It's the spittin' image of her, ain't it?"

Will turned at the sound of the familiar voice. It had been weeks since he'd seen Matt Robinson—his only friend, now that Dennington was gone. Although Matt was a year or two younger than Will, he'd grown up on the frontier and had taught Will everything he knew about how to survive. Trapping, trading, where and how to live.

They'd worked the Rockies together, then had made their way west to California. But the beaver were all trapped out now, and Matt had succumbed to the same lust that had every butcher, baker and candlestick maker heading for California in droves.

Gold fever. Will ground his teeth.

Matt whistled as he eyed the miniature. "I saw her two days ago at Sutter's Fort. Had no idea she was Dennington's kin. She don't look much like him, does she?"

Will glanced toward Dennington's just as a frazzled-looking Kate ducked out of the store to retrieve the traveling bag she'd left outside. It was a wonder no one had stolen it.

For the hundredth time in the past hour, his gaze was drawn to her trim figure and the wisps of auburn hair framing her lightly freckled face. She stole a glance at him, and he felt a queasy sort of unrest.

"I see ya've noticed." Matt elbowed him, and Will snapped to attention.

He'd been crazy to think of helping her. The last thing he needed was to get involved with another down-on-his-luck immigrant's problems. He'd done enough on that count lately, and look where it had got him.

It was time to change the subject.

"What brings you all the way to town, Matt? How's the claim?"

"It's a goin'. That's why I'm here. I thought I'd take one more shot at convincin' ya to go in with me. Whaddya say?"

Will looked hard at him, and read in his eyes what his friend didn't say. "You've heard, then."

"Heard what?"

"You know what. The whole town's talking about what a damn fool I am."

"The whole territory, more like it." Matt cracked a lopsided smile. "But you're no fool. I'd a done the same for the old Chinaman if I'd had the money."

Will snorted.

"Speakin' o' which…"

Mei Li stepped out of Dennington's store and turned up the street toward the Chinese camp on the outskirts of town. She shot Matt a tiny smile. He plucked his hat from his head and gawked at her like a schoolboy until she disappeared around the corner.

"You're sweet on her," Will said.

"Have been for months."

"You're asking for trouble, you know."

"I know."

Will grinned. "I knew there was a reason I liked you." He glanced at Landerfelt watching them through the window, and the smile slid from his face. "Seriously, Matt, if you intend to court that girl, you'd best watch your back."

Matt shook off his momentary stupor and slapped his hat back on his head. "I was hopin' *you'd* do that for me."

"Oh no. Not me. I'll be halfway to—"

"It's all gone, ain't it? The cash, your horse, everything."

Will met his friend's knowing gaze. "Yeah."

"Ya've got nothin' to lose then. Work the claim with me and we'll be filthy rich come the first snow."

Filthy rich was right.

No, that was his father's game, not his. Will had made a new life for himself here, had put his past behind him. But the gold fever and what it had done to this pristine place and the once-honest men who lived here brought it all back in spades.

"Sorry, Matt. Not interested."

"Damned if I can understand your reasonin'."

His reasons were good ones, but none of Matt's damned business. He shot another glance at the miniature in Landerfelt's store window. "Each man has to make a life for himself, Matt. On his own, in his own way."

"You're set on Alaska, then?"

He studied the image of Mary Kate Dennington's proud Irish features and bright blue eyes. "I am."

"But how ya gonna—"

"I don't know. All I know is, come hell or high water, I'll be on that ship."

It was nearly dark, and cold as any day in Dublin she could remember. Kate stood in the rain at the foot of her father's grave, her mind made up.

She was cold and wet and she bloody well deserved to be. She'd been a fool to borrow that money on the promise of yet another of her father's harebrained schemes. She knelt in the mud and placed a hand on his muddy grave.

"What were you thinking, Da?"

He hadn't been thinking, and that was the problem. Liam Dennington had been a dreamer, a risk taker. Always after that next pot of gold at the end of the rainbow.

She smiled in the dark, remembering.

A bit shaky on her feet, Kate rose as mud seeped into her boots. Exhaustion had finally caught up with her and gnawed bone deep against another familiar sensation. Desperation. She clenched her teeth and willed them both away.

Her gaze swept across the forested hillside peppered with the dying light of miners' campfires. The single street that made up the town of Tinderbox cut across it, dark and quiet.

One campfire, in particular, drew her attention. But the man hunched beside it with an oiled buckskin pulled over his head against the downpour was no miner. She watched as Will Crockett stirred up the embers with a stick.

Mei Li had been right. Vickery confirmed what the girl had said about Crockett being a trapper on his way north. He was the perfect choice for her plan. Now, if she could only muster the courage to ask him.

The soft strain of a miner's fiddle carried over the din of the rain and reminded Kate of home, though Tinderbox was certainly not like any place she'd ever seen in Ireland. It was a strange new world, and she was an outsider. That was made clear to her today by Mr. Landerfelt.

The man was pompous and, on the surface, seemed to present no particular threat, but she'd read a dangerous sort of instability in his eyes when Crockett had crossed him. Who knew what the merchant might do to protect the monopoly he seemed determined to create?

There were other dangers, too. All afternoon men had come down from the foothills where they worked their claims, just to get a look at her. It hadn't taken long for Kate to realize she was one of the few white women here. In fact, since she'd left Sutter's Fort two days ago, she hadn't seen one other woman like herself—just Indians and a handful of Chinese.

It was clear she didn't belong here. Her place was at home with her brothers. They needed her, had relied on her to care for them all the years since their mother died.

Kate had made enough just from the sale of the remaining goods in her father's store to pay for the traveling expense back to San Francisco. Selling the horse and the mule would pay for lodging and food. What then?

She supposed she could work in a laundry or at some other decent employment until she raised enough to pay the debt owed her mother's sister, and her ship passage home. But that could take months, and she'd experienced firsthand the tawdry San Francisco rooming houses built of green timbers and canvas walls. Walls that did nothing to muffle the sounds of what Kate could only imagine was going on in the next room between transient men and enterprising women.

No, she was better off in Tinderbox for now, where the memory of her father had garnered her one or two allies. She had a plan, and she'd stick to it.

A branch snapped behind her, yanking her out of her thoughts. Kate spun toward the sound.

"What are you doing out here in the rain? Christ, you're soaked through."

Will Crockett stood not two paces from her. How on earth had he crept up on her like that? Why, just a moment ago he'd been…

In the failing light, he took in her muddied garments and dripping hair. "Get back inside. It's not safe out here."

She ignored his command, wrapped her sopping shawl tight around her and started for his dying fire. She might as well get this over with.

"You should be at Vickery's." He offered her his oiled buckskin, as if it were a nuisance to do so. She took it and met his gaze.

"He gave you a bed for the night, didn't he?"

"Aye, he did."

Mr. Vickery had been more than gracious. He hadn't felt it was safe for her to stay alone in her father's cabin, and though his wife was away for a fortnight, he didn't think it improper for Kate to stay under his roof for one night. After all, he was her father's solicitor, a man Liam Dennington had trusted. Kate would trust him, too. What choice did she have?

"Go back to Ireland, Miss Dennington. Tinderbox is no place for a woman alone. A woman like you."

Like her? Just what did he think she was like? She agreed with his advice, but for reasons she was certain were different from his. In any case, Will Crockett was in for a surprise.

"I intend to go back, as soon as I might."

"Good."

"But there is something you must do for me, first."

"Me?" He looked at her, his dark eyes shining in the firelight. They were browner than she remembered. That afternoon in the store they'd seemed black as coal.

She made herself hold his gaze.

"Your father was my friend. I'll do what I can, but I'm leaving town tomorrow and don't plan on ever coming back."

As if of their own accord, his eyes washed over her body. He looked away abruptly, embarrassed, it seemed. It was the third time that day she'd caught him looking at her that way.

She pulled the buckskin tighter, conscious of her wet dress clinging to her, outlining her hips and legs. "That's exactly why it must be you, Mr. Crockett. You and no other."

He turned toward her, then, and narrowed his eyes. They were black again. Black as a Dublin night in Liffey Quay. "What exactly is it you want, Miss Dennington?"

She'd likely burn in hell for what she was about to propose, but she mustered her courage and did it anyway.

"I want you to marry me."

Chapter Three

He was the only man in Tinderbox who would have refused her. But refuse her he did, and sent Kate Dennington off to Vickery's for the night.

A few hours' restless sleep under a dead oak in a driving rain hadn't made Will feel any better about his decision. And now, in the light of day, it seemed damned stupid of him.

He'd had the exact same idea, hadn't he? To marry her for profit—his and hers. So when she'd proposed the deal, why hadn't he just said yes? He knew why. Because her doing the asking had rubbed him the wrong way.

The moment the offer had left her lips, she'd transformed herself in his mind from a hardworking Irishman's daughter in need of help to one Sherrilyn Rogers Browning, conniving Philadelphia socialite. Kate had cast him an honest, hopeful smile, but all he'd seen was Sherrilyn's mercenary little smirk.

"Crockett, you're an idiot." He shook out his oiled buckskin and rolled it into a bundle.

This wasn't Philadelphia, and Dennington's daughter wasn't a compliant pawn in one of his father's latest business deals. That chapter in his life was over. Finished.

He plucked his beaver-skin cap from the wet ground, then caught himself looking for where he'd tethered his horse. "Son of a…" He'd forgotten the mare had spent the night in drier quarters, one of Landerfelt's rented stalls down at the livery.

He slammed the cap on his head, tucked the buckskin under his arm and started in that direction. If he was lucky he could hitch a ride on the mule train to Sutter's Fort. They could always use an extra teamster or two.

It was time to get the hell out of town before he changed his mind about giving Landerfelt his due and taking Kate Dennington up on that offer.

She wasn't, by a long shot, in the same league with Sherrilyn, but she wasn't as innocent as she played at, either. He'd known that the moment he'd first laid eyes on her in Dennington's store. When Vickery told her her father was dead, she hadn't shed a tear. Not one.

What kind of woman would react like that to her father's death? A father, not like his, but one who loved a child as fiercely as Liam Dennington had loved his daughter. That little scene at the grave last night hadn't fooled him one bit. Again, no tears. Just rain. Her eyes had been as clear and cool as a predator's.

So why had he been so put off by the marriage scheme she'd cooked up? He kicked up a stone as he turned into the wagon ruts on Main Street. She'd disappointed him, that's why. He'd thought her a world apart from the one he'd come from. A world he was never going back to.

Clearly she wasn't.

Dennington hadn't talked much about Ireland or his family, except for waxing poetic about his daughter. Will had no idea if the Irishman had been well-to-do or just a common working man. Kate Dennington's plain clothes and worn-out shoes led him to believe the latter.

But a man couldn't be too sure about anyone these days. The gold rush had done one thing for California that Will did like. It made nearly everyone an equal. A rough-looking miner passed him on the street, and he knew the man was just as likely to have been a lawyer or a land-owner in his old life as he was a laborer working the railroad.

No, Kate Dennington wasn't the grieving, noble daughter he'd imagined her to be on first blush, but perhaps he'd been too hasty in refusing her offer. She was bound to marry someone if she intended to go through with her plan to keep the store.

Why not him?

He screwed up his face, remembering the one thing that didn't make sense. She'd said that it *must* be him. Him and no other. Why? What did it matter to her? Any man would do for the scheme she'd hatched.

He reached the livery just as the sun was full up. The sky was a brilliant blue, the autumn air fresh as any he'd ever breathed. It reminded him of why he loved the frontier. On impulse he turned and let his gaze wander up the hillside to John Vickery's three-room cottage.

An image of Kate Dennington's trim waist and curved hips flashed in his mind. Will allowed himself a rare smile.

''Why the hell not?''

Perhaps he'd get the money for his passage, after all, and give Eldridge Landerfelt what was coming to him.

Shading her eyes against the sunlight, Kate squinted at the charred, muddy evidence of Crockett's campfire and thanked God the trapper had refused her preposterous offer.

She must have been completely out of her mind last

night. A hundred rosaries wouldn't be enough to purge the sin of even proposing it. She'd remind herself to start on them that evening.

Pulling her still damp shawl tight about her, she picked her way carefully up the ravine separating Vickery's cottage from the rest of town. She hadn't meant to oversleep. For hours last night she'd tossed and turned, and when she finally fell asleep, she'd dreamed the most sinful things.... Will Crockett carrying her across the threshold of her father's store...sharing a slice of wedding cake with him on the porch in back. Then later, his dark eyes searing her as she turned down the sheets of their marriage bed.

"Jesus, Mary and Joseph!" She crossed herself and pushed the images from her mind.

A gust of wind blasted a pile of wet autumn leaves across her path as she turned onto Main Street. The town was bustling with activity, and a dozen pairs of miner's eyes fixed on her as she strode briskly toward Landerfelt's Mercantile.

She'd best get used to their stares. It had been no different in San Francisco, and that's where she was likely to end up. For a time, at least. She'd just have to tough it out. There was no other option. Not now.

She'd sell her father's storefront and land for whatever Landerfelt would give her. Had her foolish pride not gotten in the way, she would have done so yesterday when he'd made her the offer. She could have bargained with him at least.

Her mother would have been practical and sold. But oh, no, not Kate. She was clearly her father's daughter. She shook her head at her stupidity, then stopped dead in her tracks as a litany of rapid-fire Chinese diffused by men's shouts caught her off guard.

She fixed her gaze on the chaotic scene unfolding in

front of Landerfelt's Mercantile and Mining Supply. An overloaded wagon sat in the middle of the muddy street. Mei Li stood precariously atop the pile of supplies and mining equipment, yelling and kicking at two men who tried, unsuccessfully, to unload it out from under her.

Kate pushed her way to the front of the small crowd of miners and other townsfolk gathering to watch the skirmish.

The Chinese girl saw her, and her round face lit up. "Miss Kate, hurry!"

"Mei Li, what on earth—?"

"Wagon here with goods! Landerfelt try steal." She kicked at one of the men who'd hefted a sack of grain from off the pile. "No let him! Wagon ours."

Ours? Kate pushed closer. "What do you mean? I didn't order any—"

"Landerfelt offered me double what Dennington put down by way a deposit."

Kate frowned at the man who'd spoken: a rough-looking character sporting a long buckskin coat, well-worn gloves and chaps. She recognized him from Sutter's Fort, where she'd overnighted three days ago. He was the wagon's driver.

"You mean my father paid money in advance for these goods?"

Mei Li let out a screech.

Kate's conversation with the driver was forgotten as Mei Li let loose another tirade of what had to be Chinese curses. One of the unloaders, Landerfelt's man, grabbed her ankle. Mei Li fought to keep her balance as the man pulled her toward him, a malicious grin plastered on his face. The onlookers did nothing to stop him. What kind of men were these?

"You there!" Kate caught the ruffian's eye, and his

grin widened to reveal awful-looking teeth. "Leave her alone! She's—" The wagon driver grabbed her and jerked her back, nearly off her feet. "Let me go! What do you think you're—"

A gunshot sounded, and Kate jumped nearly out of her skin. A second later the man who'd grabbed Mei Li's ankle was flying through the air toward Landerfelt's store window. "Sweet Jesus!" Kate braced herself for the shattering glass.

The tawny-haired man she'd seen standing in the street with Will Crockett yesterday morn, scrambled atop the wagon and swept Mei Li off her feet. Kate was about to cry out for someone to stop him, but the enthralled look in Mei Li's eyes as her arms snaked around his neck stilled her tongue.

The wagon driver tightened his grip, and Kate renewed her struggle. "I said let me go, you bloody oaf!" She kicked backward at his shin, and he grunted.

"Take your hands off her or you're a dead man."

She knew that voice.

A second later the driver released her. And a moment after that, Will Crockett's fist connected with his face. A nice, clean blow. Kate winced as the driver went down.

As if such things happened every day, two onlookers dragged his limp body out of the mud and propped him against the windowless storefront of Landerfelt's Mercantile and Mining Supply.

"Y-you killed him." She took in Crockett's steely expression and coal-black eyes.

"Nah. He's just out cold. He'll be all right." Crockett's gaze fixed on her, and his eyes warmed to brown.

The scandalous dream she'd had about him mere hours ago flooded her mind, unbidden. Her face flushed with heat. "Y-you're still here."

"Yeah." His gaze washed over her, and that same queer feeling she'd had yesterday returned.

"But I thought you were gone to Alaska."

"I was. I mean I am." He took off his fur hat and played with it, then crushed it in his hands. "There's something I need to do first."

She felt suddenly overwarm, as if she'd just come down with fever. "Like…what, supposin'?"

"Well, I was thinking that—"

Shouts and the sound of hoofbeats cut short their conversation. The crowd scattered like rats in a Dublin flat. What now? Kate glanced down the street to see Eldridge Landerfelt bearing down on them on horseback.

Will stepped out in front of her, taking the brunt of the mud clods kicked up as the merchant jerked his mount to a halt in front of his store and took in the chaotic scene.

"Hell's bells, what's goin' on here?" A second later Landerfelt was off his horse, on his feet, and nose to nose with Crockett.

Kate had the same question, and waited to hear the frontiersman's answer. She stepped out from behind him, but Crockett didn't spare her a glance. His gaze was pinned on Landerfelt.

"That shipment," Crockett said. "It's mine."

"Yours?" answered Kate and Landerfelt in unison.

Crockett continued to ignore her. "That's right. Liam Dennington paid half down on it two weeks ago. I know. I was there when the money changed hands."

Landerfelt cracked a half smile. "What if he did? Dennington's dead and buried. He can't pay the balance, and she sure can't, neither." He flashed his eyes at her. "I'm doing her a favor by taking it off her hands."

He *was* doing her a favor, Kate realized. She certainly

couldn't afford to pay for the goods, and even if she could she'd just have to turn around and sell them.

"You'd pay me back my father's deposit, of course."

"Of course." Landerfelt's smile broadened. He pulled a cigar out of his jacket and lit it up, much to Kate's displeasure.

"Fine," she said, and waved the smoke away from her face. "I'd also speak with you about the store itself, and the land. I was thinking that—"

"She was thinking she'd like to keep it awhile." Crockett shot her a loaded look.

"Keep it?" For the second time in as many minutes she and Landerfelt voiced the same thought.

"She can't keep it," Landerfelt said. "It's the law."

Crockett took a step toward him, and Kate thought for sure there would be another fight. "Yeah, so I've heard. Single women can't own property."

"Or operate a business within two miles of town." Landerfelt blew a puff of cigar smoke directly into Crockett's face.

Kate braced herself for the frontiersman's reaction, but to her surprise he didn't move a muscle. His cool expression hardened. She admired control in a man. Too many of them, her father and brothers included, went off halfcocked.

"Unless the business is…well…" Landerfelt flashed his blue eyes at her again.

"I know what the law says. And I'm telling you she's keeping the store and the shipment. *We're* keeping it."

"We?" Kate had a bad feeling when she met Will Crockett's coal-black gaze.

"That's right. Mrs. Crockett here—" Will wrapped an arm around her waist and pulled her to his side "—and me."

"What?" This time she only mouthed Landerfelt's reply. The cigar slipped from the merchant's gaping mouth and sizzled in the muddy street.

"We're getting married. This morning." Crockett tossed her a cold look. "Isn't that right?"

All at once, Kate felt the world slip out from under her feet. Crockett gripped her tighter, and she was suddenly aware of his body heat, the strength of his big hand and muscled arm.

"What kinda bull is this?" Landerfelt narrowed his eyes at the both of them.

"No bull, just fact. There's nothing in town law says a married woman can't operate a business. Especially if it's her husband's business. And nothing in the law says I can't own property. I marry her and it's mine."

"W-wait a minute." Kate's head began to throb. "I thought you said—"

"I changed my mind."

"There's no preacher for miles." Landerfelt's face went bloodred. He reminded her of that boxer again. The rage in his eyes told Kate he wasn't giving up.

Out of nowhere, Mei Li's head popped in between them. "Mr. Vickery marry. He make legal." She grinned at Kate. "I help. You come now. We make ready."

"But—"

"I'll get Vickery." The tawny-haired man who'd thrown Landerfelt's crony through the window and had spirited Mei Li from off the wagon slapped Will Crockett on the back. He tipped his hat at her and cracked a crooked grin. "I'm the best man, I reckon. Matt Robinson, ma'am." He grabbed her hand and shook it until Kate thought it would break loose from her arm. "I mean, Mrs. Crockett. Back in a flash." He took off at a full run.

Kate felt as if she were outside her own body, looking down on the preposterous scene unfolding around her.

"You won't get away with this, Crockett." Landerfelt grabbed his horse's reins, then shot her a murderous look. "You, neither, you—"

Crockett grabbed the neatly pressed lapels of Landerfelt's jacket. Kate waited for him to speak, to defend her with some choice words, but he said nothing. After a few tense seconds, Landerfelt swore and pulled out of the frontiersman's grasp. The crowd parted as he jerked his mount down the street toward the livery.

"Married?" Kate stared at Crockett, openmouthed. The reality of the situation dawned on her.

"That's what you wanted, right? Get married, keep the store, make enough for your ticket home."

She nodded, dumbstruck. That's exactly what she had proposed to him last night. "Aye, but—"

"Fine. It's a deal." He grabbed her hand and shook it. Not as hard as Matt Robinson had, but firmly and with a cold intent in his eyes that made her forget all thoughts of changing her mind.

"I want the mule, the horse, and whatever we make off this wagon load. We'll sell it all today. Now, in fact."

"But the driver..." She gestured to the buckskin-clad driver who'd manhandled her and had received Will Crockett's fist in payment. His nose was bleeding. It definitely looked broken. "My father didn't pay for it all, just a deposit."

Crockett walked over to the driver, who was just coming around. The man touched a gloved hand to his broken nose and groaned.

"Don't worry. Dan, here, will wait for his money, won't you, Dan?" Crockett placed his booted foot on the driver's knee and pressed down.

"Ow! S-sure. Whatever you say, Will."

"And he'll deliver the next load to you on credit."

"What?"

Crockett put his weight into it, and the driver yelped like a dog. "Right. C-credit. No problem, Mrs. Crockett."

Wonderful. More credit. Just what she needed. Kate stood there, feeling rather weightless, as if she were in the middle of some eerie nightmare. Mei Li took her hand and pulled her in the direction of the Chinese camp.

"We make ready, quick quick. Mei Li help."

Will Crockett jammed his hat on his head and shot Kate a stony glance. "I'll leave you enough cash to get by on. Be back here in an hour, and we'll get it over with. I've got a ship to make."

Mei Li yanked the buckskin drape closed across the glassless window in the tiny shanty where she'd told Kate she lived with her father and her brothers.

"No mother, four brothers," Kate repeated. "Just like me."

She took in the assortment of unusual objects, cooking gear and other domestic possessions jammed into the tin-and-timber shack. The air was thick with an exotic pot-pourri of pungent scents. She'd never known any Chinese. Had never seen any until she stepped onto the wharf in San Francisco less than a week ago. How her world had changed since then.

"You sit." Mei Li nodded at the carpet-covered ground. "I fix wild hair."

"Wild?" She smoothed her auburn tresses and ignored the girl's well-intentioned command. "My hair's fine. Besides, it's not as if it's a real wedding."

"It real enough. Will Crockett real man. You real woman."

Kate fought a smile. Aye, Will Crockett *was* a real man. His behavior that morning had been nothing short of chivalrous. She recalled, with a bit of shameless glee, how he'd decked the wagon driver. Crockett had watched out for her. Protected her. First against the driver's manhandling, then against Landerfelt's threats.

Her stomach tightened every time she thought of it. No man had ever gone out of his way to protect her. None, save her brothers back home. And they didn't count, really. They were family; it was expected.

Aye, Will Crockett had been gallant, but in a cool, almost unfriendly manner. As if the whole affair was just an unsavory business arrangement he'd gotten caught up in. "Kate, you dolt." She shook off her girlish stupor and plopped cross-legged onto the carpet.

Mei Li frowned down at her. "What mean *dolt?*"

"Fool." For that's what she was. Of course Crockett viewed it as a business arrangement; that's exactly what it was. She needed his name to keep the store, and he needed—

What *did* he need? What was Will Crockett getting out of the bargain that was important enough to overrule his stalwart refusal of the night before? Her father's horse and a bit of coin? Surely it wasn't worth the trouble to a man in such a hurry to leave town.

"Mei Li, why do you suppose Crockett's marrying me?"

The girl ignored Kate's earlier protest and worked to tame her hair into some kind of fantastical upswept arrangement. "He like. I see it."

"No, you're wrong. Mr. Crockett doesn't like me." He'd made that clear last night. He'd chastised her, in fact, for her outrageous proposal. His censure had made her feel dirty, cheap. She recalled those dark, judgmental eyes of his and how his lips had tightened into a thin line. "No, he must have a good reason to be doing this." But what was it? He was leaving in a matter of hours. What possible inducement—

"Crockett need money. Pay for ship."

Kate twisted around so she could see Mei Li's face. "What do you mean? He doesn't have the money already?"

"Money gone. Horse, too. Pay for debt."

"He owed someone a debt?" Well, she wasn't the only one in hot water, it seemed.

Under her breath, Mei Li muttered another of her seemingly endless strings of Chinese expletives. "He pay Landerfelt. But no Crockett's debt. Cheng's debt. My papa."

"What?" Will Crockett had used the money for his ship passage to pay off the debt of a Chinese laborer?

Mei Li nodded. "Papa in big trouble. Run card game. Break law."

"A card game?"

"Only white man allowed to—"

"Don't tell me…to run that kind of business, here in Tinderbox."

The fusion of rage and frustration on Mei Li's young face was answer enough. "Game okay, as along as Landerfelt win. But he lose big to man from Hangtown. More coin than I ever see. Crockett pay back so Papa no lose job or house."

"You mean to tell me that Eldridge Landerfelt would have—? Why the bloody—"

"Yes. Him very bloody. Very bad."

Kate scrambled to her feet and peered out the small, glassless window toward town. Will and Matt were unloading the supply wagon right there in the muddy street. Miners crowded around them, shouting out offers.

It amazed her that men were willing to pay the hugely inflated prices even a fair man like her father had had to charge to cover his transportation costs. She hadn't been inside Landerfelt's Mercantile, though she suspected his prices were even more outrageous. She'd seen no customers in the place since she'd arrived yesterday.

Until that very moment. How strange…

Will Crockett plucked something from amidst the shards of broken storefront glass and ducked inside Landerfelt's. Kate waited, and in less than a minute he came out again, pocketing whatever it was he'd evidently purchased.

She eyed him, wondering exactly how much he would make in this last-minute sale of her father's goods, and if he'd keep his word and leave her with enough money to tide her over until another load could be hauled from Sutter's Fort. She also wondered whether the driver would keep his word about extending her credit.

Mei Li crowded in beside her at the window for a look. "Him good man."

None of the men Kate had known in Dublin, save her own brothers, would have exhausted their life savings to insure the livelihood of an immigrant laborer and his family. "You're right. Crockett is a good man."

"Oh. Him, too."

Him, too? She realized Mei Li's wide eyes weren't focused on Will Crockett at all. The girl was wholly captivated by his rough-looking, tawny-haired friend. "You mean Mr. Robinson, don't you?"

A tiny smile bloomed on Mei Li's lips.

Good Lord! Kate snapped the buckskin drape back into place over the window. "They're nearly done with the load, and our hour's almost up." They might as well— how had Crockett put it? *Get it over with.*

"You not ready. Dress all wrong. I fix."

"I'm fine, Mei Li. I told you, it's not a real wedding, just a wee business arrangement so I might keep the store long enough to raise some money."

Mei Li shook her head and uttered a few more choice words in Chinese. "Might as well go, then, if you no care how you look." She parted the canvas flaps of the shanty's entrance, and they stepped into the sun.

Even if, heaven forbid, it were to be a real wedding, there wasn't a man of God to be found for a hundred miles in any direction. A thousand for all Kate knew. Landerfelt had been right about that. She hadn't seen a proper priest since she'd left Ireland six months ago.

And it was that very fact which, in the end, justified her decision to undertake such a blasphemous act. Vickery's legal proceeding was one thing. But were they married in the church, well, now that was something else altogether.

She would never have considered the idea if there had been the remotest possibly of that happening. Her place in heaven was safe, she hoped, as long as she went to confession as soon as she got home, and if she started on those rosaries tonight.

As they picked their way up the street, avoiding mud holes and horse droppings, Kate felt a bittersweet sort of emptiness inside. Her whole life had been devoted to caring for her father and brothers. She'd promised herself that when the boys were grown she'd make a life for herself. Her own life. She'd find a good man to marry. One who respected and loved her.

Kate followed the wagon ruts up the street, past a stream of miners heading out of town to their claims, bearing the goods her soon-to-be husband had sold them, and considered that this was not exactly what she'd had in mind when she'd made that promise to herself so very long ago.

By the time she and Mei Li reached the middle of town, it was apparent word had spread of what was about to take place. Given the lack of women, Kate suspected there were few weddings in Tinderbox. Perhaps hers was the first.

The blacksmith stepped out of the livery, and Landerfelt's cronies out of his store. Every tradesman in town, along with more miners than she could count, gathered in the small meadow below the graveyard on the far side of town.

Will Crockett paced the wet, uneven ground, his fur hat crushed in his hands. "Took long enough," he said as she and Mei Li approached.

"I'm ready if you are." She glanced at the faces in the crowd, which closed a circle around them, but she didn't see Mr. Vickery. She hadn't seen him all day, in fact. He'd been up early that morning, long before her.

Matt Robinson appeared and, to Kate's astonishment, thrust a hastily gathered bouquet into her hands. Mei Li grinned. Crockett scowled. They weren't flowers, exactly. It was full-on autumn. November. And the chill in the air told her snow wasn't very far off.

"All right, let's do it." Crockett squinted in the direction of Vickery's cottage. "Where's that lawyer?"

Kate arched a brow, silently reiterating his question.

Matt shot them both a sheepish glance and shrugged. "He's gone. Landerfelt hornswoggled him into doin' some business for him in Hangtown."

The look on Crockett's face echoed Kate's sentiments exactly: anger mixed with a goodly dose of relief.

"But I found a ringer in the bunch who'll do a far sight

better than Vickery.'' Matt stepped aside to let a young, portly miner into the circle.

Kate didn't recognize him, nor did any of the local tradesmen, given their narrowed gazes. The man was obviously new to not only the town, but the goldfields. His clothes were new and far too clean, and his skin too white for him to have been here long. He shot a few furtive glances at the crowd, then nodded to her and Crockett.

''Who the hell is this?'' Crockett said.

''You'll see.'' Matt grinned. ''Go on, Father. Start 'er up.''

Father?

The portly miner fixed his gaze on her, pulled a small, well-worn missal out of his breast pocket and made the sign of the cross.

''Sweet Jesus,'' she breathed. For the second time that day the ground slipped out from under her. Will Crockett's big hand shot out to steady her on her feet.

In perfect Latin, tinged with an Irish accent, the priest began, *''In nomine patris, et filii, et spiritus sancti. Amen.''*

Kate dropped her bouquet.

The ceremony lasted a few minutes. Or an hour. She wasn't sure which. She was vaguely aware of repeating the vows the priest read aloud from the missal.

''No ring?'' Matt looked to Crockett, and the frontiersman shot him as black a look as Kate had ever seen.

''No,'' Crockett said.

''That's all right,'' the priest said. ''It isn't strictly necessary.''

''Fine.'' Will let go of her. It dawned on her that he'd been holding her arm this whole time. ''That's it then? We're married?''

"Aye." The priest risked a smile. "You may kiss the bride."

Kate's eyes widened at the very thought. Surely Crockett wouldn't dream of—

"Go on, Will, kiss her!" someone shouted from the crowd.

The town blacksmith shot her a lusty grin. "I'll kiss 'er for ya, Will, if ya ain't man enough."

Kate wasn't a woman who blushed easily. After all, she'd raised four brothers and had the benefit of a worldly father's adventurous tales. All the same, she touched a sweaty hand to her cheek and found it blazing.

"Come on, *Mrs. Crockett.*" Crockett grabbed her arm and pulled her through the crowd toward the livery, where her father's horse stood saddled and waiting. Evidently he'd already sold the mule.

Matt and Mei Li dogged their steps, followed by the crowd that had turned out to witness their vows.

"You're set on this dang fool Alaska thing, then," Matt called after them.

Crockett shot a stony look over his shoulder. "Damn right I am. What do you think this whole charade is about."

"I thought you was doin' it to help Miss Dennington." Matt tossed her a half smile. "Mrs. Crockett, I mean."

"*Mrs. Crockett* got what she wanted. My name. That's what they all want, isn't it? And I got what I wanted, too." He jerked her up the street, his grip tightening around her arm. "Besides, I don't think our *Mrs. Crockett* needs help. She's doing all right on her own, if you ask me."

Kate tripped in a wagon rut and, before she could react, Will caught her up in his arms. She could tell from his nasty expression that the move was purely instinctive.

Had he had time to think about it, she'd probably be lying in the mud.

"Y-you've made enough money, then," she said. His face was inches from hers, and she was conscious of her heartbeat accelerating. "F-for your passage."

Crockett's scowl deepened. "What the hell do you know about it?"

"Nothing. I just—"

He pushed her away and dug a small leather pouch out of his pocket. "Enough for a working passage, if I'm lucky. If I sell the horse in Sacramento City, there's maybe enough. I won't know till I get there." He thrust the pouch at her. "Here, it's your cut. There's still about a third of the wagonload left. Mostly things of no use out here. They're in your father's store."

"*My* store," she said, tired of his nasty attitude.

"Right. I forgot." He turned to his waiting mount.

"Go on, Will," the blacksmith called out again. "Kiss 'er g'bye. What's the matter? Y'ain't afraid of her, are ya?" A dozen voices chimed in, echoing the blacksmith's challenge.

Matt and Mei Li stood there, grinning. Kate didn't find it amusing at all. In fact, she wasn't about to stand here and be made a fool of. She turned her back on Crockett and started for her father's store. *Her* store, she reminded herself.

A second later, she was jerked clean off her feet. She sucked in a breath but had no time to exhale. Will Crockett's mouth covered hers, and it wasn't the kind of gentle kiss a man gives his new bride.

She struggled. No use. Crockett's hand snaked up her back and cupped her nape like a vise. Her last conscious thought before she gave herself up to his will and superior strength was that Mei Li's handiwork had all been for nothing. Her hair tumbled free in Crockett's hand.

And then he dropped her. "Unh!" She landed hard, on her behind, smack in the center of a muddy wagon rut.

Breathless, Kate watched as he mounted her father's horse and reined the black gelding west into the sun. Not until he was out of sight did she remember it would be the last time she would ever see him.

Her husband, Will Crockett.

Chapter Four

Mrs. Crockett, indeed. The name didn't suit her at all.

Kate swept the last of the dried mud clods out the door of Dennington's Grocery and Dry Goods and into the street. There'd been little business that morning. The fanfare accompanying the arrival of the last shipment from Sutter's Fort seemed to be over.

Most of the local miners had gone back to their claims yesterday following her spur-of-the-moment wedding to Will Crockett. The town was quiet. Almost too quiet.

Crockett had been right about what remained of the shipment. She glanced at the pile of neglected goods he and Matt had stacked against the far wall of the store. She supposed she should sort them out, display the items in an attractive manner. But who in Tinderbox would want to buy a washboard or a set of hammered tin cups or ladies' undergarments?

This was not exactly a domestic little village in County Kildare. Besides, there weren't any women to speak of to buy such things, save her and Mei Li and a few Indians. And none of them appeared to wear the kind of undergarments that had been delivered.

The wagon driver had made a bargain with Kate's father to purchase whatever was available, regardless of demand. Everything was scarce in the goldfields. Her father must have figured that, at some point, everything would sell.

The shipments had been delivered on a fairly regular schedule, as well. Once every couple of weeks, weather permitting, a new load arrived from Sutter's Fort. It was better than forty miles. A hard day's ride. But it might take the supply wagon a week, Dan the driver had told her before he'd left town.

She wondered if she'd ever see that driver again. The promises Crockett had extracted from him yesterday could hardly be enforced now that the trapper was gone. And there were a dozen other small towns just like Tinderbox sprouting up in the goldfields.

Landerfelt transported his own goods, using his own men—Jed and Leon Packett—those two ruffians who'd tried to abscond with her wagon load, and who'd harassed Mei Li. Landerfelt kept his own schedule, and would also ferry goods and mail for local miners back and forth from Sacramento City—for a hefty fee. Few could afford to take him up on those services.

Kate leaned the broom up in the corner and wiped a thin sheen of perspiration from her brow. The day was cool, but she was warm from work. Her gaze drifted over the clean shelves and newly scrubbed floor. Aye, it would have to do.

All she could do now was wait. Crockett had left her a bit of coin, and there were enough jarred goods, salted meat and flour left over for her to get by on until the next shipment arrived. If anyone knew how to stretch the ingredients for one meal into a dozen, it was Kate.

Mei Li had been a big help to her. Kate had discovered that the girl and her father, Cheng, had ministered to her own father when he'd first taken ill. At least he'd had friends here in this strange and wild place. People who'd cared for him.

She'd been lucky that Vickery and Mei Li had extended their friendship to her. Vickery had offered to house her until she was able to sail for home, but Kate had declined. His wife was expected back soon, and Kate couldn't imagine Mrs. Vickery would take kindly to a stranger in her house.

Besides, the cabin her father had fashioned into a store had a tiny room in the back with a bed, a place to cook and a wood-fired stove. It was a far sight better than where she and her brothers lived near Halfpenny Bridge in Dublin. No evidence of rats, at least. Only field mice and a few harmless insects that wandered in from the forested hillside butting up to the back of the cabin.

Kate walked to the window and gazed across the street at Landerfelt's Mercantile and Mining Supply. The man himself hadn't shown his face since their altercation in the street yesterday morn. Perhaps with Will Crockett gone, this rivalry was over. Surely there was enough business for two stores, Landerfelt's and hers, in a growing town like Tinderbox. She hoped there was, for as long as it took to raise enough for her passage home and to clear her debt.

A rap at the storefront window jarred her from her thoughts. She peered out the now sparkling glass and saw Mr. Vickery's worried eyes squinting back at her.

Lord, she must look a fright! She snatched the old rag tied about her waist in apron fashion and tossed it behind the counter, then smoothed her hair as best she could. "Mr. Vickery," she said as he stepped into the store. "How nice to see you."

He removed his bowler but didn't return her smile.

"Miss Dennington—um, Mrs. Crockett, I mean." His frown told her he didn't think much of what she'd done to protect her assets.

She bit her lip. "Won't you please call me Kate?"

"Very well, Kate. I've just come by to check on you. I wish you'd stay at the cottage. It's not safe for you here at the store. Mrs. Vickery will be back from San Francisco soon, and I'm certain she'll share my concern for your safety."

"I appreciate it, truly I do. But there's no need to worry. I'm perfectly fine here."

In truth, now that she'd been here a couple of days, she didn't feel any more uncomfortable alone in the store or on the street than she had in certain sections of the grindingly poor neighborhood she'd been raised in.

"I've braved the streets of Dublin alone from an early age, Mr. Vickery. I'm quite capable of watching out for myself."

He studied her face for a moment, searching, perhaps, for signs of feigned confidence. She drew herself up and squarely met his gaze. Well, perhaps some of it *was* feigned.

"Yes, I believe you are. And I'd have expected nothing less from Liam Dennington's daughter." He smiled, finally, then visibly relaxed.

Kate was pleased. She needed allies, and suspected Mr. Vickery was a good one to have.

"You're nothing at all like the first Mrs. Crockett."

"The *first* Mrs. Crockett?" Kate's eyes widened of their own accord. "You mean, Will was married before?" She'd never considered that possibility. He didn't seem at all the kind of man who'd have a wife. Well, not a real wife.

"What happened to her?"

"Happened?"

"I mean…she *is* dead, isn't she?" The look on her face must have betrayed the split second of fear that shot through her mind.

Mr. Vickery dismissed her concern with the wave of his hand. "Of course she's dead. You don't think he would have…" He shook his head as if she was supposed to understand. "…if she weren't?"

"Oh, no, of course not." Kate shook her head, too, and looked properly shocked at the very thought. Though, judging from her brief experience with Will Crockett, his good deed to the Chinese family aside, she wouldn't have put it past him to have had a wife in one place and have no qualms about marrying another he would never see again.

She offered Vickery a seat on the wide window box and pulled up a stool beside him. She encouraged him to go on with his tale.

"Right. Well, yes, she died of cholera. Not six months after Crockett brought her West."

"So he's from the East then. New York?"

"Philadelphia."

"Ah." Kate hadn't a clue where that was. The only place she knew of in the eastern part of America was New York.

"Sherrilyn Rogers Browning was her name. They say she was a beauty."

"Really." Absently Kate smoothed her well-worn dress and tucked a tendril of frazzled hair back into place.

"With a taste for luxury and fine things."

"And yet she wed a fur trapper?" That was too far-fetched to believe.

"Well, yes, I guess she did."

"Just how do you know this, Mr. Vickery? Did Crockett tell you?"

"Oh, my, no. He's not the kind of man who talks about his family."

Kate hadn't gotten to know him well enough to either agree or disagree.

"Matt Robinson told me."

"Ah, the infamous Matt Robinson." She smiled, recalling his swashbuckling behavior of the day before. "He's quite the colorful character."

"Oh, quite." Vickery leaned in close, as if he were about to tell her something of great import. "Rumor has it Crockett's the son of a very wealthy man. Someone important—in politics or banking maybe—back East. No one really knows."

Six months at sea packed aboard a ship with immigrants of every imaginable background and social status, Kate had gotten quite good at picking up languages and at judging people's circumstances from their speech.

More than once she'd detected a sort of refinement in Crockett's voice and manner, though he seemed to bend over backward to cover it up, obliterate it. He worked hard at being something he was not. Why?

Kate rose from the stool and gazed out the window at the clear autumn sky. It didn't really matter, did it? Will Crockett was gone for good, and so much the better. He was right, after all. She had what she wanted. Why, then, did she feel so despondent?

After Mr. Vickery said goodbye and tottered off down the street, Kate turned back to the window and stared blankly after him, her thoughts consumed by what she'd learned of Will Crockett.

Trailing a finger across her lips, she recalled their kiss. It had been her first. She was twenty-two and had never been kissed. Not until yesterday morn when Will Crockett made her his wife. He wasn't really her husband, she reminded herself. It was purely a business arrangement. It's not as if he'd left her. He'd planned to leave all along.

She glanced up the street and, to her surprise, saw the portly priest turned miner who'd married them the day before. Father Flanagan, newly arrived in Tinderbox to make his fortune. A fortune he'd use to build a church, a parish, here on the frontier.

Crossing herself, Kate offered up a silent plea for God to forgive her sin. Sweet Jesus, she'd actually married him! In the church. No matter that it was out in the open, under the clear blue sky. She'd said the vows before a priest, before God.

It *was* a real marriage, despite the fact that Will Crockett was on his way to Alaska, and that soon she, too, would take to ship and sail for home.

Will stood on the levee in Sacramento City in the shadow of the *Golden Eagle* and resisted the urge to draw the miniature out of his pocket. Why the hell he'd bought it, he didn't know.

The painted image of Kate Dennington surely hadn't changed in the ten minutes since he'd last looked at it. All the same, the keepsake was in his hand before he knew it, her blue eyes and proud Irish features staring up at him.

''You're an idiot, Crockett.'' He jammed it back into his pocket as the men huddled around him on the levee waiting to board the riverboat turned to stare. Shrugging, he swore silently under his breath.

He'd been hard on Kate yesterday, and regretted his bad behavior. He'd been angry, not at her so much as himself. He was attracted to her, and that was the problem.

The way she'd pushed through that crowd of men and come to Mei Li's defense yesterday morning in town had surprised the hell out of him. The woman had grit. He admired that, along with those blue eyes of hers.

Absently his hand moved to the pocket housing the miniature. At the last minute he fisted it at his side and mouthed a silent curse.

Kate Dennington wasn't his concern. So why did he have second thoughts about leaving her? She was a woman alone in a town full of ruffians and gold diggers. So what? From what he'd seen of her, she was damned capable of taking care of herself.

Besides, he had plans. And those plans didn't include a woman in them. Women were trouble. Sherrilyn had taught him that little lesson. Kate Dennington was trouble, too. That chaste kiss of hers proved it. How long had she practiced it, and with whom? She was good, all right. Very, very good.

He would live the life he wanted, the life he'd imagined while shut up for days on end in the private schools his father had insisted he attend. California was spoiled for him now, by the gold and the greed.

But Alaska…now she was something a man could build a life around. Untamed, unspoiled. The adventure of a lifetime. His gaze focused again, and he realized with a start it was fixed on Kate Dennington's blue eyes.

That damned miniature must have jumped out of his pocket and into his hand! He gripped it until the silvered edges cut into his palm.

It was no kind of life for a wife, or children. Not his, or anyone's. Something dark and bitter balled in his gut as an image of Sherrilyn, her face white in death, her lips blue, crashed into his consciousness.

Will jammed the miniature back into his pocket and

eyed the restless crowd. Where in hell was that livery
hand? It was an hour past the appointed time the man said
he'd meet him. He'd offered a fair price for Dennington's
gelding, and Will needed every cent he could get his
hands on to buy that working passage and make a new
start.

The steamer headed north sailed day after tomorrow
from San Francisco, right on schedule, so a riverboat
stevedore had told him. The *Golden Eagle* was boarding
passengers now for the day-and-a-half trip downriver to
the port.

Will was out of time. "Damn." He turned and calmed
Dennington's horse, who grew more agitated as the crowd
on the levee began to board.

He'd bribed that same stevedore to sneak him on the
second before the riverboat pushed off. He could be
caught, but that was a chance he was willing to take. The
bribe had been less than the fare by half.

Will scanned the faces of the men crowded around him,
desperate to find that livery hand. It was a damned fair
price, so where the hell—

"Leon told him once the husband was gone—some
trapper or other—they was gonna burn her out."

Will froze as his gaze fixed on the rough-looking miner
who'd spoken.

"No kiddin'?" The greasy-haired man beside him
laughed. "Well, hell, wouldn't be hard to do. They don't
call it Tinderbox for nothin'. One match and the whole
town'd go up."

Will dropped the gelding's reins and put a gloved hand
on the miner's shoulder.

"Hey, mister, wait yer turn."

Will spun him around to face him, and the miner went
for his knife. "We're all in line, here."

Will reached for his gun. Son of a—he'd forgotten he'd lost it to Landerfelt. "Burn who out?" he said, and locked gazes with the man.

The miner frowned but stayed his hand.

"Leon Packett told you this?" Will didn't think Packett was capable of saying anything, for at least a day or two after Matt had launched him through that store window. "Burn who out?" he said again.

"That Irish gal." The miner turned to his greasy friend. "What's her name, you know it? That wagon driver we seen up Horseshoe Bar last night was the one told us."

"That's right. Said some Leon character told him his boss don't take kindly to no furreigners puttin' him outta business."

"You heard this last night from Dan Dunnett?" He'd give that wagon driver more than a broken nose the next time he saw him.

"Dunnett. That's right." The miner narrowed his eyes. "What's it to you? You know the lady or somethin'?"

Will shot them both a dark look. "Yeah, I know her."

Perhaps there were rats, after all.

Kate sat up in bed and strained her eyes to see in the dark. There was no window in the small living quarters of the cabin-turned-store. She'd left the door propped open between the two rooms, and a thin sliver of moonlight played across the rough-hewn floorboards.

Wait! There it was again. A kind of scraping sound. She narrowed her eyes and listened, but all she heard were the crickets outside. Still, if she did have rats, she'd best take care of them now. They could clean out an entire month's worth of grain in one night if you let them go unchecked.

She swiveled quietly out of bed and touched a toe to

the floor. Lord, it was cold as ice! She groped in the dark for the chair on which she'd draped her dress and shawl but couldn't find it. And if she lit the lamp she'd scare the vermin back into hiding.

Something creaked from the next room, and Kate froze in place. All the hairs on her nape prickled. She held her breath and listened harder. If it was a rat, it was an awfully big one.

As quietly as she could, she slipped a hand between the bed's straw mattress and ropes. Her fist closed over the cool steel of the percussion cap pepperbox that had been her father's pistol since she was just a sprite. Vickery had given it to her along with a single-barrel flintlock rifle and what few other valuables her father had in his possession when he died.

When she'd left Ireland she hadn't known a pistol from a dead bolt, but six months at sea with a shipload of strangers, some of them military men, had taught her much. She'd cleaned and loaded the small, six-barrel pistol last night, just in case, never imagining she'd have to use it so soon. Brandishing it in front of her, she inched on tiptoe toward the open door.

She'd be all right as long as she didn't trip over anything. Her eyes adjusted slowly to the dark. But the cold! She shivered almost uncontrollably. Her feet were like ice, and the thin wool of her shift provided little protection against the chill air.

Well, if it *were* rats she'd feel awfully stupid. Sliding up beside the open door, Kate peeked slowly into the moonlit store. All was quiet. She could swear that something, or someone, was in there. Or had been a moment ago.

She scanned the floor and countertop, and the half-empty shelves for scurrying rodents. Nothing. Perhaps she'd been mistaken, after all. It wouldn't be the first time she'd dreamed of vermin or insects creeping up on her. The Dublin tenement had been full of them.

Her nose wrinkled as she caught a whiff of kerosene. How strange. She'd filled the lanterns that afternoon but could swear she'd sealed the fuel tin. She stepped into the store, squinting toward the corner where her father had housed his tinned goods.

Two distinctly human footfalls sounded to her left. Without a second thought Kate whirled, leveled the pistol at the sound and fired. The blast shattered the silence.

A second later the intruder was on her. A scream rose up in her throat as he wrestled her to the floor, fighting for possession of the gun. His knees dug into her spread thighs and pinned her to the splintery floor.

"Let me go, you bleedin' bastard!" The pistol jammed as she tried to fire again. No other choice left to her, she hit him with it—a sideways swipe in the dark that grazed his head.

"Son of a bitch!"

That voice! She could swear it belonged to—

He grabbed her wrist and squeezed so tight tears came to her eyes. She dropped the pistol, and in one quick move he pinioned both her arms above her head.

"Sweet Jesus!"

"Wrong. Guess again."

His face was inches from hers. She could barely make out his features in the milky light but felt his breath hot on her face, and the tease of soft fur against her bare arms.

"Crockett!"

"Good guess. Give the lady a gold star."

"Of all the—" She struggled beneath him, but was no match for his size and strength.

Crockett jerked her arms higher, forcing her back to

arch and her breasts to press upward into his chest. His body radiated heat like the pig-iron furnaces in Clancy Street back home.

"Are you done, now?" He relaxed his grip on her, and she yanked her wrists free.

"Done with what? And get off me!"

He rolled off her, and she scrambled to her feet.

"Done trying to kill me. There's a law against that kind of thing, you know. A wife kills her husband—well, that's a hanging offense here in Tinderbox."

"Husband, indeed!" She dashed to the lantern sitting on the countertop and lit it as Crockett got to his feet. An open window explained the cold, and how he'd gotten in. She swung it closed and latched it tight. "What the devil are you doing here?"

The soft lantern light played across his even features and reflected back at her from those black eyes. "I could ask you the same thing. You're supposed to be at Vickery's."

"Oh, aye, and let ruffians break into my store in the night and steal me blind, I suppose?" She stepped toward him with the intent of chewing him out. Just who did he think he was, letting himself in and—

His gaze raked over her shift-clad form, and for the barest moment she read something in his eyes that made her heart stop. In a flash, she retrieved her shawl from the other room and pulled it tight around her body.

She could swear he was grinning somewhere under that stony expression of his. She took in his muddied boots and garments and his wild hair, which looked as if it hadn't seen a comb since he left Tinderbox.

"Shouldn't you be on the riverboat?"

His eyes grew cold again. "Any man in his right mind would be. But I'm not, am I?"

"But your ship, the steamer north... I thought that you—"

"There's another one in a month. And that one I'll be on, come hell or high water. Bet on it."

"A month!"

He was supposed to sail now, this week, and be gone forever. That had been their bargain. That's what he'd said, what everyone had been telling her for days. She wouldn't have married him at all had he meant to stay on.

"What, exactly, do you intend to do for the next month?"

He moved toward her, his gaze pinned on hers. The tiniest spark of fear balled inside her. She backed toward the door leading to the street. "Su-surely you don't think to..."

A dozen random thoughts raced through her mind. She realized that she knew nothing about him, only what little Mei Li and Mr. Vickery had told her. He could be anyone—a criminal, a murderer or...

He reached for her and her breath seized up in her chest.

"Stand aside."

"W-what?"

His dark eyes narrowed, and she realized he wasn't looking at her, but past her at the door. She breathed again and scooted sideways out of his light.

"Looks like there's plenty to do around here for a month."

"What do you mean?" Her gaze followed his and when she saw what he'd been eyeing she gasped. "Someone's tried to jimmy the door!"

Crockett fiddled with the loose latch. "You haven't seen Leon Packett around here, have you? Or his brother, Jed?"

Landerfelt's men. The ones Will and Matt had thrashed the day before. Well, almost two days now. It was well past midnight. "No, I haven't seen them. Why?"

Crockett shook his head. "Damned stupid." The self-deprecating edge in his voice surprised her.

Then she noticed the blood. "You're hurt." Without thinking, she reached out and touched her finger to his temple.

"Yeah. Thanks." He brushed her hand away. "Lucky your aim is as bad as your judgment."

She felt bad about the incident. Nevertheless, it would have been his own fault had she killed him. What was he doing snooping around, looking for Jed Packett? She supposed she should be grateful. Clearly someone had been in the store.

She sniffed the air, remembering the kerosene. Padding to the dark corner, she peered at the open tin. She knew she'd closed it after filling the lamps. It wasn't the kind of thing she'd forget to do.

Voices sounded from up the street, drawing their attention away from the fuel. Torchlight played off the glass of the storefront window, and a second later Matt Robinson's concerned eyes peered through the glass. Two others huddled beside him, their guns drawn.

Crockett opened the door. "What's wrong?"

"We was just about to ask you—er, Mrs. Crockett—the same thing." Matt eyed Crockett's rumpled clothes and the blood trickling from his temple. "We heard shots."

"Just an accident." Crockett retrieved her father's pepperbox from the floor. "Miss Denning—Kate, I mean, was cleaning her pistol."

"At two in the mornin'?" Matt cocked a tawny brow

at the both of them. It was clear he didn't believe it. "You two okay?"

"Fine," they both said in a strained show of unity.

Matt Robinson wasn't buying any of it, but the cautionary look in Crockett's eyes kept him from probing further.

"That's that, then." Matt tipped his hat to her. "We'll be gettin' back to bed." As he turned to leave, he shot Crockett a wicked grin. "So, ya decided not to go, after all."

Crockett's face hardened. He grunted some unintelligible response and kicked the door shut behind them.

Kate had had enough.

In a confrontational pose that had always garnered excellent results when questioning her brothers, she crossed her arms over her chest and tipped her chin at him. Crockett looked at her as if she were some mildly amusing annoyance.

"What now?" she said.

His gaze flashed on her bare feet. "I think it's time we both got some sleep. I'll just—"

"No. I want to know why you're back, and exactly what your intentions are."

He stared at her for a full ten seconds before answering, those black eyes fixed on hers. By God, if he thought he was going to intimidate her, let him think again.

"My reasons are my own business," he said evenly. "As for my intentions..." He broke their deadlocked stare. "It's a month till the next steamer north. You need protection, and I could use more cash. I'll stay and work the store, until we both make enough to get the hell out of here."

He wasn't asking her, he was telling her. And there was

something about his tone, a certain overconfidence, that she didn't like.

"I don't need protection."

He twirled her father's pistol around his little finger and cast a glance at the jimmied door latch. "All right. Suit yourself. I'll be gone in the morning." He slammed the pistol on the counter and turned to leave.

"Wait. I—"

There were a dozen good reasons she should boot him out and slam the door behind him. And a dozen more why she shouldn't, not the least of which was the fact that he was right. She did need protection. And it might not hurt to have a man around, either. Much of the store's stock was so heavy, the mining equipment in particular, she couldn't lift it even with Mei Li's help.

He looked at her, one dark brow arched in question, his hand on the broken door latch.

"I...I guess that would be all right," she said. "But the cabin's too small for us both. You'll have to sleep outside."

In Dublin she'd lived with her father and four brothers crowded into a basement flat smaller than this by half. The cabin was a palace by comparison.

No matter. It was just a tiny lie. One of many, she suspected, she'd be forced into over the next month. She'd save them all up and when she got home she'd have a nice long confession with her parish priest.

"That suits me fine." Crockett yanked the door open and stepped into the night.

"Good night, then, Mr. Crockett."

He slammed his fur hat onto his head and winced. The spot where she'd hit him had swelled to the size of an egg. "Good night *Mrs. Crockett*." The words hung there between them as a bitter look twisted on his face.

She watched him as he stormed up the street, and had the gnawing feeling she was destined to burn in hell after all.

Chapter Five

Crockett's Grocery and Dry Goods.

"Got a ring to it, don't it?" Matt gathered up the borrowed stencils and horsehair paintbrush and stood back to admire his handiwork.

"Not particularly." Will stared at the drying paint and ground his teeth.

The only other building he'd ever seen his family name on was built of hand-hewn granite and the finest imported marble one could buy. His mood darkened just thinking about it.

"Glad you decided to stay, Will."

"I told you, I'm not staying. It's just temporary."

"Oh, right, I forgot."

He caught Matt's mischievous grin and was tempted to wipe it off that silly face of his.

"See ya around, then." Matt waltzed up the street toward Cheng's, whistling a bawdy miner's tune.

Will swore.

Aside from the fact that he was out of his mind to have returned last night, two good things had come of it. He'd saved Dennington's daughter's hide. Again. And he'd foiled Landerfelt's little plan, which gave him immense satisfaction.

He grabbed the homemade ladder leaning up against the store, swung it under his arm and started around to the back porch of the building he now owned. Before he turned the corner, he shot a glance across the street.

Landerfelt glared back at him, an unlit cigar crushed between his teeth, through the new pane of glass installed in his storefront window earlier that day. God knows where he'd got it, and what he had to pay to get it here.

On impulse, Will tipped his hat at him and smiled. Hell, yes. If he was going to be here another month, he might as well glean as much twisted pleasure out of the situation as possible.

Speaking of which…through the open side window of his new enterprise—the window he'd climbed through last night—he spied Kate behind the counter bargaining with two scraggly-looking miners.

He stowed the ladder and moved up close to the sill to watch her. Her back was to him. His gaze strayed lazily over the curve of her hips and the plump swell of her derriere.

His mind fixed on the image that had kept him awake half of last night…Kate standing in front of the lantern in her threadbare shift, the curves of her naked body silhouetted in the soft light. He recalled the feel of her struggling beneath him on the floor, her thighs pinned open by his, her breasts crushed against his chest.

Snap out of it, Crockett.

He reminded himself that their arrangement was a business deal. Not unlike the one his father had concocted with his last bride. This time the stakes were much lower, of course…a couple of steamship tickets and some cash…but the intent was the same.

To make money.

And the second Mrs. Crockett appeared to be quite good at it, from what he overheard of her dealings with her two most recent customers.

"Don't be tellin' me my business, now." She placed a brass weight on the tendering scales, as he'd shown her that first day, then fisted her hands on her hips. "There. That's the price. Take it or leave it."

The miners grumbled but completed the transaction. Goods and gold were exchanged. Kate swept the precious tender into the old leather pouch Dennington had used to safeguard his money, and stuffed it into her skirt pocket the instant the miners left.

Will slipped past the open window and chucked his rawhide gloves on the back porch before stepping into the living quarters flanking the store. Kate had been busy in the short time he'd been gone. The cabin was spotless. So tidy he hardly recognized it.

"There's a shelf in there needs fixing," she called out when she heard the scrape of his boots across the split timber floorboards. "By the stove."

It had been like that all morning. She'd roused him in the gray dawn, rattling off a list of chores that would take six men a week to complete.

"I'll get to it," he said. "When I'm ready."

His reply was met with icy silence on the other side of the wall separating the cabin's living quarters from the storefront. Though he couldn't see her from where he stood, he felt her blue eyes burning into him.

The tiny brass bell he'd hung over the storefront's door tinkled to life. One of the first things he'd done that morning was repair the busted front door latch. He'd be paying a visit to the Packett boys later today on that account.

Mei Li blew across the threshold with an armload of stuff, eyeing the newly installed bell. "Okay, Miss Kate. I ready to start." Will recognized Cheng's old abacus sticking out from under her arm.

"Good," Kate said. "It won't take long if we work together."

In the day and half he'd been gone, these two had grown thick as thieves. What exactly were they up to? Will sidled up to the doorway and peered into the store.

Mei Li set the abacus on the counter and surveyed the hodgepodge of items left over from their last shipment. None of it was good for much, in Will's estimation.

Kate ran a hand over the carved ivory balls of the Chinese counting device, then handed Mei Li a paper Will recognized—the inventory list Dan the wagon driver had delivered along with the shipment.

Mei Li thrust the paper back at her. "You read list. I count."

"But—"

"Faster this way."

Under the counter Mei Li found the inventory ledger she'd created for Liam Dennington months ago. Will recalled that the Irishman had rarely used it. Dennington hadn't been one to keep track of his stock, or his profits.

"You read," Mei Li said. "I count. Then you write— here." She nodded at the ledger.

While Mei Li sorted goods, Kate studied the list and the ledger, her expression as grave as Will had ever seen it. He wondered what she was thinking. Their situation wasn't all that bad. Dan would be back in a week with new stock.

"Okay, I ready."

Will watched as Kate ran a hand over Dan's chicken-scratch writing. Her gaze fixed on the list, but it was as if she were feeling the words on the paper rather than reading them. Mei Li looked at her expectantly.

Then it dawned on him.

Kate Dennington couldn't read.

A split second later she saw him, lurking there in the doorway. She slapped the list onto the counter. "What the devil are you doing there?"

"Watching." He stepped into the store.

"Watching? Watching what?"

"You."

She made a derisive little sound and turned her back on him. "Don't you have chores?"

"They can wait."

Mei Li shot him a quick glance, then slipped toward the front door. "I come back later. Husband and wife talk now."

"She's not my—" the brass bell signaled Mei Li's swift departure "—wife."

Kate flashed angry eyes at him, grabbed the list and the ledger off the counter and yanked open a drawer.

In three strides Will was behind her, his hand clamped over her wrist. "Not so fast."

"Let me go!"

"Let's see that list."

She jerked free of his grasp and slammed the list and the ledger onto the counter. "I've work to do. I'll just—"

"Read it to me." He gripped the edge of the counter, hemming her in as she tried to slip past him. "Read it."

"No."

Anger, and something else, flashed in her eyes. In the privileged world he'd been raised in everyone could read and write. But things were different here on the frontier. She was different, too. Perhaps he'd misjudged her.

"Mei Li could help you with that, you know. I could even help you, if you wanted."

"With what?"

He nodded at the list on the counter. "Reading."

Surprise registered in her eyes, then vanished just as quickly. "I don't need your help."

He knew she'd say that. In fact, he would have been disappointed had she not. "Suit yourself. It doesn't matter to me if you can't read."

"I never said I couldn't read." She tried to move past him again, and again he blocked her escape. "It's just that…" Her face flushed crimson. "It's none of your business."

She was right, it wasn't. "Fair enough." He was sorry he'd embarrassed her. That's not what he'd meant to do. Besides, what did he care if she could read or not? "But why the inventory?"

"It's necessary."

"For what? What does it matter? The goods come in. We sell them. Period."

He pressed closer, and she looked away, refusing to acknowledge his invasion of her personal space. He told himself his proximity to her didn't affect him, either, but it did.

All at once he was aware of a hundred tiny things about her. The shimmering wisps of auburn hair grazing her neck, her freckled cheeks flushing under his scrutiny. He leaned closer still, dangerously drawn to her lips, which were pursed in that prim, defiant manner he was beginning to admire.

''To keep track of the profits, of course.'' At last she met his gaze, her blue eyes ice. The hint of vulnerability he'd perceived a second earlier had vanished.

''The profits,'' she repeated, as if he hadn't heard her the first time. Her expression hardened before his eyes. ''Yours and mine.''

''Yours and mine?''

''Exactly.'' She pushed past him, and this time he didn't stop her. ''We shall count every item sold, and at the end of each day, we'll divide the profits between us in equal shares.''

It was always about the money, wasn't it? First his father, then Sherrilyn. Now her. ''What, do you think I'd cheat you?''

''You might.''

The brass bell over the door tinkled to life again, and he bit back the comment he was ready to let fly.

Kate's eyes widened. ''Mr....Landerfelt.''

Will spun toward the door, a hand on his empty holster. ''What do you want?''

Landerfelt stood in the doorway, smirking. ''I'm here to offer *Mrs. Crockett,* here, a deal.''

''What kind of deal?'' Kate started toward him. Will grabbed her arm, and she shot him a nasty look.

''She wants to go home. I'm prepared to send her.''

''What do you mean?'' Will said.

''I'll buy her passage. Half now, half later.''

''You will?'' Kate jerked out of his grasp.

''Whoa!'' Will grabbed her again, and this time he wasn't letting go. ''In return for what?'' As if he had to ask.

Landerfelt grinned. ''For the store, of course.''

* * *

"Done!" Kate could hardly believe it.

"Good." Landerfelt turned to leave. "I'll just have my boys—"

"No deal, Landerfelt."

Will's grip on her tightened, and she twisted around to stare at him, incredulous. "What do you mean, no deal?"

His black eyes bored into Landerfelt's back, as the merchant turned to face him. "Just what I said."

"You can't mean that." Kate tried to wrest her arm from Will's grasp, but his fingers only tightened around her flesh. "You're hurting me. Let go!"

"I do mean it." His gaze was riveted to Landerfelt's, his expression stone.

"But—"

"The store's mine, and everything in it. The land, too."

"No. You don't mean that." She shook her head, not wanting to believe he'd do this to her. "It's mine. It was my father's. I only married you to—"

"For the money." He shot her a bitter look and let her go. "Don't remind me."

Didn't he understand her predicament? Why was he being so unreasonable? He'd made enough off their last shipment to have made their short-lived arrangement worth his while. Why would he prevent her, now, from securing the funds she so badly needed?

"Come on, Crockett. You don't give a hoot about this place—or her."

Landerfelt was right about that. Last night she'd thought differently, but now she could see Will Crockett was only in it for the coin. Looking at him now, she wondered how she could have ever thought him chivalrous.

"You want to see the little lady dealt with fairly. I can understand that." Landerfelt stepped toward him, but Will raised a cautionary hand and the merchant froze in place. "All right, then. I'm a fair man."

"Right." Will snorted. "And my father's a saint."

What was he talking about? And what on earth was he thinking? It was clear to her, now, that Crockett meant to cheat her, somehow, out of what was rightfully hers. He'd never intended to keep to their bargain.

She must think of a way out of this, and fast. "It's a grand offer, Will." She forced herself to smile at him. "In fact, I'd be willing to split—"

"I told you. The land and the store are mine, and I'm not inclined to sell them. Not just yet." He wasn't even looking at her. His gaze was locked on Landerfelt's. "And sure as hell not to him."

Crockett had lied to her—about everything.

An ill feeling welled inside her. She was in this alone, now, and it was up to her to get herself out again.

As the two men stood there, glaring at each other, Kate had a fearful premonition she'd never see Ireland again.

Kate didn't speak to him for three days, and that suited Will fine.

They'd worked together in silence, side by side, with occasional help from Matt and Mei Li, making minor repairs to the cabin and readying the store for the next shipment.

The inventory was done, the ledger updated, and what additional profits they'd made divided. His and hers. Exactly as Kate had demanded. It was all about the money, and as soon as they'd made enough, he was out of there.

Will spun the loaded cylinder of the Colt he'd just acquired in a street trade with a passing miner, then glanced skyward, squinting against the rain pummeling his face. Sleeping outside, he'd been soaked to the skin for two days now. It was November, and the weather had changed for good.

Along with his plans.

He stuffed the pistol into his belt and sloshed across the muddy street toward the store. They hadn't made a sale all day, and Dan Dunnett was late. It would be rough going from Sacramento City to Tinderbox in this downpour. He'd give the wagon driver another two days before he set out to find him.

Kate was behind the counter when he blew across the threshold. "Wipe your muddy boots! I've just scrubbed the floor."

Now this was a surprise. "So I take it we're speaking again."

She glared at him with those icy eyes of hers.

He thrust a hand inside his pocket and gripped the painted miniature he'd purchased the day they'd married. He'd been wrong about the artist. The portrait didn't capture the hard-edged contempt that had graced her expression ever since he'd declined Landerfelt's offer.

He kicked his boots off in the corner and hung his dripping jacket on a peg near the door. His hair was plastered to his face. He wiped it from his brow and considered her position.

She was as stubborn as Dennington's old mule, for sure. But not wrong to be angry at him, given what little she really knew of Eldridge Landerfelt's character.

His own bottled-up anger had stopped him from explaining his actions to her that day. But sleeping in a wind-whipped tent in the rain the past three nights had dampened his pride, if not his bitter mood. If they were going to work together for the next few weeks, this standoff had to end. And he'd end it now.

"You're wrong, you know."

Grabbing a rag and a tin of linseed oil, she ignored his statement and proceeded to polish the counter.

"About Landerfelt—and me."

She shot him a quick glance but didn't respond.

"Sure, he might have paid you half now. Half of what he would have convinced you was the passage—and he would have been lying, by the way."

Her hand froze on the counter, and she met his gaze.

"Two, three hundred dollars, if you were lucky. He would have packed you off to Frisco, and that'd be the last you'd ever see of him or the rest of what he owed you."

He watched her mind working, wondering if he was telling her the truth.

"How do you know?"

"I just do. Landerfelt's a bad egg. You'll have to trust me on that."

"Aye, trust you. What a fine idea." She started polishing again, putting her back into the long strokes.

The rain beat on the tin roof. He glanced out the window at his tent, which had collapsed and now had a small creek running through it, and swore.

"You'll catch your death." She nodded at the other room. "Go in by the stove and warm up."

For a second her eyes warmed to the blue portrayed in the miniature. He caught himself recalling their kiss again. Her soft lips. The smooth skin at the nape of her neck.

"You sure?"

"Go on before I change my mind and toss you out."

He fought an unconscious smile as he squished across the floor in soaked socks. She was back to treating him like an errant child again. Probably the way she treated her younger brothers. She had four of them, to hear Mei Li tell it. It was better than silent contempt, he supposed.

She followed him into the next room and lit the lamp on the table. It was nearly dark, the sky gone black with storm clouds. Something was about to happen. He could see it her eyes, read it in her puffed-up demeanor. The old Kate was back. He didn't know whether to be happy about it or not.

"Have you eaten today?"

"No. You?"

"Just some hardtack this morning." She shrugged. "I can...cook something, if you like."

"That'd be good." He eased onto a stool flanking the potbellied stove and warmed his hands. It was the first time she'd offered to cook for him. He'd eaten nothing but wet jerky for days. The store was nearly out of food-stuffs, and she'd kept him so busy with chores he hadn't had time to hunt. He wondered what she'd been eating the past few days.

A chill gripped him. Damned rain. He inched closer to the stove.

"Here, you're soaked through." She tossed him a blanket from off the bed. "Strip off and I'll draw you a bath."

"What?"

"A bath. Hot water? Soap?"

"You want me to—"

"Aye." She opened the door leading to the back porch and, fighting the wind, dragged Dennington's old copper tub into the cabin. "Besides, you'll not stay here with me, smelling like you do. You could use a wash."

His eyes widened of their own accord. "You want me to stay here? With you?" He glanced at the neatly made bed.

Their gazes locked. For the briefest moment he knew she was thinking the same thing he was. Her freckled cheeks flushed, and it wasn't from the heat of the tiny room.

"Not *here,* you fool." She looked away and busied herself searching for the bucket.

"Over there." He pointed to it under the table flanking the wall.

"You can sleep in the store." She met his gaze again, and again he was surprised by the change in her. "Well, you can't sleep out there, now can you?" She nodded toward the forested hillside back behind the cabin.

"Hey, wait a second." Was that his tent washing away down the ravine?

"You'll sleep in there—" she nodded at the other room "—and I'll be in here. With the door closed," she added.

In her eyes he recognized a hint of the same vulnerability he'd read in them the night he'd surprised her in the dark.

"Just until the rain stops, mind you." She tossed her cloak around her shoulders and went to draw water from the rising creek out back.

He sniffed at his clothes, wondering if he really did smell bad. He couldn't remember the last time he'd had a real bath, with soap and hot water. It sounded damned good. At the least it would warm him up. If she was game, so was he.

The standoff was over.

Will watched as she readied the tub and collected some linen. Two buckets of boiling water later, Kate stood in the doorway leading to the store. "Go ahead." She nodded at the steaming tub. "I'll find you some soap."

Before he could ask her if she was planning on stepping out while he bathed or staying and scrubbing his back, she disappeared into the store.

Fine. It didn't bother him any. He listened to her rooting around in the near dark of the store as he stripped off his wet clothes and hung them to dry across a chair he'd pulled close to the stove.

"I'll not wash those filthy rags you call clothes," she called from the other room. "You'll have to do that yourself."

"Okay by me."

She breezed back into the room, a bar of lye soap in hand, just as he was stepping into the tub. Her eyes went wide as saucers as she took in the whole of him.

It dawned on him that she might have expected him to bathe in winter woolen long johns, as some of the miners did in the spirit of killing two birds with one stone. She didn't realize he never wore them.

"Jesus, Mary and Joseph." She dropped the soap—it skittered toward him across the floor—and she was out of the room like a shot.

The last thing Will heard as he sank into the hot water was the brass bell over the front door tinkling off its hook.

Chapter Six

W**hat a ninny!**

Kate pulled Will's buckskin jacket up over her head, shielding herself from the downpour as best she could and dashed up the street toward the Chinese camp.

She had four brothers, for God's sake. Had witnessed hundreds of baths in the tiny kitchen of the Dublin tenement in which she and Michael, Sean and the twins had grown up.

No matter how hard she tried to think of something else—anything else—the image of Will Crockett standing naked in the lamplight filled her mind's eye.

She'd burn in hell for an eternity for the sinful thoughts that had raced through her mind a moment ago. Thoughts that no decent girl should be thinking. She wondered if the priest who'd married them heard confessions.

"Ow!" She tripped over a piece of scrap lumber as she neared the encampment at the edge of town. Her boots were soaked through. Main Street was a river of mud.

She wouldn't have let a dog live outside in this weather. Inviting Will to sleep under her roof—their roof—had been the only Christian thing to do. Besides, last night she could swear she'd heard someone trying to get into the cabin. Through the back door this time, two strides from where she slept.

She supposed he was right about Eldridge Landerfelt, too. The merchant would certainly have tried to cheat her, had Will agreed to his latest offer. Kate didn't know much about either man, but after three days stewing on it, her instincts told her Will had called it right and that he was only trying to protect her. Why was another matter all together.

Soft lantern light and strange music greeted her at the Chinese encampment. She burst through the door of Mei Li's shanty without so much as a knock. Foul weather always precluded the normal courtesies here in the wild.

"Miss Kate!" Mei Li sprang to her feet.

"Mei Li. I—I'm sorry to trouble you, but—"

"No trouble." She handed a bowl of what looked like rice to an old Chinese man who remained sitting on the patchwork of carpets covering the ground. "Here, you sit."

"No. No, I can't stay. I'm just here to beg a favor." She smiled at the old man. Mei Li's father, she presumed. He arched a gray brow at her in response.

"My papa," Mei Li said.

"Mr. Cheng." Kate extended her hand to him.

The old man ignored it. "You wet."

"Oh, aye." She realized she was dripping all over their carpets, which were surprisingly dry given the torrent outside. "Sorry." She whipped the buckskin jacket from around her shoulders.

"Husband's coat too big." Mei Li snatched it from her and placed it on a hook over the door. "Look funny on you."

"I—I left in a hurry." That was the God's truth. "I didn't have time to find my cloak."

Mei Li's father sat silent, cross-legged, studying her as if she were some oddity. Kate tried her best to politely ignore his scrutiny.

"Where Crockett?" Mei Li said.

"In the cabin. B-bathing."

The girl's brows shot up. "Good. He stink like beaver."

Their eyes met, and Kate battled a smile. Her newfound friend did not mince words.

Mr. Cheng rose abruptly with the all the grace of Kate's childhood image of a Chinese emperor. When she was a girl her father had spun fantastical tales of the Orient and places far removed from their dreary life in Ireland. Liam Dennington had never been there, of course, but Kate didn't care. The stories seemed real enough.

Cheng nodded at his daughter, donned a black slicker and moved toward the door. The shanty was so tiny Kate had to squeeze into the corner to let him pass.

"Goodbye, Mrs. Crockett."

"Oh, I'm not really—" She bit her tongue. No matter what she was in her heart, in the town of Tinderbox she was Will Crockett's wife. "Goodbye."

Cheng slipped outside into the rain.

"Papa go round up brothers for supper."

"Oh, right. Supper." She'd nearly forgotten. "That's why I'm here, actually."

Mei Li snatched up the rice bowl her father had left on the carpet. "You want eat? Here, take." She thrust the bowl at her.

"Oh, no. That's not what I meant." Kate pulled her father's old money pouch from the deep pocket of her dress and plucked a few coins from its depths. "I'm out of flour. Out of everything, really." She offered the coins to Mei Li. "Our new supplies haven't arrived yet, and I thought perhaps you'd sell me some—"

"No. No sell." Mei Li squatted beside a beat-up trunk. "You borrow." She lifted the lid and inside Kate spied a surprising array of foodstuffs, some of them wildly exotic. A game bag hung above their heads. Mei Li grabbed it and drew a fat hare from its depths. "Here, you take."

"Oh, no. I couldn't."

"Yes. You take." Mei Li thrust it at her. "Crockett replace tomorrow."

It did look good. She'd hardly eaten a thing the past few days. She'd sold most of their remaining flour and other grains from the last wagonload. And she couldn't really remember the last time she'd eaten meat. Panama, perhaps. "You're sure?"

Mei Li gave her the hare, along with an armload of other items from the trunk. "Go home. Cook for husband. He work hard."

He *had* worked hard. In fact, Will had done everything she'd asked of him. "Thank you. I'll replace the meat tomorrow, and the rest of the goods as soon as—"

"When driver come."

Kate smiled. She felt lucky to have the girl's friendship in such a wild and unfriendly place as Tinderbox. Back home, Kate's best friend had lived next door. She was older and married with two small babes.

Kate reminded herself that she was married now, too.

Mei Li pulled Will's jacket around Kate's shoulders and pushed her out the door. Squinting into the blackness, she called after her. "It dark. Bad men out. You run."

Aye, it *was* dark. Like pitch. No moon, not even a bit of starlight breached the angry mass of storm clouds raging overhead. The downpour had dulled, at least, to a light, steady rain. If she was careful, she wouldn't get too wet on the walk back.

Only a few campfires twinkled on the wooded ridge surrounding the town. Most of the transient miners had moved on to their claims in the foothills. Kate knew they'd be back when their supplies ran out. She was counting on it.

Crudely painted white letters, proclaiming a ramshackle patchwork of boards and tin Mustart's Livery, stood out in the dark. She slowed her pace, her gaze washing over the words. Mei Li had told her what they said, along with all the other signs in Tinderbox.

Will had seen plainly that she couldn't read. It shouldn't have embarrassed her, but it had. It still did. If he'd been anyone else she wouldn't have cared. But there was something about him—a certain edge of sophistication hiding under all that buckskin and fur, and the way her illiteracy had seemed to shock him—that had made her feel small and out of place.

She'd wanted to learn to read but was never able to take the time away from her chores for schooling. Perhaps she could learn now. Oh, the things she'd read if she could!

"Nice night, ma'am."

The disembodied voice startled her nearly out of her skin. Kate froze in her tracks. "Who's there?"

"Just us," said another voice, this one behind her. She spun toward it. "No need to be frightened, ma'am." The man stepped closer, and she squinted into the blackness to make him out.

"Jed Packett, ma'am."

"And Leon."

Landerfelt's men. Her heart beat the tiniest bit faster and her mouth went dry. The Packetts had done nothing concrete to incite her fear. All the same, panic gripped her so tight she could barely breathe. On instinct, she sidestepped out of the circle they seemed to be closing around her. "G-good evening, gentlemen."

"Looks like ya got a load there." The dark shape that was Jed Packett sloshed toward her in the mud. "Let me help."

She grasped her bundle tighter. "No, I'm fine. Truly."

"Aw, come on, Miz Crockett," Leon said, closing in. "All's we want is to—"

A revolver's hammer clicked behind her, and Kate froze. The Packetts stopped dead in their tracks.

"Evening, boys."

The familiar voice registered in Kate's mind, and she breathed again.

Will moved up beside her in the dark, slipping a possessive arm around her shoulder. "All you wanted was to…?" She could just make out the glint of polished steel in his hand, and wondered where he'd gotten the pistol.

"Nothin'," Jed said. The brothers inched backward. "Just sayin' g'night, is all."

Will's arm closed tighter around her. "I've got something I'd like to talk to you boys about. Tomorrow."

"Fine, Will. Tomorrow, then." The Packetts didn't wait for any customary parting words. Jed sloshed down the street toward Landerfelt's Store, dragging his brother with him.

Kate drew a breath of cool night air and audibly exhaled.

"You okay?"

"Aye."

"Here, let me take those." She heard the revolver's hammer click back into place. Will stuffed the weapon under his belt and grabbed the armload of goods from her.

"Thank you."

"What the hell were you doing out here alone, anyway?" He started for the cabin, and she followed.

"I was just getting some things for supper—from Mei Li's."

"Damned stupid. You should have waited for me."

"I—I guess I should have, but—" She nearly had to run to keep up with him. Mud sucked at her soaking boots.

He stopped short in front of the storefront, and she nearly collided with him. The rain had stopped, she realized. All at once a sliver of bright moonlight peeked through the breaking clouds.

Will's expression was hard as stone, his eyes black as coal. "Don't ever go out alone at night again. Understand?"

His gaze was riveted to hers, and had she wished to look away she would not have been able. In this light, in this place, he looked as dangerous as the Dublin thugs back home who murdered men in their sleep for a few shillings or a sack of food.

Kate nodded her compliance. "All right."

He grabbed her arm and pulled her up the steps to the store. "Come on, *Mrs. Crockett.* Let's eat."

Will sat at the table, skinning the hare with his buck knife, and watched Kate sort through the groceries she'd brought back with her.

Damn fool woman. If he'd known she was going to go traipsing all over town in the dark he would have stopped her. She arched a fiery brow at him as she peeled a couple of turnips, as if she knew exactly what he was thinking.

"I went to Mei Li's." She flicked the peelings into a bowl, then shot a quick glance at the wet floor and his clean shirt steaming by the stove. "What a mess you've made."

He shrugged. "You should have stayed and helped me."

For an instant their eyes met, and he perceived a warring host of emotions raging behind hers. Against her will her cheeks flushed crimson, but he could see her grit her teeth behind those tightly pressed lips.

She hacked at the last turnip and promptly changed the subject. "Where did you get those?" She nodded at the new wool britches he was wearing, and the flannel shirt.

"Borrowed 'em from the store's stock."

Again she glanced at his shirt dripping by the stove, and he'd stake his life she was wondering what he wore under the borrowed clothes. Nothing, in fact. And the new wool made him itch like hell.

"You'll have to replace them tomorrow," she said curtly. "And that hare."

"Fine by me." He'd borrow Mustart's shotgun. He needed to bring in some meat, anyway. And he could use the time alone. He wasn't used to spending this much time with anyone, least of all a woman. It was a nuisance having to look out for her, but he'd given his word, and he wouldn't go back on it.

For a split second, out there in the dark, when he saw the Packett boys creep up on her... Will swore silently under his breath, resisting the jumble of random emotions pressing in on him.

"Hmm?" Kate looked up from her work, an absent, faraway look in her eyes. Her hair had come undone again from her jaunt in the rain, and a few damp tendrils clung to her freckled face.

For a moment he could almost imagine she was really

his wife. The kind of wife he'd thought he married the first time. The kind who loved her husband.

"Nothing," he said, and slapped the newly skinned hare onto the cutting board before her.

She snatched the buck knife out of his hand and proceeded to cut the meat into incredibly small pieces.

"Quarter it," he said. "Or cook it whole."

"Whole? You're daft."

He noticed she'd set a pot of water on the stove to boil. The frying pan was still hanging on the wall, and the flour she'd borrowed sealed tightly away in a tin.

"This rabbit will feed us for half a week at least. Longer if we stretch it with turnips."

"Half a week? Half an hour you mean. I could eat the whole thing myself in one sitting."

She shot him a pithy glance. "Aye, I expect you could." She tossed a spare handful of meat into the pot along with the turnips. "Over my dead body."

He fought a smile that came out of nowhere. Watching her bustling about between the stove and the table, he thought of his short life with Sherrilyn.

Her short life, he reminded himself. His smile faded.

Sherrilyn had hated the frontier, had hated him for dragging her West. They'd had plenty of money at first, but she'd gone through it the first month. He recalled their lavish hotel meals, the food she'd ordered but hadn't touched because she said it was badly prepared or of poor quality.

Kate looked hard at the turnip peels that, in Sherrilyn's world, would have gone into the trash. She bit her lip, considering, then tossed them into the pot along with the rest of what was to be their meal.

A meal that Will would never forget.

"You're not eating," she said a few minutes after she'd

ladled a helping of the boiled meat and turnips into his bowl.

He pushed the muck around with a spoon. The hare was tough as shoe leather and the turnips mush. He hadn't seen her use even a pinch of salt, let alone any of the fragrant herbs Mei Li had given her.

He watched as she sipped the weak broth and picked gingerly at a few bits of meat. "So, this is the kind of thing you eat back home in Ireland."

"Lord, no. We rarely had meat as fine as this. When we did, it was usually a bit of lamb that Michael bought with extra wages." She shot him a half smile. "Or that Sean had pinched."

"Michael and Sean. Your brothers?"

"Aye. Along with the twins, Patrick and Francis." Her eyes sparkled in the soft lamplight. "But we call him Frank."

"You miss them."

A softness he'd not seen before washed over her features. She looked uncharacteristically fragile to him all of a sudden. "I do," she said.

Will listened as she related a story about how the five of them had once surprised their father on Christmas with a leg of lamb they'd bought with their savings.

"A whole leg! From the butcher in Entwistle Street. Can you imagine?" She put down her spoon and waited for his reaction.

At first he didn't answer. He was recalling another Christmas, years ago in Philadelphia when he was a boy, shortly after his own father had made his fortune.

The Clearys had lived under them in a basement flat for as long as Will could remember. Dennis Cleary had been just his age. They were best friends until Will's father bought a house in a posh section uptown.

After that, Will wasn't allowed to see Dennis anymore. Dennis wasn't the *right sort* of boy, his father had said. The Clearys weren't the right sort of people for them anymore.

Meaning they had no money.

Looking at Kate, he realized he'd been wrong about her intentions. She was nothing like Sherrilyn. How could she be?

"No, I can't imagine," he said at last.

Pushing the onslaught of memories from his mind, he grabbed their bowls before Kate could take another bite of the awful stew. "But I can imagine a better supper than this dreck."

"Dreck?" She followed him outside and let loose a tirade of cuss words he didn't even realize she knew as he poured the contents of their bowls into a rusted tin pail Dennington had used to feed stray dogs.

"Vickery's hound'll love it, if he can get to it before the coons do."

"Vickery's—" Kate reached for the pail, and he caught her hand.

"There's plenty of food, Kate." He looked at her in the moonlight and read a desperate sort of panic in her eyes that he'd seen there once before, on the first day he met her.

Her hand was rough, chapped from water and hard work, and seemed so very small in his. "Trust me," he said. "The woods are full of game. I'll hunt tomorrow. Besides, the wagon will be here soon with more grain than we could eat in a year."

She looked into his eyes, and he knew she struggled to believe him. Until tonight he hadn't realized how far off the mark his first impressions of her had been. He squeezed her hand and willed her to hold his gaze. "There's plenty of food, Kate."

Slowly she drew her hand away, and he could tell from the way she absently smoothed her hair and straightened her dress that she was embarrassed. "All right then."

He held the door open for her and followed her back inside.

She shot a backward glance at the pail. "But Vickery's dog best get here quick. That stew wouldn't last a minute on a stoop in Clancy Street."

"Speaking of Clancy Street, didn't your mother ever teach you to cook?"

"Of course she did."

"Could have fooled me." He grabbed the frying pan off the wall, a tin of flour and the last of the butter she'd been hoarding all week. "Bring me the rest of that meat."

"Oh, so you're going to cook now, are you?"

"*Aye,*" he said, mimicking her Irish brogue. "I'm going to cook."

She stood by him at the stove, arms crossed, a skeptic's smirk and an arched brow conveying her disbelief. "Well, this I've got to see."

"Pull up a chair, Kate, and prepare to be amazed."

She *was* amazed. And stuffed as a Christmas goose.

Kate cleared the last of the dishes from the table and carried them out to the back porch where Will was finishing the washing up.

The rain had dulled to a light drizzle, and pockets of starry sky peeked at her through the fast-moving clouds. The porch was awash in moonlight, the air cool and thick with the scent of wet pine. All her senses came alive, and for the first time in months she felt relaxed.

She told herself it was this wild and beautiful place that

stirred her blood, that her feelings had nothing to do with the man standing beside her washing dishes.

"Truly, Mr. Crockett," she said to him. "I've never tasted anything so good. Well, except for Michael's leg of lamb."

"Tell me about him."

"Michael?"

"All of them. But Michael first." She handed him the frying pan, and he swished it around in the pail of dishwater. "He was the one your father sent for. Why didn't he come?"

She wondered when he'd get around to asking her that. No one had asked, up until now. Not even Mr. Vickery. "Michael couldn't come. I wouldn't let him."

"*You* wouldn't let him." Soft lamplight streamed through the cracked door onto the porch, illuminating Will's amused expression.

"That's right. And with good reasons."

"Such as…"

"A new job, a new wife and a babe on the way." Already born, she realized. Oh, how she'd love to see the wee thing. "Surely you don't propose he should have left them?"

"No."

"He'd wanted to bring them, but—"

"No, you're right." His voice had an edge to it Kate had never heard before. "You made the right decision."

Had she?

Will handed her the frying pan, and she dried it, wondering how her brothers were faring without her. They had Michael's wife, Hetty, to care for them now. But the girl was young and a bit fragile in Kate's estimation, and had her own wee babe to look out for.

"You're sorry now, aren't you?"

"Hmm?"

"That you came. That you…" She looked up and caught a hint of remorse in Will's dark eyes. "That you married me."

Listening to the sound of the rain on the tin roof of the porch, her mind raced over the events of the past week. Had she to do it all over again, decide a course of action, she honestly didn't know what she'd do.

"No, Mr. Crockett, I'm not sorry."

He stared at her, silent, and for all the world she wondered what he was thinking.

"Are *you?*"

He shifted on his feet, and she could tell by the sudden stiffness in his demeanor that he was uncomfortable with the question. She felt embarrassed and wished she hadn't asked it. It was clear to her what his answer would be.

He tossed the dirty dishwater off the porch and nodded toward the dark stand of trees spread out behind the cabin. "It's a hard life here. No place for a woman."

She nodded, recognizing this was his way of sparing her feelings. He *was* sorry he'd married her, but he was too much of a gentleman to say it. His response was a polite confirmation of his distaste for the whole situation.

Regardless, her pride got the better of her. "Not nearly as hard as at home," she said.

"You can't mean that."

"I do mean it. What do you think I do all day in Dublin, Mr. Crockett? Sit on my behind and sip tea and eat bonbons from a fancy tin?"

"I don't know. Maybe. Some women do."

"Perhaps the women you know."

His face twisted into a scowl, and she feared she'd struck a nerve with her retort. Mr. Vickery had told her Crockett's wife had been well-to-do.

Obviously Will Crockett knew nothing of her life back home. She wondered what her father had told him of her. There was no imagining. When Liam Dennington had a few pints under his belt, he was prone to notorious story-telling, much of it made up.

Still, Crockett's attitude irked her. "Besides," she said, "there are plenty of women here, and children, too." None here in town, perhaps, but she'd seen several on the long wagon ride into the foothills.

"Miwok and Chinese, you mean."

"Aye, mostly."

"It's different for them."

"Is it now?" She'd never heard anything so daft. "Why? Mei Li works all day. I work all day. And at night she takes care of her family." Kate was separated from her family, but she would take care of them if they were here. "She cleans and cooks. And I clean and—"

They both heard the distinctive wheezing of John Vickery's fat corgi as it barreled around the corner of the cabin and made straight for the pail of Kate's rabbit and turnip stew.

"Cook?" He arched a brow at her.

She slapped the wet dish towel she'd been absently wringing across the porch railing to dry. "It's a sin to waste food like that." She watched, disgusted, as the corgi inhaled the stew. "There might have been hungry children at the Chinese camp would have liked it. Did you think of that?"

"I don't think—"

"Aye, that's the God's truth." The man was impossible! She jerked the cabin door wide and started inside.

"Wait a minute."

"Do you know what it's like to watch a child starve to death, Mr. Crockett?" She crossed herself, remembering a grindingly poor family who'd lived across the street from them in Liffey Quay. "Or die in the cold winter from lack of a decent roof over his head?"

He grabbed her arm and she spun toward him, sick of his manhandling, her free hand already balled in a fist. Her breath caught in her throat as she saw the stinging fusion of pain and rage shining in those coal-black eyes of his.

"Yes, I do know. I know exactly what it's like." His grip tightened around the soft flesh of her arm, and for a moment she feared he was really going to hurt her.

Their eyes locked, his darting briefly to her readied fist, as if daring her to strike him. With a shock she realized he wanted her to do it. Lord, he *did*. But the anguish she read in his face unnerved her and made her wonder if his motive was something beyond having an easy excuse to rough her up.

"Then," she said quietly, "you know why I was upset about the stew."

His grip loosened, but she made no move to extract herself from his control. "I—I'm sorry," he said. He released her, and she spent an awkward moment tidying her hair and smoothing her skirt as he locked the back door. When he turned toward her, he was in control again, eyes hard, jaw tight.

She didn't know how or why they'd come to angry words, but she suspected it was her own doing. "It's my fault. I provoked you. I've always had a fierce temper. It's best you know about it now."

"Doesn't matter. We'll be out of here in a couple of weeks."

"Aye, I suppose we shall." She should thank God she had a way out, a way home. Home was where she belonged. Not here in the wilderness, wed to a man she hardly knew. "Good," she said.

"My sentiments exactly." He grabbed his dry clothes off the chair back by the stove and one of the blankets from the pile on her bed. "If you need me…" He paused in the shadowed doorway leading into the dark store.

She nodded, understanding that again he was just being polite. She made ready to extinguish the lamp, then remembered something. "Mr. Crockett," she said on impulse.

He turned, his face half in darkness, half in light. It suited him, she thought. He was, after all, a man surrounded by no small amount of mystery.

"Who was the child? The one who died."

He stood there, silent, watching her, his expression stone. Her heart pulsed steady in her chest, the rain on the roof echoing its beat. Somewhere in the distance a dog barked. Mr. Vickery's corgi, no doubt, his vigor renewed from a belly full of stew.

Resigned to Crockett's silence, and intrigued by the past he seemed so intent on guarding, she extinguished the lamp and moved blindly toward the bed.

To her surprise, he continued to stand there in the doorway, soft moonlight lending a ghostly cast to his hardened features.

"Dennis Cleary," he whispered in the dark. "My best friend. He was the child."

Chapter Seven

Time away from her should have done him good.

It didn't.

He'd only worried about her, alone in the store all day. Will maneuvered his horse down the steep, manzanita-and-pine-choked ridge above Tinderbox, snaking his way back to the cabin. He'd left before dawn that morning, anxious to get an early start on replacing the game Kate had begged from Mei Li two days earlier.

Foul weather had kept him from venturing out sooner, but today he'd woken to clear skies and a thin crust of frost on the ground. It reminded him that winter wasn't far off, and the last ship of the year would leave San Francisco for Sitka in three weeks' time.

Two good-size pheasants swung from his saddle horn. A borrowed shotgun, a steady hand and a bit of luck had insured they'd have something decent to eat for the next couple of days. He'd have taken a deer or a pig if he'd seen any, but he hadn't. Maybe next time.

Will reached into his pocket to retrieve the painted miniature of Kate, and studied it for the third time that day. Even away from her, she was still in his mind.

And under his skin.

A fragile sort of peace had settled in the narrowing chasm between them. A chasm that, for a score of reasons, Will was determined to keep from closing all together.

Their candid conversation of two nights ago hadn't been repeated in the days since. All the same, he had an unsettling feeling that Kate's understanding of him had grown in that time.

He'd gotten to know her better, too, despite his wish not to. She'd surprised him in any number of ways. But most surprising of all was her matter-of-fact acceptance of her fate, of the poverty she'd grown up in and was determined to return to, as soon as she made enough money for her fare.

He didn't understand her at all.

The town was in sight. He made out Vickery's cottage on the opposite hillside, smoke curling black from the chimney and twisting a lazy path across the reddening sky. Sunset came early this time of year. He urged Dennington's gelding faster.

Dan Dunnett's raspy voice made his ears prick as he unsaddled the horse and tethered it to a pine behind the cabin. The supply wagon was finally here. About damned time. Will had just about resigned himself to the fact that Dunnett had broken his word. Good thing for Dan he hadn't.

He rounded the corner of the building and saw that the wagon was nearly empty. Kate flashed him an annoyed look as she toted a heavy sack of flour toward the store. He moved to help her, but Cheng beat him to it. The old man was surprisingly agile for his age.

Will shrugged at her. "Looks like you're doing fine without me. Wagon's almost unloaded." He raised the dressed pheasants, expecting her praise.

She didn't even acknowledge them. "We just started. Mr. Dunnett only arrived a moment ago."

"What?" He followed her inside, scanning the half-empty shelves of the store. Nothing new had been brought inside except the bag of flour Cheng deposited behind the counter. "Where's the rest?"

"There isn't any more. What Dunnett brought is in the wagon." She arched a fiery brow at him, as if it were his fault.

He shot back out to the street. "Dunnett!"

"Yo. Over here."

Will spotted him kneeling beside one of the wagon's wheels. "Where's the rest of the shipment? If you've sold it to Landerfelt, I swear to God, I'll—" He jerked Dunnett to his feet.

"Whoa! What the—"

Ignoring Dunnett's protest, Will hauled him to the middle of the street, prepared to give him the beating of his life.

"That's all there is, Will! I swear it!" Dunnett threw up his hands in defense. "I went to the fort, like always. But most everything I usually get was already sold."

"Sold? To whom?"

"Merchants."

"You're lying." There weren't any merchants in Sacramento City. At least none big enough to buy out half the goods traded at Sutter's Fort.

"He's right." Kate's hand lit on his shoulder. "I heard it this morn from the blacksmith."

"Two men from back East," Dunnett said. "Huntington and… Who the heck was the other one?"

"Hopkins." Kate continued to glare at Will until he released his hold on the wagon driver.

"Yep, that's the one," Dunnett said. "Buying up everything. Waitin' on their own shipment, too. Comin' by clipper, folks say.''

Will grunted. He'd actually met Collis Huntington when he was a youth. The businessman had spoken at Will's school, and afterward had been entertained by Will's father in the parlor of their Philadelphia town house.

He bit off a silent curse and balled his fists at his sides, surveying the paltry contents of the wagon.

"It doesn't matter," Kate said, and pushed past him to continue with the unloading.

"It *does* matter."

"Mr. Dunnett's promised us another load straightaway. Only this time he'll meet the river barge on the levee. Hang the fort—he'll go straight to the source." She shot him a haughty look. "It was my idea."

"That's not the point." Will jerked the last sack of grain from the wagon and hauled it inside.

Kate dogged his steps. "It's a good plan. If the weather holds, God willing, we'll have new supplies next week."

"Merchants." He ripped his buck knife from its sheath and slashed open the grain sack. "Swindlers more like it."

"You're in a foul mood." Kate nudged him aside and planted a measuring scoop into the dried barley.

"And you're not?"

She shrugged.

"We'll never get out of here at this rate."

"Of course we will. We'll just have to work harder."

He watched as she arranged the rest of what Cheng brought in from the wagon into a surprisingly nice display. Nothing seemed to daunt her. She took it all in stride: the recent foul weather, competition for salable goods, even Landerfelt's threats.

She was tenacious as hell, he'd grant her that.

His anger cooled.

"There." She stood back and surveyed the neatly arranged shelves. "'Twill do for now."

A wisp of auburn hair strayed across her freckled cheek, which was flushed ripe as an autumn apple from the cold. Without thinking, Will brushed it off her face.

"It'll do," he said.

For a moment their eyes met, and he found himself wondering what it would be like if she were really his wife. Not just in name, but in all the things he'd once thought possible between a man and a woman.

Her blue eyes widened, almost imperceptibly. He could swear she'd read his mind.

"Finished!"

They both jumped at the sound of Cheng's voice, and the moment was lost.

"Aye, right." Kate composed herself and turned quickly toward him. "My thanks, Mr. Cheng. Oh, and wait—" She retrieved one of the pheasants from the counter where Will had dropped them, and offered it to the old man. "To replace the hare."

Cheng held the bird aloft and grunted satisfaction.

"Thank you, too, Mr. Crockett." She glanced at the other pheasant lying on the counter. "And...you'll show me a proper way to cook it, I trust."

"Yeah, sure." He paused. "Mrs. Crockett."

Kate met his steady gaze. Letting his guard down, he smiled. She blushed, and this time he knew it wasn't from the cold. Before he had time to think about what it meant, she had dashed outside again.

Will watched her through the storefront window as she thanked Dan Dunnett for the load. The wagon pulled away, horses snorting and livery clanking. Kate shaded her eyes against the brilliant sunset and watched it as it rumbled down the street.

"Your wife is an unusual woman," Cheng said.

A thousand reasons why he should resaddle the horse and get the hell out of there pronto flashed across Will's mind. All of them vanished as Kate Dennington Crockett turned toward the store and smiled at him through the glass.

They hadn't had a customer all day. Until now.

Kate hopped off the stool behind the counter and smiled cautiously at the Indian woman staring through the window at an infant's matinee jacket perched on one of the store's half-empty shelves.

Kate pointed at the jacket and nodded her head.

"Uh-oh," Mei Li said.

"What's wrong?" Kate cast the Chinese girl a quick look as she pulled open the front door. "Come in. Please." She waved the Indian woman toward her.

"Miss Kate, you cannot!" Mei Li said.

"Why not?"

The Indian woman hesitated. It was then Kate noticed she wasn't alone. A Miwok man moved up beside her and placed a protective hand on the woman's shoulder. Her husband, if Kate had to venture a guess.

Both were dressed in soft-looking deerskin and moccasins, the woman's double-fringed apron elaborately decorated with bits of seashell and colored rock.

She'd seen many Indians on her journey to Tinderbox, but had never had the chance to speak to any of them. She'd take that chance now. Besides, they might have something interesting to trade.

"Won't you come in?" She gestured to the open door. "We've got grain and tinned goods and—"

"Hold it right there!"

Kate looked past the Miwok couple to see Eldridge Landerfelt jogging toward them from across the street, rifle in hand.

"I told you," Mei Li whispered, inching closer. "You in big trouble now."

A high-pitched squeal startled them all.

The Miwok woman's hands flew to the shoulder straps of what Kate had thought was a rucksack. The woman turned her back to her husband so he could tend to—Lord, it was a babe!

The wee thing was wrapped in soft furs and strapped to the Miwok woman's back. What a clever idea. The infant began to squall in earnest, his tiny arms flailing. On impulse Kate reached out to quiet him.

"What the hell do you think you're doing?" Landerfelt skidded to a halt in the dust, his rifle leveled at all of them.

The Miwok man stepped quickly in front of his wife and child, into Landerfelt's line of fire.

"Go on," Landerfelt said, and gestured with his gun. "Git!"

The Miwok man glared at him for a long moment, then took his wife's arm.

"Wait a minute," Kate said. "You don't have to leave if you don't wish to."

"The hell they don't."

The infant's cries grew louder. Landerfelt winced. The Miwok woman looked frightened, her husband angry.

"Come inside, Miss Kate." Mei Li tugged at her arm, but Kate ignored her.

"They're my customers." Kate looked pointedly at Eldridge Landerfelt, then smiled at the couple. "Please, you're very welcome to come inside."

Men gathered in the street—the blacksmith, some miners Kate recognized, and Jed and Leon Packett. Where the devil was Crockett when she needed him?

The Miwok man looked hard at her, and Kate gestured again to the open door. Finally he nodded.

Landerfelt flicked the hammer back on his rifle and glared at the Miwok man. "One step, boy, and—"

"And what?" Will appeared in the open doorway behind Kate, his revolver cocked and pointed directly at Landerfelt's chest.

Kate sucked in a breath.

"Go back inside." He flashed her an angry look.

"These people," she said, ignoring his demand. "I think they'd like to trade for—"

Will grabbed her arm and jerked her backward, nearly off her feet. "I said go back inside."

Mei Li shot past them into the store. Kate's face grew hot with rage. Her arm burned from Will's viselike grip. What, did he think her a child? That she couldn't decide for herself whom she would serve and whom she would not?

She knew very well why Eldridge Landerfelt was standing in the street pointing a weapon at the unarmed Miwok family. Indians weren't allowed to do business in Tinderbox. Nor were they allowed to bear arms anywhere in the territory.

They were stupid laws. As ridiculous as the one that prohibited Kate from owning her own business, which is what got her into this whole mess with Will Crockett to begin with.

"Fine," she said, and wrenched out of his grasp. "I'd thought you were different from the likes of him." She flashed her eyes at Landerfelt, then back to Will. "It's clear you're not.'' She brushed past him into the store, then thought better of backing down. She whirled on him.

His face turned to stone. His eyes grew icy black, as menacing as she'd ever seen them. The Miwok couple stood frozen in the street, the husband's gaze riveted to Will. Landerfelt hadn't moved a muscle. His rifle was still cocked, his expression cool.

In a move that stunned her, Will grabbed the matinee jacket from the shelf behind her and thrust it toward the Miwok man. He said something to him in his own tongue. After a moment, the man accepted it, nodding. He handed the tiny garment to his wife, who clutched it to her chest as if it were made of gold.

Landerfelt's scowl deepened. Will held his pistol steady, trained on the merchant's chest. He said something else in Miwok that Kate couldn't understand, but from the tone of it, it sounded like a farewell.

The Miwok nodded again, responding in an even tone. He shot Landerfelt a steely glance then turned away, pulling his wife with him.

Kate breathed.

The couple moved down the street toward the edge of town, and the blacksmith and miners who'd paused to watch went about their business as if nothing had happened. Only Jed and Leon Packett remained in the street, edging up behind their employer.

''Best keep that little wife of yours in line, Crockett.'' With a gentle click, Landerfelt released the firing mechanism on his rifle.

Will said nothing, but Kate could feel his wrath. She wasn't certain who it was directed at. He holstered his revolver, turned on his heel and leveled an angry look at her as he brushed past her into the store. He was gone out the back before she had the presence of mind to react.

This was not how she'd expected her day to go.

Landerfelt smiled at her, slung his rifle over his shoulder and sauntered back across the street, Jed and Leon Packett in his wake. The brothers looked around at her as she closed the door, and a premonition of something evil coiled inside her.

"You crazy, you know that?" Mei Li shook her head, muttering something in Chinese.

Kate plopped down on the stool behind the counter. "Aye," she said. "I must be."

Another day gone, and only a handful of miners had made purchases in the store. Landerfelt's business had fallen off, too, despite the fact that he had more to sell.

The weather was turning again. Will swore as he glanced at the white sky and turned the fur-trimmed collar of his buckskin jacket up against the wind. It would be at least a week before Dunnett returned from Sacramento City.

Kate joined him outside on the street, a wicker basket in hand. "Can you mind the store for a bit? I won't be gone but an hour."

He eyed her cloak and well-worn gloves. "Where are you going?" It wasn't like her to leave the store in the middle of the day.

"Up the hill." She nodded at the forested hillside above the town, where Vickery's cottage peeked out from thick stands of pine and madrone. "For berries. Mei Li says there are lots of them, just on the other side, in a sunny spot where the trees thin out."

He knew the place. It was nearly a mile from town, and the hill was steep. "It's too far. Besides, the weather's turning."

"Looks as good as any day in Ireland to me." She

pulled her cloak tight and buttoned it at the neck. "And a good stretch of the legs will do me good."

"It's too late for berries. They'll all be gone by now."

"I guess I'll find out, won't I?" She shrugged and started up the street.

Damn her! Just once, he wished she'd listen to him. Yesterday when Landerfelt had threatened her and the Miwok couple, Will practically had to drag her back into the store to keep her from getting her head shot off. She had no idea just how dangerous that situation had been. Had she persisted, and had he not been there...

Christ, he couldn't watch her every minute, could he?

She shot him a backward glance from up the street, not missing a step. So, she expected him to stop her, did she? Well, he wasn't about to. Let her slog up that hill alone and see how she liked it when she got to the top and found nothing but dried brambles picked over by birds. It might even rain. It would serve her right if she got soaked.

He kicked wide the half-open door to the store and marched inside, slamming it behind him. The brass bell flew off its hook and clanged to the floor.

What was wrong with him?

She wasn't really his wife. It was a simple business arrangement, nothing more. He wasn't responsible for her. Or for anyone. That's how he liked it. That's how it had to be.

His gaze flicked across the shelves, over rows of gold pans, bags of flour and rice, across to the carefully folded stacks of women's and children's clothes.

Will couldn't look at them.

He swore under his breath, grabbed Dennington's rifle and locked the storefront door. Thirty seconds later he was out the back and saddling the gelding that grazed in the small enclosure he'd constructed for it just beyond the cabin.

On his way down the street he saw Landerfelt chatting outside the livery with a slick Hangtown moneylender, Brett Zundel, who leaned casually against the building whittling big curls of pine off a piece of scrap wood with his knife. It was no secret Landerfelt owed him money. Big money, to hear Matt tell it. Zundel flashed him a disinterested look as Will trotted past.

It didn't take him long to catch up to Kate.

Will maneuvered the gelding up the ravine on the opposite side of town and reined him to a halt beyond a fat pine, about fifty feet from where Kate had stopped to chat with John Vickery. Their conversation didn't last long. After a few minutes the lawyer tipped his hat to her, and Kate continued up the hill.

"Afternoon, Mr. Crockett," Vickery said, as Will guided the horse up the slope in Kate's wake a minute later.

Will nodded.

"I had wondered where Miss—er, Mrs. Crockett—was going all alone, and so close to dark. There's been talk of a grizzly out near Spanish Camp giving folks trouble."

Will had heard the rumors, but Spanish Camp was miles from Tinderbox. "Berries," he said, and kept moving.

"Oh, right. Berries." Vickery cast him one of his annoyingly nervous little smiles. "Well, uh…very good, then. I'll, uh, just be…"

Will didn't wait for the lawyer to finish his sentence. He clicked his tongue and the gelding picked up speed. Kate proceeded up the hill at a brisk pace, not looking back. A moment later Will lost her in the trees.

Didn't matter. He'd cut right, across the slope, and meet

her at the top. He didn't want her to see him. Not yet. He was curious as to how she'd do on this little—what had she called it?—stretch of the legs.

It was sure to be that. The slope was so steep even the horse was having trouble. Will leaned forward in the saddle and urged him up the hill.

Kate Dennington might have come halfway across the world on her own, but that had been different. She'd traveled with an older couple as escort for most of the journey—so Mei Li had told him. True, she'd braved San Francisco on her own, and had made her way to Tinderbox unharmed. But traveling by riverboat and buckboard manned by seasoned guides and crowded with other passengers was one thing. Traipsing off alone in the California foothills was another.

At the top of the ridge he dismounted and proceeded on foot, leading the gelding along a game trail to the small clearing where he thought Kate would emerge from the trees.

"What the—?" To his astonishment, she was already there.

Quickly he tethered the gelding where he stood and crept forward. Kate hadn't seen him. She set the berry basket on the ground and clutched a spindly madrone as she caught her breath.

The sky overhead grew dark, and it wasn't because the sun had gone done. Another storm was on its way. Will could smell it on the wind whipping at the fringed hem of his buckskin jacket.

He moved silently along the ridgeline below Kate, just inside the cover of the trees. Twenty feet. Ten. Wind rustling the last of the crisped autumn leaves clinging to oaks and madrones covered the crunch of his footfalls.

When he could almost reach out and touch her, he

stopped. She stood an arm's length in front of him, still as a statue, her arm looped lazily around the madrone, her cheek pressed up against its smooth, dappled surface.

She was looking at something. Or someone.

He followed her gaze across the clearing spread out below them on the other side of the ridge. Just as Mei Li had promised, a tangle of elderberry bushes choked the hillside.

Will did a double take.

The Chinese girl, her skullcap missing and her waist-length, jet hair free, stood in the clearing twisted in Matt Robinson's awkward embrace.

Kate clutched the madrone tighter, her gaze riveted to the lovers. When the two kissed, her knuckles went white. Will allowed his own gaze to travel slowly over Kate's features. That wild auburn hair, which he knew was soft. Her trim waist and lush hips.

He found himself wondering, not for the first time, if she was a virgin. Remembering their one kiss, the ripe blush of her freckled cheeks, the fusion of shock and interest he'd read in her eyes when she'd seen him naked.

Kate Dennington was untouched. He was sure of it. The day they'd married he'd thought her unschooled kiss was feigned. Looking at her now, he knew it wasn't.

Will inched closer.

A heady blend of lavender water and soap invaded his senses. Wisps of loose hair danced in the wind on the nape of her neck. He wondered what she'd taste like if he kissed her there.

A gust of wind slapped him in the face, and he jolted out of his stupor. What the hell was he thinking? He shouldn't be having these feelings. Not here, and not for her. Cool raindrops on his face shocked him to his senses. On impulse he grabbed her arm.

"Jesus, Mary and Joseph!" Kate jumped like a startled kitten and whirled toward him.

"Whoa! It's just me."

The panic in her eyes iced to anger as she recognized his face. "Of all the—" She jerked out of his grasp and thumped his chest with a fist. "What the devil are you doing creeping up on me like that?"

"I wasn't creeping, I was just—"

"Following me. Why?"

He started to speak, then thought better of it. Why had he followed her?

"Well?" She crossed her arms over her chest and arched a fiery brow at him. The wind whipped at her hair and cloak. He'd never seen her look more beautiful.

For the briefest second, he knew why he'd come, and so did she.

"It's…" Struggling for an explanation, he nodded toward the clearing where Matt and Mei Li continued to kiss, oblivious to the rain and their presence. "It's them."

"Them?"

"Yes, them. You've got a put a stop to it. The townspeople won't stand for it." It was true. They wouldn't.

Kate's eyes widened. "*I'm* to put a stop to it? I'll do no such thing. He's *your* friend. You put a stop to it."

"Me? As if I could. That little vixen down there—"

"Mei Li has nothing to do with this. It's *his* fault." She gestured toward Matt. "Everyone knows it's men who…who…"

"Men?" A hundred tiny incidents from his first marriage crashed across his consciousness. Sherrilyn had taken seduction to a new art form, had used it to manipulate him from the very beginning.

"Aye, men!" She thumped his chest again. "The sisters taught me all about it. How—"

"The sisters?"

"Aye, at St. Stephen's, back home. Our parish priest says that when a man gets the devil in him, there's no tellin' what he'll do."

"Oh, so it's the devil, now?"

"Aye." She tipped her chin at him. "And don't be actin' like you don't know what I mean."

He knew exactly what she meant.

An overpowering urge to kiss her charged every nerve in his body—past reason, past all concern for consequences and far past restraint.

"To the devil, then," he said, and pulled her into his arms.

Chapter Eight

Never had she dreamed of such a kiss.

Kate gave herself up to Will's crushing embrace and, in a haze of desire and confusion, opened her mouth to his questing tongue.

His hands were everywhere. Cupping her behind, stroking her back, pulling her tight against him. No matter that she wore three layers of wool, her body responded to his touch as if he stroked her bare skin.

His scent intoxicated her—a heady rush of leather and wood smoke and sweat. His tongue was hot glass, his lips commanding. The roughness of a day's beard growth burned her face, but she didn't care.

Her arms slid easily around his neck, and her cloak, which she'd unbuttoned during the climb, slipped to the ground. Somewhere at the edge of her awareness, she realized it was raining. Will lifted her off her feet and backed her against the tree.

Icy raindrops pelted her face, cooling her skin but not her ardor. Will groaned as he rolled his hips into hers, spreading her legs with the motion. Thunder cracked overhead.

"W-wait." Her eyes flew open as she felt the hard length of him press against her.

Lightning flashed. His eyes were slits, his expression a feral union of power and desire.

"Stop," she breathed, and pushed weakly against his chest. God help her, she knew she didn't mean it.

Will's body went rigid, as if heeding her command of its own accord. He opened his eyes, blinking against the rain. The wind whipped at his long, dark hair.

Their gazes locked, and in that moment Kate knew what it was to want a man, to crave his touch, his kiss, the feel of his body hard against her own.

"Sorry," he said, and eased her feet to the ground, releasing her. He raised his palms in a gesture of apology, his eyes darting from hers, as if he were suddenly embarrassed.

A flurry of erratic feelings twisted inside her. This wasn't supposed to happen. He was a stranger, their marriage a sham. *In name only.* That was their bargain. He had plans, and she, obligations. In little over a fortnight they'd quit this wild place, never to see each other again.

Why, then, did her stomach twine into knots as he backed away from her?

"I—I'll get the horse." He ran a hand through his hair as rain sluiced down his face.

"You go on," she said. "I'll walk back."

Another flash of lightning lit the darkening sky.

"You're soaked. Wait for me."

"I'm fine." She snatched her cloak and the borrowed basket from the ground. "Besides, Mei Li and I can—" She glanced at the clearing where the couple had stood not a minute before. "They're gone."

"They're smart." Will cast her a hard look. "Wait here. I'll be right back."

The second he disappeared into the trees, she fled down the hill. Not because she didn't want to ride double with him on the gelding, pressed up against him, clutching him tight.

But because she did.

Two minutes later Will cut her off, reining the horse directly into her path. Kate had no choice but to stop.

"I told you to wait."

"Aye, but—"

"Get on." It was an order, not a request. He held a hand out to her, his expression stone. The passion she'd read in his eyes just moments ago had vanished. She felt like a fool.

"Put your foot in the stirrup—" he slipped his own booted foot out of it to make room for hers "—and I'll pull you up."

She obeyed, and a second later plopped onto the gelding's back, her wet skirts twisted beneath her. It was anything but comfortable. Before she had a chance to adjust her position, Will kicked the gelding into action.

Kate swore.

She looped her arm through the basket and held on to him as gingerly as possible, affording herself just enough leverage to keep her seat.

In silence Will maneuvered the gelding down the hill toward town, his demeanor icier than the weather.

The rain continued into the next afternoon. Will counted four days since Dan Dunnett had hightailed it back to Sacramento City for another load of goods. No telling when he'd return.

Not that it mattered. The brass bell overhanging the store's front door hadn't sounded all day. The whole town, in fact, was dead quiet. Too quiet.

Will watched as Kate counted the coins in Dennington's old cash box for what had to be the fourth time in as many hours. Her fingers flew over the carved ivory beads of the abacus Mei Li had taught her to use.

"Well?" he said, and snorted. "Has it miraculously doubled since you last counted it?"

She shot him a pithy glance, and proceeded to reweigh the gold dust she kept secreted away in the leather pouch in the pocket of her dress.

"We'll never get out of here. Not at this rate." He strode to the window, restless, and looked out on the empty street.

"There's enough to get us both to San Francisco, and nearly enough for part of one sea passage. But that's all."

He didn't want to think about it.

"We'll sell the horse in the city, and my father's rifle, too. With that, we'll have—"

"Give it a rest, Kate."

"I'm not giving up."

He turned on her, primed with a snide retort, but the fire in her eyes stilled his tongue.

"We've a bargain," she said, and slammed the lid of the cash box closed. "I mean to hold you to it, Mr. Crockett."

Twenty-four hours ago he'd held her in his arms, had kissed her with a hunger and a ferocity he hadn't realized he'd been leashing until that moment.

And she'd kissed him back. Willingly. Wantonly.

But today it was back to Mr. Crockett, and skirting around each other, being polite, taking care not to meet the other's gaze. As if it hadn't happened.

He wished to hell it hadn't.

"I don't go back on my word," he said evenly.

She arched a brow at him, her way of saying she didn't

trust him. She was right not to, he supposed. If he had any kind of sense, he'd saddle the horse, grab the cash and go.

A cynical grunt formed in his throat. He didn't have any sense. That was the problem. If he had, he wouldn't be here now. He'd be halfway to Sitka, a free man. No ties. No responsibilities weighing on his mind.

She flashed a glance at him, wondering what he was thinking. Watching her tidy up the counter, he ran a hand across his smooth chin. He'd shaved that morning, and now he asked himself why. Was he hoping for a repeat of yesterday's excitement?

Kate busied herself around the store, and he allowed his gaze to follow, drinking in her features. Those down-soft lips, freckled cheeks, the curve of her neck as she reached for a tin resting on a high shelf.

There was nothing remarkable about her looks. At least that's what he kept telling himself. All the same, he felt an uncomfortable tightness in his groin as he watched her.

By accident she brushed a pile of neatly stacked garments to the floor. Will was there in a second, stooping to retrieve them. She knelt at the same moment, and their hands brushed in the exchange.

Neither of them moved.

Her face was inches from his, her lips parted, her breath soft and warm on his cheek. Her eyes widened ever so slightly. He looked into their sea-blue depths and knew if he kissed her now, he wouldn't want to stop.

"Tell me something," she whispered.

At that moment, he'd tell her anything she wanted to hear.

"Why did you do it?"

"Do what?" He inched closer, aware of her rapid

breathing, the acceleration of his own heart rate, of the tension wound so tight between them it threatened to snap.

"Give over the wee jacket to the Miwok man." Slowly Kate drew the stack of fallen garments—baby clothes, he realized—from his grasp. She rose, and he with her.

A jumble of raw emotions gripped his gut, constricting his throat. He started to answer, then thought better of it.

"It was a good and decent thing you did, Mr. Crockett. For the babe, I mean."

He turned away and stared out the window, eyes unfocused, a barrage of dark memories blasting across his muddled mind.

"You were married before," she said matter-of-factly. Will didn't answer. "Mr. Vickery told me. He said that your wife—"

"She died."

"Aye, he told me that as well. I'm sorry."

He fisted his hands at his sides, remembering the flat white light of the winter sky on the day it happened.

"She…" He shook his head, then spun on her. "The frontier's no place for a woman—or a baby." Kate jumped as he jerked the tiny garments out of her hands and stuffed them onto a high shelf, out of her reach.

"So you've said before."

He stormed across the room, then turned and started to pace. "Damned this weather! No wonder we've had no business."

"The frontier's really no different than anywhere," Kate said, ignoring his change of topic. "Aye, there are strange animals, deadly weather and other dangers. But illness can strike a man, or a woman, anywhere. What happened to your wife could have happened—"

Will froze and leveled his gaze at her.

Kate's mouth clamped shut.

"Mention her again and the deal's off."

Shock registered on her face.

Before he could say more, the bell over the storefront door jingled to life, startling them both. Kate smoothed the skirt of her dress and quickly turned to greet the customer.

"Mrs. Crockett."

Vickery.

Will snorted. Perfect timing. He was ready to wring the lawyer's twiggy white neck. Somehow Vickery had found out he'd been married before, and that his wife had died. Will didn't have to think hard to figure out who'd told him.

"Oh, good day, Mr. Crockett." Vickery looked almost surprised to see him. "Still here, I see."

Will grunted.

Vickery carefully closed what had to be the only umbrella for a hundred and fifty miles, and tucked it under his arm next to a parcel wrapped in oilskin. "Just this morning I was speaking with your friend Mr. Robinson, and—"

"The two of you are damned chatty these days, aren't you?" He planned to wring Matt's neck while he was at it.

"Mr. Robinson and I? Well, yes, I guess—"

"Forget it." Will started for the back room, thinking to grab his slicker, saddle up the horse and go for a hard ride. To hell with the weather.

"I—I'm just here to remind you about tonight."

Will turned.

"Oh…yes. That's right! I nearly forgot." Kate moved toward him, forcing a smile. "Mrs. Vickery's returned. We're invited to supper this evening."

"Supper?" He stifled a groan.

"Aye. Yesterday afternoon as I passed their cottage, Mr. Vickery mentioned it to me."

Vickery nodded, with a measure of enthusiasm that seemed overdone, given Will's icy reception of him. Kate nodded, too, and clasped her hands together, waiting for his response.

"You go ahead. I'm going out for a while. Don't know when I'll be back." He started to turn and caught the disappointment in Kate's eyes.

For a moment no one said a word. He wondered how long it had been since she'd sat down to supper in a real house, with another woman for company.

He swallowed the curse forming in the back of his throat and exhaled. "What time?"

Kate's face lit up.

"Seven o'clock," Vickery said, and smiled.

"We'll be there!" Kate walked the lawyer to the door, and held his parcel while he opened the umbrella.

"Oh, I nearly forgot." Vickery nodded at the oilskin-wrapped package in her hand. "That's for you, from Mrs. Vickery."

"For me?" Kate shook it, grinning like a child on Christmas Eve.

From across the room, Will narrowed his eyes at the mysterious gift. "What is it?"

"Oh, it isn't much, really. Just something Gladys can't use anymore. She thought Ka—er, Mrs. Crockett—might like it."

"Thank her for me, will you?" Kate clutched the package to her chest. "And please do call me Kate."

"Thank her yourself, tonight." Vickery opened the door, the brass bell sounding his departure. "Seven o'clock, then."

"Aye, on the dot." Kate closed the door, then whirled

toward Will, still clutching the gift. "Do we have a time-piece?"

"Jesus, Mary and Joseph!"

Kate wrestled with the hooks of her corset, which she'd relaced three times before it felt snug enough, given the tight-fitting lines of the two-piece gown laid out on her bed.

Mrs. Vickery's present.

Gingerly she ran a hand over the shimmering, midnight-blue silk, not believing for a moment the gown was a castoff, as Mr. Vickery had implied. What woman in her right mind would give up such a treasure?

She slipped into the cambric-lined skirt, then the stiff bodice, and fastened as many of the tiny hooks that ran up the back as she could reach. Perhaps she'd don her cloak, run up the street and ask Mei Li to fasten the rest. The sky had cleared, and it promised to be a fine night.

Will had gone down to the blacksmith's. Something about beaver traps he'd lost to Landerfelt in the incident with Cheng. He wanted to buy them back, she supposed, to take with him to Alaska. Not that they could afford to buy anything right now.

Footfalls sounded on the back porch.

He was back!

The storefront door was bolted, and Will had made her lock the back door as well when he'd gone out. She'd draped the one window in the cabin's living space and couldn't see out to the porch, but she recognized Will's familiar knock.

"Just a minute," she called, and hastily retwisted her hair into a knot and pinned it on top of her head.

There was no looking glass. Not that she'd ever had one at home in Dublin. All the same, she wished for one now. She had no idea how she looked, and it was the first time in her life she'd ever worn an evening gown.

She suspected her father would roll in his grave if he saw her like this. Her brothers would probably laugh. As her hand closed over the back door latch, she peered down at her breasts, pushed high from the tightened corset and half-bared in the sinfully low-cut gown.

"God forgive me," she breathed, adding another rosary to the penance she'd yet to start on.

"What's the hold up?"

She sucked in a breath and yanked wide the door.

Lantern light spilled onto the porch, illuminating Will's face. He never finished the sentence. Kate stood rigid, waiting for his reaction, watching his expression change from annoyance to surprise to something else all together as he swept his gaze over the lines of the gown.

"Is it awful?" she said, unable to contain her anxiety.

She held the door open and he nearly tripped into the room, his eyes darting from her bosom to her face, then back to her bosom again.

"It is, isn't it?"

He started to speak, then stopped.

"I'll have to wear it, regardless. Mrs. Vickery gave it to me."

"That's…what was in the package?"

Kate nodded. "I know I don't do it justice. All the same, I—"

"No. No, it looks fine on you."

He was probably just being polite again. She was suddenly embarrassed. Their gazes locked, and she felt a slow heat radiate from his eyes, which had gone a warm chestnut-brown in the lamplight.

All at once she recalled his hands on her, stroking her

back, grazing her breasts, molding to the curves of her behind. Perhaps he wasn't being polite at all.

"I...I couldn't manage all—" she gestured to her back, struggling to get the words out "—the hooks."

She felt her cheeks blaze as she turned her back to him, unable to hold his simmering gaze a second longer. For a moment, he didn't react, and she thought perhaps he would refuse to help her. Then she felt his fingertips graze her bare back as he gently fastened the remaining hooks in place. Her skin prickled with anticipation.

"There," he said. "All done."

She couldn't bear to face him yet, and busied herself clearing up the oilskin wrapping and string strewn across the bed. "What do you plan to wear?" she said absently.

"Who, me?"

"Aye." She wound the string into a tiny ball and placed it and the oilskin on one of the shelves over the stove.

"What's wrong with this?"

She turned and surveyed his garments: greasy buckskin trousers, flannel shirt, and his well-worn fringed and fur-trimmed jacket, which he took off and hung on a hook by the door.

"That's fine for everyday. But I thought, perhaps, since..." She looked down at the fine silk dress, then immediately dismissed the thought. "You're right. It doesn't matter. What you've got on is grand."

"You want me to change?" He moved toward her, studying her face, making her more uncomfortable than she already was.

She shook her head. "No. Besides, you've nothing else to wear."

He nodded at the door leading to the darkened store.

"I could borrow something from the inventory. Like last time."

"True. But don't dress up on my account. It really—"

"Just give me a minute." He lit another lamp and strode toward the store, flashing her a half smile before he pulled the door closed behind him.

It was the shortest minute of her life. While he was gone Kate pulled at the bodice of the gown, trying to work it higher. No good. It wouldn't budge. She hiked up her skirts, making certain her dark wool stockings were fastened tight, then smoothed the blue silk over her legs again.

This was all a bad idea. What, did she think she was Cinderella going to the ball? Yesterday she'd all but let him take her right there in the woods. In the rain. And now tonight, here she was, parading around in front of him in a wicked dress, her breasts thrust up like ripe fruit ready to pick.

"How's this?" Will stepped into the room, working a tie around a stiff collar pinned to a white shirt. He wore black trousers, which fit a bit tight around the hips. Struggling with the tie, he tossed a matching black suit coat across the bed.

"Here, let me help you."

Her father had never worn a tie in his life, but Kate had seen shop girls tying them on manikins in high-priced store windows in Dublin's Grafton Street.

"I've got it," Will said.

To her astonishment, he tied it perfectly on the very first try. And with no looking glass to guide him. She approached him slowly, marveling at the way he took on the air of a gentleman in the new clothes.

"You're not really a fur trapper, are you?"

"What?" He'd been preoccupied with the tie, and hadn't noticed her scrutiny until just now.

On impulse she took one of his hands in hers and ran a finger over his scarred palm. He allowed it, though she felt him tense under her touch.

"From the traps?" she said, tracing the line of a scar running the length of his forefinger.

"Yeah. What of it?" He narrowed his eyes a bit, and the warmth she'd seen in them moments ago iced over.

"And this?"

He flinched as she ran her finger across the wicked-looking scar on his cheek. He moved her hand away, his jaw tight, his lips thinning to a hard line.

"Was it a bear? A fight, perhaps. Aye, a fight."

His expression grew increasingly wary, and Kate knew she'd struck a chord in him. Since the day she'd met him, she'd had the strangest feeling he was something more than the man he made himself out to be. His discomfort fueled her curiosity and made her overbold.

"But not here in the wild. In a pretty drawing room somewhere. Say…Philadelphia."

The murderous look in his eyes startled her. Unconsciously she stepped back.

"You don't know what you're talking about." He ripped the tie from around his neck and hurled it to the floor.

She'd been wrong to prod him like that. She was sorry, now, that she'd done it.

"I'll take you to Vickery's on the horse. And the loose-tongued bastard can walk you back himself."

"But—"

He grabbed her arm and pulled her toward the back door. "Come on. Where's your cloak?"

"Let me go!" She jerked out of his grasp, her own anger rising.

"Damned supper parties. I came out here to get away from them, not—" He stopped, swearing under his breath, and batted at the garments hanging on pegs near the door, apparently searching for her cloak.

She saw it lying on the chair by the table and snatched it up. "I'm sorry if I reminded you of your old life. I didn't mean to make you angry."

"I'm not angry. I'm just not going."

"Fine. I understand."

"No, you don't."

"Aye, fine then, I don't." She'd learned not to argue with him when he was in a foul temper. She wrapped the cloak around her shoulders, wishing she'd never brought the subject up. "But I won't be carried to the Vickerys' and dumped on their doorstep like a child. I'll walk, thank you, and I'll be perfectly fine on my own."

"The hell you will."

"You swear too much." She strode to the bed, reached under the mattress and yanked out her father's pistol.

"So do you."

"Me?" She turned on him.

"Watch that thing." He nodded at the six-barrel pepperbox. "Yes, you. On the horse, yesterday."

She remembered. "That was *your* fault." She pocketed the pistol and made for the door.

"It's dark. You're not walking over there alone."

"Watch me," she said, and didn't look back.

Chapter Nine

She didn't understand him at all.

Kate stormed down Main Street in the dark, cursing herself for not thinking to carry a lantern. No matter. The night was clear and cold. Stars flickered in the velvet sky, and a splash of moonlight lit her path.

Behind her she heard a door slam and the brash tinkling of a bell. Will meant to follow her. That was grand. Let him.

At first, his chivalry had thrilled her. But now that she knew him better, she realized his protective behavior wasn't fueled by any particular feelings he held for her. He was simply being a gentleman. And gentlemen didn't allow women to dash off unaccompanied on a dark night in a place as wild as Tinderbox.

In her heart she felt strangely disappointed.

She marched on toward the edge of town, passing the clearing where they'd married, and where young Father Flanagan said the mass on Sundays if the weather was good. Behind her she heard the sucking sound of Will's boots in the mud.

She turned onto the path leading down into the ravine and out again, skirting the miner's camp near the graveyard where her father was buried, and where she'd first asked Will Crockett to marry her.

The Vickerys' cottage lay just up the hill. Warm lantern light peeked at her through thick stands of trees. Kate quickened her pace.

As she climbed out of the ravine, skirts hiked to her knees to protect her gown, a branch snapped to her left. She froze, remembering what she'd heard about bears and other dangerous creatures. A shape lurched toward her in the dark. A second later, her father's pistol was in her hand.

The shape stopped dead, wheezing.

A rush of heavy footfalls, snapping twigs and the unmistakable click of a Colt revolver, told her Will was right behind her. His hot breath on her hair a second later confirmed it.

The shape hiccuped loudly.

Will yanked her behind him and leveled his revolver at the man.

"Howdy, Will," the shape said, and hiccuped again. "Miz Crockett."

Kate blinked to adjust her eyes as the man tripped forward, wavering on his feet. She breathed in the strong odor of whiskey, sweat, and other awful smells that made her nose crinkle.

"Son of a—" Will clicked the revolver's hammer back into place. "Is that you, Floyd?"

Kate took a step back, covering her mouth and nose with her hand.

"Uh…*hiccup*. Yep. It's me."

Floyd Canter was one of the local miners who seemed to be permanent fixtures in Tinderbox. Kate had no idea how these men lived. They didn't appear to be doing any mining, only drinking and card playing at the nightly game Mei Li's father ran at the Chinese camp.

"Go to bed, Floyd," Will said. "You're drunk."

Kate pocketed her father's pistol. Before she could proceed up the hill, Will's hand closed over her arm like a vise.

"Come on," he said, and pulled her along with him.

She knew better than to argue with him. All the same, she refused to be treated like a child. "I didn't need your help. It was only Floyd."

"Next time it might not be."

His stride was longer than hers by half, and she had to practically run to keep up with him.

"I have a weapon and I know how to use it."

Will snorted and stepped up his pace, practically dragging her up the hill. Her cloak caught on downed branches. At one point she stepped in a hole and nearly lost her footing. Will's grip on her tightened.

As they reached the cottage, Kate dug her heels in and jerked her arm backward against his grip. "For pity's sake, stop!"

To her surprise, he obeyed.

"Just let me catch my breath a bit."

The light from the Vickerys' cottage illuminated his hard features and those dark eyes she knew had the power to both heat her blood and chill her heart.

"So," she said, "what's it to be, then?" He released her and she felt the circulation return to her arm. "Are you stayin' to supper or not? I want to know before we get to the door."

They both turned at the sound of rattling hardware coming from the Vickerys' front porch. A bright wash of lamplight illuminated the surrounding woods as the cottage door opened.

"Mr. and Mrs. Crockett! Look, John, they're here!"

Kate squinted against the light silhouetting the enormous woman wedged in the doorway. The mystery of why John Vickery's wife could no longer use the elegant silk evening gown was solved.

"Do sit down." Gladys Vickery indicated two chairs opposite each other at the small dining table Kate remembered from her first night in Tinderbox under the Vickerys' roof.

She marveled at the table setting. Never in her life had she eaten off a table draped in cloth, white linen at that. China and silver sparkled. Crystal goblets reflected the candlelight. Perhaps she was Cinderella after all.

"I'd hoped that gown would suit you, and it does. You look lovely in it, my dear." Mrs. Vickery beamed. "I haven't been able to wear it for years now."

Kate wondered that she'd ever been able to wear it at all. Even on Kate it was tight. She couldn't imagine even a young Mrs. Vickery squeezing into it.

"It's too dear, really, Mrs. Vickery. After tonight I'll return it to you."

"Oh, gracious, no. I won't hear of it. It's yours now."

Kate thanked her for her kindness.

Will beat them all to the table and, to Kate's surprise, he pulled out a chair for her to sit down. There'd been a tense moment on the front porch when she wasn't certain if he intended to join them for supper or not. Stealing a glance at him as she settled into the chair, she could see that he was resigned to the evening, though clearly not happy about it.

Mr. Vickery hung up Kate's cloak and joined them at the table. Will held out Mrs. Vickery's chair for her, too, and it creaked as she sat. Kate stifled a smile as he tried, in vain, to scoot the enormous woman closer to the table.

Squinting at Will behind his spectacles, Mr. Vickery said, "Don't fret about it, Mr. Crockett. It would likely take three of you to move her."

"Oh, John!" Mrs. Vickery let out a titter, apparently not offended by her husband's remark.

Will mumbled a gracious response and took his seat.

"Well now, here we all are!" Mrs. Vickery swept her napkin into her lap and Kate followed her lead. The food was already laid out under covered dishes, and in a whoosh of passing plates and clanking silver, Mrs. Vickery doled out large portions to them all.

The food looked marvelous, and Kate was starved. Will seemed to relax a bit now that they were here and seated. She didn't understand what all the fuss had been about. The Vickerys were nice people, and it was generous of them to invite Will and Kate to share their food and finery.

"The very moment I returned from San Francisco," Mrs. Vickery said, "John told me about your arrival, and that you and Mr. Crockett had married."

Kate smiled at her. "Aye, it all happened quite fast. You see, I had no idea my father had…"

She'd tried not think about his passing, had fixed all of her energy on getting home. But tonight as she'd passed the graveyard on her trek up the hill, Kate was reminded of how much she'd loved her father, despite all his faults.

"We were all so sorry." Mrs. Vickery lifted a fork and pointed it at a pile of mashed potatoes. "Mr. Dennington was a fine man. As is Mr. Crockett." She flashed Will a tiny smile. "I'm so glad you two found each other. And so quickly, too!"

"Well, I didn't really have a ch—"

"Oh, do try the butter beans. I carried them all the way from San Francisco in my bag."

Will sat silent, his expression unreadable. Mr. Vickery shot Kate a tight smile, then poured them all a tiny bit of wine. Mei Li once mentioned that the Vickerys made it themselves from the elderberries up on the ridge.

Kate grasped her fork, then stopped. There were *two* of them. Why on earth were there two forks? She couldn't tell which one Mrs. Vickery was using to shovel mashed potatoes into her mouth.

She looked to Will for help, raising her brows in question while discreetly fingering each of the forks at her place setting. Will grabbed the outermost fork at his place and nodded once to her. Kate followed suit.

As they ate, Mrs. Vickery jabbered on about every imaginable topic. Her trip to San Francisco, the progress of the railroad, rumors of new gold strikes and how much she loved it here in California, despite the hardships.

Kate marveled at how comfortable Will seemed with all the finery. He grasped his crystal goblet with authority, used each piece of silver as if he normally ate with a half-dozen utensils instead of one or two.

The black wool jacket and snow-white shirt suited him. He'd apparently retrieved the tie he'd shucked off in the cabin. It fit snugly around his starched collar, finishing the ensemble.

His jet hair was combed back off his face. Kate remembered running her fingers through it when he kissed her yesterday on the ridge. He seemed an entirely different man tonight.

Will glanced up and caught her staring. His eyes swept over her figure, lingering for a second on her breasts. Perhaps he wasn't so different, after all.

"The royal-blue suits her eyes, don't you think, Mr.

Crockett?" Mrs. Vickery paused her fork in midair and waited for Will's response.

Kate met his gaze and waited, too. For all the world she wondered what he was thinking.

"Yes," he said evenly. "It does."

Mr. Vickery forced a smile, Mrs. Vickery tittered in delight, and they went on with the meal. When their plates were clean, Mr. Vickery whisked the dishes away, dealt clean ones like a deck of cards, and Kate discovered what the second fork was for.

"Raw greens," Mrs. Vickery said, unveiling another dish. "It's French, you see."

Kate had never been to France, nor had she ever in her life eaten raw greens. She was already full, but continued eating so as not to upset their hosts. Will didn't miss a beat.

A half hour and several additional helpings later, just as Kate was concluding that Mrs. Vickery might never stop eating, the woman put down her fork and said, "Have you chosen any names for children yet?"

Will's face drained of color.

"Ch-children?" she said.

"It's never too early to plan these things, you know."

"Gladys," Mr. Vickery said, "I don't think—"

"We weren't blessed with any ourselves. It would be so nice to see little ones scampering around town."

Will drew himself up in his chair, his back stiff, his expression hard. He'd barely said a word all evening. This was three times now that talk of infants or children seemed to agitate him.

"Gladys," Mr. Vickery said again, this time emphasizing each syllable.

Mrs. Vickery looked from her husband's pointed expression, to Will's stony one, then back to Kate. Clearly the woman had no idea of the circumstances under which Kate and Will had married. Mr. Vickery must not have told her. Either that, or she chose to ignore the facts.

"You do want children, of course?" Mrs. Vickery said.

Kate felt suddenly overwarm in the small room. Will was staring at her, waiting.

"Aye. Of course I do. It's just that…"

"John tells me you have four brothers, and that you're the oldest."

"That's true," Kate said, thankful for a reprieve from the topic.

"Well, then, you've had plenty of practice raising young ones."

Desperate to change the subject, Kate said, "Michael's the eldest boy. He's married now. Then there's Sean, and the twins, Patrick and Frank."

"Twins! How wonderful."

"Y-yes," Mr. Vickery said. "Your father told me all about them."

Kate looked down at the fine china place setting and crystal goblet tinged pink from the Vickerys' elderberry wine. "I miss them," she said. "More than anything."

"Oh, of course you do, dear!"

"No." She shook her head. "You don't understand."

None of them did. How could they? They were here, free, in a world of their own making. And she was here with them, sipping wine in a fancy dress, while Michael and Sean slaved in a damp, Dublin storehouse for wages they'd have to split with their mother's sister until Kate returned with the money to pay off their debt.

"They should come here, to California," Mrs. Vickery said. "To live here with you and Mr. Crockett. Why, when the store gets going, you could build another—"

"It's late." Will drained his wine goblet and returned it to the table. "We'd best get back."

"Yes, you're quite right." Mr. Vickery scrambled for his pocket watch. "Oh, dear me, yes. Nine o'clock. Time for bed."

"No, don't leave yet!" Mrs. Vickery wrapped her sausagelike fingers around Will's wrist. "I haven't told you the most interesting news of all."

Mr. Vickery's spectacles slipped down his nose as he frowned at his wife. Under the table Kate felt the lawyer's foot kick outward. Mrs. Vickery squealed.

The exchange wasn't lost on Will. "What news?" he said, gently extracting the woman's fingers from his wrist.

"You won't believe it! There's a new bank to be chartered in San Francisco. On Montgomery Street, right near the wharf."

Mr. Vickery kicked her again. Kate felt the whoosh of his boot under the table. Mrs. Vickery ignored him.

"You'll never guess the name of the banker. It's the oddest coincidence." Mrs. Vickery looked pointedly at Will. "They say he's terribly rich. And he's come all this way from…Philadelphia, I think, just to open a bank."

Will's lips thinned. He rose from the table, crushing his linen napkin in his fists. Kate rose with him. Mrs. Vickery prattled on as Will strode to the door and retrieved Kate's cloak. He handed it to her and she quickly put it on.

"Thanks, Vickery," Will said to the lawyer, who dogged their steps out onto the porch.

Mrs. Vickery was still struggling to get up from the table, when Kate turned to wave goodbye.

"Don't you want to know the name of the banker?" she called after them.

Kate turned to Will, but he'd already vanished into the night. She saw him pacing amidst the trees just below the cottage, waiting for her to join him for the walk back to town.

Chapter Ten

Philadelphia businessman Coldwell Crockett opens doors on San Francisco's newest bank...

Will ran a finger over the smudged print of the letter sheet Matt Robinson had begged off a mule team driver who'd passed through town at dawn.

A single page printed on both sides, the letter sheet was the frontier's answer to a newspaper. Passed from hand to hand, they were often months old by the time they arrived in Tinderbox. This one was dated a week ago.

Will crushed the sheet into a ball and tossed it into the creek.

"It's true, then." Matt wiped his brow with a gloved hand and settled on a nearby log. "Vickery's wife was right."

Will jerked his ax free of the stump he'd been using to split firewood and continued hacking spindly branches off a downed madrone. "Makes no difference to me."

"No?"

Will swung the ax with a vengeance and nearly took his own foot off as the blade shattered the madrone into pieces the size of matchsticks.

"Could have fooled me."

He shot Matt a warning glance but knew it wouldn't do any good. In a nagging contest with a score of seasoned biddies, Matt Robinson would win hands down.

"He's your father—and rich as Midas, ain't he? Why not just ask him for the money?"

Will checked his swing at the last second, the ax poised in midair.

"Just a thought." Matt shrugged.

Will had thought about it, too. All night in fact. He'd lain awake on his bedroll in the store, listening to Kate's erratic breathing, the sounds of her tossing and turning in a fitful sleep.

Last night when Mrs. Vickery had asked her about her brothers, the pain he'd read in her eyes nearly undid him. At that moment he would have done anything to have sent her home, or anything to have kept her. He wasn't sure which.

He finished the stroke and cast the ax aside. "Stop thinking, Matt, and start loading wood onto the skid."

"Nope. You're on your own there." Matt rose and yawned. "Time I hightailed it back to the claim. Been in town too long."

"Town? Down at the Chinese camp, you mean." He worried about Matt's infatuation with Mei Li. Nothing good could come of it. Not in a place like Tinderbox.

"Maybe." Matt grinned. "You oughtta come back to the claim with me. Offer's still open, you know."

"No thanks."

"Suit yourself. But your bride ain't no closer to gettin' home than she was when she got here. And you ain't no closer to Alaska."

Will ignored the comment and backed the gelding up to the skid.

"Where is she, anyway?"

"Kate? Down the clearing at Flanagan's church service. Hang on, boy." Will clipped the gelding's livery into place.

"It ain't a church service, it's a *mass*."

"I know what it is." He'd gone once or twice with Dennis Cleary when they were boys.

"Them Irish Catholics sure got some strange customs."

"And the Chinese don't?"

Matt grinned. He mounted his horse and reined him east toward the claim he'd staked three weeks ago. "See ya, partner."

"Watch your back out there."

"Always do." Matt dug his spurs into his mount's side and disappeared up the hill into the trees.

A half hour later Will was still loading the skid. And still no closer to a decision about what to do. Time was running out.

A branch snapped on the hill below him. He whirled in the direction of the sound, his hand poised an inch from his holstered revolver.

"It's just me."

Recognizing Kate's voice, he relaxed. She climbed the last few feet to where he was working, picking her way carefully around granite boulders and downed tree limbs.

He had a sudden image of her in the midnight-blue gown, her breasts thrust high and half-bared, her waist nipped in, her hips lush and round. She'd been a vision. He'd had a hell of a time keeping himself from staring.

Still, he preferred her this way, in her plain wool dress, her auburn hair loose, her cheeks flushed ripe as cherries from what she'd call a good stretch of the legs.

"You shouldn't be up here," he said as he shucked a glove off and wiped the sweat from his brow.

She stopped to catch her breath, surveying the skid, the gelding and the pile of split wood. "I can help."

Every day they spent together, Will felt the weight of his convictions lessening. Up until now, the only women he'd known well had been either fortune hunters or those so delicate they'd never survive the kind of life he intended to live. Sherrilyn had been both. Will swallowed hard, remembering. Kate Dennington was, perhaps, neither.

And that scared the hell out of him.

"I don't need help," he said, and jammed the glove back on his hand.

"Everyone needs help at some time or other."

He eyed her, wondering what she meant. The gelding fidgeted, and the skid shifted on the hillside. Kate grabbed the bridle to still him.

Watching her take in the scenery, absently stroking the gelding's neck, breathing deep of the fresh air, Will could almost believe she belonged here, that she loved wild things and wild places as much as he did. That she was cut out for the kind of life he meant to lead.

But last night in the dark on the way to Vickery's cottage, when a man sprang at her from the brush, Will's breath had seized up in his chest. It didn't matter that it was only Floyd Canter three sheets to the wind and harmless as a flea. It could just as easily have been one of the Packetts or some other unsavory character intent on doing her harm.

Will ground his teeth remembering that split second of panic when he wasn't sure if he could reach her in time, and if he did, if he'd be able to protect her.

"That man Mrs. Vickery mentioned last night," Kate said, wrenching him from his thoughts. "The banker."

Will's gloved hand froze on a length of firewood. "What about him?"

"He's from your home, isn't he? Philadelphia."

"What of it?"

Kate shrugged. "I just wondered if you knew him. You seemed…agitated when Mrs. Vickery brought it up."

"No. I was just ready to leave."

"Ah."

He knew she didn't believe him, but he let the lie stand.

"You never speak of your family."

"No reason to mention them." He positioned the last armload of firewood onto the skid and looked around for the rope he'd brought to tie it down with.

"Here," she said, retrieving it from behind a stump. "Tell me about them."

"Who?"

"Your family."

Why did she care? What did it matter? Her prodding irritated him. "My mother's dead. I was an only child. There's nothing more to tell."

He tossed the rope over the skid. To his surprise, Kate caught it with one hand. She secured the load as if she was used to such things, using knots any seaman or teamster would be proud of.

"And your…father?" she said.

His gaze flew to hers.

"Are you very much like him?"

Her expression was open, her eyes wide. It was likely an innocent question. But maybe not. He reminded himself that his first wife had mastered just such a look when it suited her purpose.

It dawned on him that Kate might have known all along Coldwell Crockett was his father. Maybe she'd seen his bank when she passed through San Francisco three weeks ago. Maybe she'd even met him.

He recalled their conversation the night she'd asked him to marry her. He'd asked her why. Why him? *It must be you,* she'd said. *You and no other.*

A dozen possibilities occurred to him. All of them made his gut twist. She stood beside the gelding, eyes wide, her face flushed and innocent, waiting for his answer.

"No," he said tersely. "We're nothing alike."

He snatched the gelding's reins out of her hand and mounted. Kate seemed mildly surprised when he didn't immediately offer her a hand up.

"I…I'll walk back," she said.

"You do that." Will dug his heels into the gelding's side. As he maneuvered the skid down the hill, he could feel her eyes on him.

He never looked back. He wasn't even tempted.

The man was completely unpredictable.

One minute he'd dog her every step, refusing to let her out of his sight unescorted. And in the next breath he'd vanish as if he didn't give a whit about her.

Kate started down the hill, following the path the skid had carved in the damp earth, pondering the events of last night and this morning.

Clearly, any mention of Will's past irritated him. Her first week in Tinderbox, Mr. Vickery had told her it was rumored his father was someone influential, a politician or a wealthy banker.

A Philadelphia banker.

Newly arrived in San Francisco.

It seems Mrs. Vickery had hit the nail on the head. Kate's own instincts and what she'd witnessed of Will's behavior confirmed in her mind the truth of it.

Yet she couldn't imagine what circumstances would drive a banker's son west with his new bride to take up a life as a fur trapper.

No. Will had been adamant. *We're nothing alike.*

Unless there had been some falling-out between father and son. Such things weren't uncommon. Her own brother Michael had not been on the best of terms with their father when Liam Dennington had sailed for America. Michael accused him of abandoning them, but Kate hadn't seen it that way at all.

Kate had understood her father's dream of a better life for them all. But not Michael. He was the practical one. More like their mother. Cautious, and disapproving of anything risky.

As she tromped down the hill in Will's wake, Kate wondered what Michael was doing now, this very minute. She liked to think of him home with his wife and child, sitting down to Sunday dinner with her brothers. A dinner as fine as the meal she'd had last night.

Now there was a fantasy. Sunday or no, she knew Michael—and Sean, too—would be working. Likely for next to nothing. There would be no Sunday dinner. Not tonight, not next week or next month. Not until she returned with coin enough to reimburse her mother's sister the loan.

Kate's fists balled so tight her nails dug into her palms.

Dragging her from her thoughts, Will's voice, calm and sure, carried through the trees below. She saw him as she approached the creek behind the cabin, talking to the gelding as he shooed him into the corral he'd built last week.

Will didn't see her, and began unloading firewood from the skid onto the back porch. On impulse Kate paused in the shadow of a pine and watched.

He dropped his suspenders and peeled off his shirt. To her surprise he wore nothing underneath. Her gaze trav-

eled the chiseled lines of his darkly furred chest, and fixed
on the hardened muscles of his back and arms as he hefted
load after load from the skid. She'd felt those arms around
her, and had a dizzying recollection of his strength
and heat.

Will Crockett was a hardworking man, and an honest
one. He'd done everything she'd asked of him, and more,
without complaint. She knew he didn't have to. Nor was
he obliged to stay with her, beyond the fact that he'd
given his word.

But he had.

And it shocked her to realize it wasn't gratitude she felt
twisting her stomach into knots. It was something else.
Something she'd felt yesterday when he kissed her, and
again last night when his gaze had washed over her body
in heated waves. She couldn't name the feeling. It was
something raw, visceral, beyond admiration or desire.

Without warning, Will looked up from the skid and
caught her staring. Their gazes locked, and all at once
Kate knew what the feeling was.

In the chill gray hour before dawn, Kate woke to the
sounds of boot scuffs, creaking floorboards and the squeak
of the back door opening and closing again.

Blinking the sleep from her eyes, she sat up in bed and
shivered. The fire in the potbellied stove had gone out in
the night, and it was cold as a tomb in the cabin.

She could hear Will moving around on the back porch.
Swiveling out of bed, she grabbed her shawl from the
nearby chair and touched a toe to the cold floor. Lord, it
was ice!

What on earth was Will doing up so early?

Kate tiptoed to the window, lifted the drape and peered
out. As her eyes adjusted to the dim light, she saw him,

standing just inside the corral saddling her father's gelding.

There was no telling what he was up to. He'd hardly spoken to her since yesterday morn when she'd met him on the hillside to offer him help with the firewood.

Her questions about his family—his father, in particular—had angered him. He'd spent all of yesterday afternoon in silence, finishing small tasks around the cabin and store, fixing odd things that were damaged or broken.

Will closed the corral gate and led the gelding to the back porch, where his bedroll and a loaded saddlebag sat waiting. The edge of a tin gold-pan poked out of the top. A shovel and a short sledgehammer she recognized from the store's inventory were already tied across the gelding's rump.

With a shock she realized he was leaving.

Not bothering to dress, Kate tossed the shawl over her shoulders and stepped barefoot onto the icy porch. The chill air breached her thin shift in an instant.

"Where are you going?" she asked.

Will cast her an apathetic glance as he grabbed the rest of his gear from the porch and secured it to the gelding's livery. "East. To work a claim."

"What claim?" He'd not said anything to her about a claim. She stepped to the edge of the porch, pulling her shawl tighter.

"Robinson's. It's not far. A half-day's ride at most."

"But when did you—"

"Yesterday." He mounted the horse and adjusted his gear.

Kate could hardly believe it. Will had never tried to hide his bare tolerance for the droves of men who'd come to California lusting for gold.

"You told me nothing of this," she said.

"I'm telling you now."

His manner was cool, the tone of his voice just short of antagonistic. Almost as if he wanted her to pick a fight with him.

"Why?" she said, willing him to look her in the eye. "Was it because of something I said yesterday on the hill. Or Mrs. Vickery's—"

"It has nothing to do with that." At last, he fixed his eyes on hers. They were cold. Dead. She'd never seen him like this before.

"I know we haven't made near the money we'd hoped, and that time's running out for you."

She did the calculations in her head. His ship was due to leave in just over a fortnight. Three weeks at most. She'd have to be gone by then, too, or she'd not make it out till spring.

"This'll be quicker. I'll work the claim with Matt. Get enough gold to get us out. That's what you want, right? To go home?"

"Aye." She nodded but knew in her heart it was a lie. Were it not for her brothers, were it not for the debt, she'd never go back. Not now.

"I won't be gone long. A few days. A week at most."

She recalled the conversation they'd had the night he'd cooked the hare. He didn't want a wife. Or a family. That was made clear to her on numerous occasions, even if he hadn't said it in so many words.

"Cheng's sons are in town for a while. Railroad construction's on hold."

"Aye, I met one of them the day before yesterday. The eldest, I think."

"Cheng'll keep an eye on you while I'm gone. He'll send one of the boys 'round at night to sleep here on the porch."

She'd seen Will march up the street toward the Chinese camp late yesterday, and wondered why he'd spent so long there. He viewed her as a troublesome responsibility, one he likely hadn't thought through when he'd agreed to their bargain.

"All the same, keep that pistol handy, and your father's rifle by the bed."

She nodded, silent, dazed over this change of events.

"When I get back, we'll leave for San Francisco. Be ready."

He didn't wait for her to respond. Clods of mud splattered her shift as he dug his heels into the gelding's sides and the horse took off up the hill.

For the second time in as many weeks, Will Crockett was gone.

Chapter Eleven

"Forty-eight, forty-nine, fifty." Kate trailed a finger along the stack of tightly nested gold pans.

"Same as yesterday, Miss Kate."

"I know." She'd only counted them again to keep her mind occupied.

In the day and a half since Will had left to work Matt Robinson's mining claim, not one customer had visited the store. Kate peered out the window at the empty street and wondered what they were going to do.

"New strike in south," Mei Li said.

"Aye." She'd heard the news that morning from the blacksmith. "Near the place the Miwok call Mokelumne."

"Much gold there. Many men go."

"So they say." She hoped for all their sakes that Matt Robinson's claim would be even a fraction as bountiful.

The steady stream of immigrants and transient miners she and Will had counted on for business had all but vanished. Most, she suspected, had been lured south on rumor of the new strike.

Those who did pass through Tinderbox spoke of the thriving businesses—mercantiles, hardware stores, groceries—springing up overnight in Sacramento City. Competition for goods was fierce, and Dan Dunnett still hadn't returned.

To Kate, the silence that had descended on Tinderbox was almost eerie. She had Mei Li for company, and the Vickerys, too. But yesterday morning as she'd watched Will ride away, an overwhelming sense of aloneness had gripped her.

Which was ridiculous.

She'd traveled for months on her own before she'd even heard of Will Crockett. She'd always been independent, had never relied on anyone. Yet his absence weighed on her.

She missed him. It was as simple as that.

"No sad face," Mei Li said. "Husband come back soon."

Kate snapped to attention. "I—I'm not sad. I was just…thinking."

"Of Crockett."

"No, not at all."

"I think, too. On *my* husband."

"Husband? You mean you and Matt—"

"No, not real husband. Not like Crockett."

Kate's eyes widened in response. Given the circumstances of her union with Will, she would hardly describe him as a real husband.

"Matt Robinson husband of heart."

"Oh, I see." An image of Mei Li and Matt together, kissing, that afternoon on the ridge flooded Kate's mind. "You love him something fierce, don't you?"

"More than anyone know."

"And he loves you."

Mei Li nodded, a mischievous grin blooming on her face. Kate followed her as she all but floated across the room, stopping in front of their small inventory of women's undergarments.

"How do you know? That he loves you, I mean?"

"He say words, up on ridge by berries." Mei Li's black eyes lit up, remembering. "I say back."

"Ah." Kate recalled Will's possessive kiss that very afternoon, and her own unbridled response to it. A kiss very much like the one she'd witnessed between Matt and Mei Li, though she and Will had exchanged no such tender words. They'd argued, in fact. And he'd been more aloof than ever in the days since.

"What will you do?" She knew if Mei Li and Matt married here in Tinderbox, Landerfelt and some of the other townspeople would make trouble for them. Mixed marriages were frowned upon even here on the frontier.

Mei Li pulled a corset from the stack of undergarments and held it up against her tiny frame. "We leave. As soon as Matt find gold."

"You're leaving? But your father, your brothers—what will happen to them?"

"Nothing." Mei Li studied the hooks and laces of the corset and frowned. "How this work?"

"Nothing? You can't just leave them." She snatched the corset from Mei Li's grasp and unfastened the front hooks. "Here, like this."

Mei Li wrapped the corset around her, over her baggy blue tunic, and fastened the front hooks according to Kate's instruction.

"How will your brothers get on without you?"

"Same as always. They work railroad. Papa run card game. Life go on."

"But they depend on you. To cook and clean and take care of them."

Mei Li stepped to the window. Light reflecting at an

angle allowed her to see her reflection in the glass. "I not servant, and they not children."

"Aye, I suppose not." For the dozenth time that day Kate thought of her brothers back home. She reminded herself that the youngest, Patrick and Frank, *were* children. "You won't miss them?"

"Every day." Mei Li twisted the corset on her torso, grimacing. "This tight. Feel like prisoner."

Kate stared past her into the empty street and thought about her years growing up. "Aye, but one gets used to it."

Mei Li swore as she struggled out of the corset and dumped it unceremoniously onto the counter. "Wise man once say, 'Free woman make happy home.'"

"Hmm?" She hadn't been listening. Mei Li repeated the proverb, and Kate smiled. "Perhaps he's right." Though it didn't seem right, no matter how badly she wanted it.

She knew she had to drive these wild dreams from her head once and for all. She had to go back. Her brothers needed her. Even if they didn't—if there were no debt, if Frank and Patrick were grown—what reason had she to stay?

She closed her eyes and conjured the feel of Will Crockett's mouth on hers. He'd wanted her, and she him. But he didn't want to keep her. That fact was clear as day.

"Maybe tomorrow we make visit."

Kate's eyes flew open. "W-what visit?"

"To claim. Good idea you see husband."

"It's not a good idea. And I don't need to see him. Besides, he just left yesterday."

Mei Li snatched the corset and stuffed it back into the pile of women's underclothes. Under her breath she whispered another of her proverbs, one Kate did not take kindly to.

She started for the back room and Kate followed. "That's nonsense. And this has nothing to do with—"

The bell over the storefront door tinkled to life, and Kate's response died on her lips. "Afternoon, Mrs. Crockett."

She turned, the hairs on her nape prickling at the southern drawl. "Mr. Landerfelt."

Eldridge Landerfelt stood in the doorway, dressed to the nines, sporting new snakeskin boots, his hat in hand. He smiled charmingly at her, his trademark cigar notably absent.

"Just thought I'd stop by to see how you're getting on. What with your husband gone and all."

Kate started toward him but felt an insistent tug at the back of her skirt. She looked back at Mei Li, who stood just inside the living quarters, out of Landerfelt's sight, frowning.

"It's all right," she whispered, and turned her attention back to the merchant. "I appreciate your concern, but I'm fine, thank you. My husband will be back in a few days."

"Will he now?" Landerfelt strolled to the counter and ran a manicured finger over the tendering scale. "You sure about that?"

"Of course I'm sure. What do you mean?"

"There's a whole lot of gold to be had down south. Maybe he won't be comin' back."

Kate stiffened. "He's not in the south. He's gone east, just a half-day's ride, in fact. I expect him back—"

"East? There ain't no gold east. Everyone knows that. He must be putting you on."

She frowned. "Putting me…on?"

"Lying." Landerfelt grinned. "Men have been known to lie now and then to their wives."

A dozen good reasons why she shouldn't listen to him warred with seeds of doubt. All the same, in her heart she knew Will Crockett wasn't a liar.

"What do you want, Mr. Landerfelt? As you can see, I'm very busy."

He looked around the nearly empty store, eyeing their remaining inventory of odd items. "Not much business to be had, I'm afraid. For you or me."

"Aye, that's true."

"Maybe we should throw in together. Just until your, uh, husband gets back." He raked his eyes over her in a way that made Kate feel uncomfortable.

"You're not serious."

"Sure. Why not? Your inventory's low and so's mine. But together we have a decent stock."

Mei Li had told her that just yesterday Landerfelt had sent the Packett boys off to buy more goods in Sacramento City. It was true his inventory had also suffered from new competition.

"But what good is stock when there aren't any customers?"

"There are," Landerfelt said. "They just ain't here."

Kate eyed him, her brows furrowed into a frown. "Go on."

"Here's what we do. We load up the wagon with—"

"*Your* wagon? The one with the bright yellow wheels? I thought it had gone to town with the Packetts."

Landerfelt shrugged. "So we borrow Vickery's wagon. We'll load it up good, drive south a couple hours to where the spur road from Sac City comes in. Hundreds of men'll be on that road, headin' south to the new strike."

Landerfelt was right. From what Kate had heard, what

they'd all heard, there would be scores of men on that road. Scores of would-be customers.

"We'd go just for the day, you mean. Not overnight?"

"Hell, no. Just for the day. You and me. What do you say, Kate?"

It wasn't a half-bad idea, she had to admit. The only bad thing was the man who proposed it. Kate wavered.

What if Landerfelt was right? What if Will didn't intend to come back? What if he *had* gone south, and not to Matt Robinson's claim at all? What if he dug a fortune in gold and decided to keep it for himself? He'd be gone to Alaska, and she'd still be here, waiting for him to return.

"Psst!"

Kate turned at the sound and spied Mei Li peeking through the doorway at her from the back room, beckoning impatiently with wide dark eyes. Landerfelt spotted her and frowned.

"I'll just be a moment," Kate said to him, and hurried into the back room.

Mei Li pulled her into the corner by the bed, out of Eldridge Landerfelt's sight. "One more thing wise man say."

"Oh, the wise man again, is it? Go on, then, tell me." Kate looked into Mei Li's troubled eyes and had a bad feeling she already knew what it was.

Pulling her close, Mei Li whispered it in her ear. "'Beware of weasel who come to henhouse smiling.'"

Will hefted another chunk of barren granite and, with a grunt, tossed it toward the front of the cave. He collapsed, breathless, against the damp rock wall and felt blindly for his pickax amidst the rubble surrounding him.

"Let's take a break, partner." Matt grabbed the lantern and crawled toward him on hands and knees.

"No. We keep digging."

"Key-ryst, Will. I'm soaked to the skin. So are you."

"Doesn't matter." He blew hot breath into his hands to ward off a chill. It was cold as an arctic winter in the cave where Matt had staked his mining claim.

"If I'd a known you was gonna work me to death, I might not a asked ya to go in with me."

"Too late now."

Matt laughed, and the sound echoed eerily in the dark, wet confines of the cave. The lantern provided minimal light. Their kerosene supply was low already—Will had taken half of what was left in the store—and to conserve, Matt had adjusted the flame as low as it would go without going out all together.

"So, ya reckon we'll be rich men before the week's out?"

Will made a derisive sound in the back of his throat. "Don't count on it."

"What is it with you and money?"

He didn't answer.

"I known ya a long time, partner, and in all those years not once did ya want to make anything more a yourself than a sorry-assed fur trapper livin' from hand to mouth and movin' from place to place."

"That's what *you* do, isn't it?"

"For me it's all right. But for you…seems a waste to me, is all, seein' as how smart ya are."

He laughed at that. "I'm not so smart as you think." If he was, he wouldn't be here right now, cold and wet and tired, poking around in piles of rock. "And another thing…just because a man chooses to make his life on the frontier doesn't mean he hasn't made anything of himself."

"Well, ya know what I mean."

He knew, all right. A man's success was measured by the size of his bankroll, no matter what contemptible things he'd done to grow it. Or here in California, by the weight of his gold pouch.

"I just need enough to get out of here," Will said, and swiveled around onto his knees.

"Yep. Me, too."

He shot his friend a questioning look. "Where are *you* going? No farther than a day's ride from a certain Chinese camp, I'll bet."

"You'd lose that wager, partner. I'm leavin' and takin' her with me."

"Mei Li?"

"Who else? We're gettin' married."

"What? Are you out of your mind?"

"Might be." Matt pulled the lamp closer and drew with his finger in the coarse sand lining the rock floor of the cave. "Cape Mendocino, the Injuns call it. It's on the coast. We're goin' there, me and Mei Li, as soon as you and me strike it rich."

"But—"

"I know what you're gonna say, so just save it. There's Russians there—a whole settlement full of 'em. Imagine that. And Mexicans and Injuns. Chinese, too. All kinds o' folks. That's why we're goin' there."

He understood now. "No one will think anything of a white man married to a Chinese girl."

"Told ya you was smart."

Will laughed. "I *was* right. You are out of your mind."

"Maybe so, but I'm a happy man, Will. A happy man." Matt shot him a loaded look. "Which is more than I can say for some."

"Meaning?"

"You know what I mean. What the heck are ya gonna

do with her? Put her on a clipper outta Frisco and wave goodbye? Just like that?''

''That's the plan.''

''Ya know what? I was wrong. You're dumb as this here rock.'' Matt chucked a piece of rubble toward the pinpoint of bleak light marking the cave's entrance twenty feet away from where they hunkered on the wet rock floor.

Will didn't bother arguing the point.

''Don't tell me ya don't want her. I've seen how ya look at her when ya think no one's lookin'.''

He did want her. That was the problem.

Ignoring Matt's comment, he grabbed his pickax and sledgehammer and crawled toward the back of the cave where he'd been working. They'd been digging around in here all day, and had next to nothing to show for it. A few tiny nuggets culled from a quartz vein. That was it.

What he needed to do was concentrate. Something he hadn't been able to accomplish for more than five minutes straight since he'd left Tinderbox the morning before.

Since he'd left *her*.

Two exhausting days and a cold, hard night in between thinking about Kate hadn't done him any good. It had cleared his head about one thing, though. He was dead wrong about her knowing his father.

The notion had gripped him that afternoon when she'd questioned him on the hillside, and had roiled inside him unchecked, fueled by ugly memories of his first marriage.

He shook his head and swung the sledgehammer. The reverberation as it connected with solid rock burned all the way up his arms. ''You're an idiot, Crockett.''

''Hmm? What's that?'' The sound of Matt digging six feet away from him abruptly stopped.

''Nothing. Forget it.''

Matt pulled the lantern closer so he could see Will's face. "Thinkin' ya shouldn't a left her?"

"She'll be all right. Cheng and his boys will keep an eye on her. Mustart and Vickery, too."

"A lawyer, a blacksmith and a bunch a Chinese railroad workers. Let's hope Landerfelt don't get any more bright ideas while you're gone."

The truth of it was he *was* worried about her, but less so than he might have been a week ago. She had grit, and she was smart. And he knew at the first sign of trouble Cheng would send one of his boys to fetch him back to town.

Still, he cursed himself for being so damned hotheaded. It wasn't the first time he'd gone off half-cocked without thinking things through.

He told himself it was the shock of his father's arrival in California followed by Kate's probing questions that had driven him to the edge. But he knew in his gut there was more to it than that.

He was beginning to care about her. And a whole hell of a lot more than a man who was simply trying to help out a dead man's daughter should care. That was the problem. And had been since the day he first saw her in Dennington's Dry Goods, holding her own against the biggest swindler in town.

Two days he'd been gone from her. Two short days, and he missed her more than he'd ever missed any woman. Had Matt not been watching him like a hawk, Will knew he'd slip the painted miniature out of his pocket to have one more look at her.

Not that he needed a picture to remind him how blue her eyes were, how those unruly wisps of auburn hair curled on the nape of her neck. A neck he'd tasted. Skin so heated and soft he hadn't been able to resist running his tongue along her throat as he'd fondled her breasts and ground his hips into hers.

"So, we're takin' a break, then?"

Matt's voice echoed off the cave's walls and snapped him back to reality.

"W-what?"

"Ya stopped diggin', so I thought maybe—"

"No, you go ahead. I'll keep working." Damn, why couldn't he get his mind off her? He didn't want a wife, or a family. He wasn't cut out for it, and it didn't fit his plans. He was getting the hell out of here as soon as possible. As far away as he could get.

"Suit yourself, then." Matt shrugged, dropped his pickax and crawled toward the pinpoint of light at the cave's entrance. "I'll see if I can rustle us up somethin' to eat."

"You do that. Thanks. I could use something."

Yeah, like a swift kick in the rear end. Will shook his head at his own fool behavior these past weeks and redoubled his grip on the sledge. A granite boulder wedged between the cave's narrow walls made it impossible for him to retreat deeper.

I don't need her. I don't want her.

He swung with all his might and landed the blow, cleaving the boulder in two.

"You're sure about this?" Kate eyed the bay mare with trepidation. "She's awfully big."

"Crockett big man. Need big horse." Mei Li pushed her toward the blacksmith, Mr. Mustart, who stood ready to help her mount.

"What's her name?"

"Dunno," Mustart said. "Been boarding her here three weeks now, ever since Crockett lost her."

"Lost her to Mr. Landerfelt, you mean?" Kate glanced up the street where Eldridge Landerfelt shouted orders at two men tying a tarp over the wagonload of goods he hoped to sell on the road south of town.

"That's right. Damn shame, too." Mustart beckoned her forward. "Okay, grab on to that horn there, put your knee here, and I'll boost you up."

Kate did as she was told, and a few seconds later was in the saddle. It was none too comfortable, especially with her skirts twisted beneath her. She'd only ridden a handful of times. Twice when she was little and they still lived in the country, and once in Clancy Street, when her father had bribed a teamster to let her sit atop one of his Clydesdales while it clip-clopped down the street.

"Crockett's been by to see her near every day since, making sure she was doing okay."

"She's a fine animal." Kate patted the mare's neck.

"Can't believe Landerfelt loaned her to you. Don't reckon he's ever done a favor for anyone 'round here, that he didn't get something in return for it." Mustart shot her an innocent look that appeared far too practiced for Kate's liking. "If you know what I mean."

"I know exactly what you mean, Mr. Mustart. And I can tell you that Mr. Landerfelt got plenty in return for the use of his horse."

"Too much." Mei Li glared up the street at him.

They watched as Eldridge Landerfelt settled onto the high seat of Vickery's modified buckboard and snapped the reins. The wagon rumbled toward them.

"If we're lucky, he'll sell the goods we've given him for a lot of money."

"We lucky if he come back at all," Mei Li said. "I think you make bad deal."

"So he's heading south then, toward the strike. Must

be some deal, Mrs. Crockett.'' Mustart shook his head as Landerfelt approached. ''First time I ever seen him do anything himself—without those Packett boys to fetch and carry for him. He must be desperate.''

''We're all desperate, Mr. Mustart.'' She looked at Mei Li. ''Are you ready?''

''Plenty ready. Clear sky, fast horse. We make good time. Be at claim by noon.''

Kate looked at the flawless sky. It was the best weather they'd had since she'd arrived in Tinderbox. Mei Li had talked her into closing the store for a day and riding up to Matt Robinson's claim.

Why she'd agreed, she didn't know. She told herself she was going because she didn't want Mei Li traveling all that way alone. Mr. Cheng and his sons would have a fit if they knew about it. They'd left town early that morning to pick up some day work hauling lumber.

Mei Li was going. Her mind would not be changed. Kate had tried to talk her out of it, halfheartedly. In the back of her mind, no matter how much she wanted to deny it, Kate knew the real reason she'd agreed to go had little to do with seeing that the girl had a proper escort, and everything to do with seeing Will. If he was really there. If he hadn't lied to her, as Eldridge Landerfelt had implied.

Kate looked up as the merchant reined his team of hired oxen to a halt in front of them. Will's mare started when she saw him, and it was all Kate could do to keep her from bolting.

''Whoa, girl,'' Mustart said, and grabbed the mare's bridle. ''Easy now.''

''She doesn't like me much.'' Landerfelt grimaced at the mare. ''Can't imagine why.''

''I can,'' Mei Li whispered loud enough for Kate to hear.

"Sure you won't change your mind and come with me?" Landerfelt grinned at her, and Kate felt as if she'd just made a pact with the devil.

She'd thought about his offer all last night. On the one hand, she desperately needed the money that could be made by taking the goods south to where they'd find ready customers. On the other hand, she didn't trust Eldridge Landerfelt as far as she could throw him.

Mei Li had cautioned her about entering into any kind of arrangement with him. So had Will, on several occasions. But Will Crockett was gone, and Kate had a feeling he wasn't coming back. It was up to her now, to do what she thought best.

Landerfelt had wanted her to come with him. A fifty-fifty proposition. But she had no intention of riding off alone with a man the likes of him. They'd settled on seventy-thirty if he went alone—seventy percent of the profits for him and thirty for her—and Kate had given over to him what was left of the store's inventory.

She'd also talked him into loaning her Will's mare while he was gone. Landerfelt didn't know, of course, that she and Mei Li intended to ride into the foothills to Matt Robinson's claim. If he had, he'd never have agreed to the deal.

"No," she said. "I won't be changing my mind, Mr. Landerfelt."

"Suit yourself." He flicked a couple of mud clods off his new snakeskin boots before raking his eyes over her again. "So, it's riding lessons for you, is it?"

"Aye."

"I wish you'd wait for me to get back. I'd teach you myself."

"Thank you," she said. "But Mr. Mustart, here, will be a fine instructor."

"Oh, right. Riding lessons." Mustart showed all his teeth in as lying a smile as Kate had ever seen. She owed him for that, and for his discretion.

"Well, I'll be seeing you, then. Tonight most likely. Tomorrow for sure." Landerfelt tipped his hat to her, snapped the reins, and the oxen moved on. They all watched as the wagon rumbled south down Main Street and onto the bumpy road leading out of town.

As soon as the merchant was out of sight, Mei Li raced into the blacksmith's shed to retrieve their loaded saddle-bags and the rifle Kate had inherited from her father.

Mustart fastened the bags onto the mare's saddle, stuffed the rifle into the saddle holster and boosted Mei Li up behind her. "I still don't like it, you two riding out there alone. Crockett'll have my head if finds out I knew about it."

"We'll be fine, Mr. Mustart. And don't worry, he won't find out. I've a grand lie all prepared." Another to add to her growing list. Her next confession would likely take all day. Kate crossed herself for good measure.

"You're not back by dark, I'm riding out after you."

"Don't worry, we'll be here." Kate snapped the reins, and the mare lurched forward. She instantly grabbed the saddle horn to steady herself.

"Maybe riding lesson not bad idea," Mei Li said. Kate ignored her.

Mustart waved, and they returned the gesture. On the outskirts of town they left the road, reining the mare east up the wooded hillside toward Matt Robinson's mining claim. Kate didn't know whether to hope Will was there with him, as he'd said he'd be, or not.

As they took to the rugged trail, Mei Li began to sing in Chinese. If Kate had to venture a guess, she'd bet her last gold piece it was a love song.

Chapter Twelve

"Looks like we been skunked."

"After all that? The digging and hauling and—" Will stared at the gold pan, blinking the grit out of his eyes, as Matt gently swirled the mixture of mercury, water and crushed rock.

"Yep. Nothin' but quartz."

Will ground his teeth and counted to ten, controlling the frustration boiling up inside him.

Men dug up fortunes all around him, every day, poking around streams, caves and washed out tree roots. He'd never wanted to do it. He'd have starved to death first.

It was *her* fault. She'd driven him to it. "Here, let me see that." He grabbed the gold pan and tilted it so the sun shone directly on the beads of mercury.

"Ain't nothin' there, Will. I'm tellin' ya."

He'd abandoned his principles and had stooped to the kind of get-rich-quick scheme he loathed. He deserved to fail.

"We could always try up west o' that—"

"Shut up, Matt." Will thrust the pan at him, grabbed his pickax and started for the cave.

"It ain't my fault, ya know."

"It's nobody's damned fault." Nobody's but his own. He had two weeks left. Two. After that, there'd be no getting out—for him or for her.

On hands and knees Will scrambled back into the cave, dragging the pickax behind him. Matt called after him, shouting something unintelligible, but Will ignored it. Gripping the ax, he narrowed his gaze on a thick quartz vein running along an untouched wall of the dimly lit cavern.

Matt's voice—a lot closer now—interrupted. "You'd best get out here, partner."

Will swore, trying out a couple of the Irish words he'd heard Kate use that day on the ride down the hill from the elderberry patch. Tossing the ax aside, he scrambled back out of the cave, squinting against the sunlight. "What is it now?"

The words froze in his throat, as his gaze fixed on the bay mare—his mare—grazing in the clearing where he and Matt had made their camp.

Landerfelt. It had to be.

Will's pistol was in his hand before the thought even registered. He whirled left, then right. And stopped dead. Matt and Mei Li stood in the shade of a massive oak.

"What the hell?" He marched over to them, holstering his gun on the way, and scanned the trees for signs of others. He saw no one. Mei Li was going on about something, using her hands when her English failed her.

Matt saw him coming. "You'd best hear this." He turned his attention back to Mei Li. "Go on. Tell him."

The girl's eyes grew wide as saucers as Will approached. She shook her head quickly. "No. You tell."

"Tell me what? And what are you doing with my horse? Landerfelt's horse."

"He loaned it to 'em," Matt said.

"Them? You mean—?" Will shaded his eyes against the sun and scanned the tree line again, this time for Kate. He felt his mouth go dry and his heartbeat quicken.

"She ain't here."

A stab of disappointment twisted inside him. "Good. She ought to be in town where she belongs. Speaking of which—" he turned to Mei Li "—what are you doing out here on your own?"

"I not alone. Not at first. Miss Kate come, too. But—"

"Where is she?" A vision of her lying dead at the bottom of a ravine flashed hideously across his mind.

"On trail to Sac City. Men come and—"

"What men?" He grabbed Mei Li. "What happened? Did they hurt her? Is she—"

"Whoa, partner." Matt peeled Will's hands from Mei Li's narrow shoulders. "She's fine. It's just that they was on their way here to pay us a visit, when Mustart sent a couple o' town boys out after 'em."

"Why? For what?"

"Dunnett drove his wagon plumb off a cliff near Spanish Camp. Busted a wheel. Stuff scattered everywhere."

"Our new stock, you mean?" It was half paid for already, damn it. Not that it mattered, since business in Tinderbox had dropped off to nothing.

Mei Li tugged at Will's sleeve. "Miss Kate go back with men. I think bad idea, but she stubborn as mule. I come here, fetch you."

"Which men? Who were they?"

"Floyd Canter," Matt said.

"The town drunk?" Will bit back a string of swearwords.

"Yes, that him." Mei Li wrinkled her nose in disgust. "And other man I not know. Never see before."

Will snatched Matt's rifle off his bedroll next to the dead campfire. "I'm borrowing this."

"Take it."

"Here. This, too." Mei Li pulled Kate's pepperbox revolver out of the pocket of her long, blue tunic.

"You keep it. But I'm taking my horse. She's a damn sight faster than Dennington's old nag." He grabbed his buckskin coat and fur hat off the boulder where he'd left them, vaulted onto the mare's back and thrust Matt's rifle into the empty saddle holster. "She take her father's rifle?"

Mei Li nodded.

At least that was something. One smart move on top of two stupid ones—thinking to ride out here in the first place, and going anywhere with Floyd Canter. He reined the mare west into the sun, then turned in the saddle. "You said Landerfelt loaned you the horse. Why?"

Mei Li bit her lip and looked to Matt, her eyes widening.

"Well? Spit it out."

"You ain't gonna like it, Will."

Mei Li took a tentative step toward him. "Miss Kate make deal with Landerfelt. He borrow wagon and ox, take store goods south to new strike."

"Whose goods?"

"All he have left. And Miss Kate's, too."

"She let him?" Will couldn't believe it.

Mei Li nodded. "For share of profit, and loan of horse. No choice, she say."

"What do you mean?"

Matt slid an arm around Mei Li's shoulders. "Seems your wife didn't think you'd be comin' back."

"If I was smart I wouldn't."

"But you ain't smart." Matt grinned. "Now is ya?"

Will snapped the reins, and the mare sprang into action.

"I'm right behind ya," Matt called after him, "as soon as I get Mei Li home."

"What about horse?" Mei Li ran alongside the bay mare, waving at Will. "I no take back, Landerfelt plenty mad."

"I'll give him something to be mad about." Will dug his heels into the mare's sides and she shot west into the woods toward Tinderbox.

He plucked the painted miniature from his pocket and squeezed until its sharp-edged frame drew blood from his palm. If he stayed mad at her long enough, it might just stave off the fear twisting in his gut.

Kate put a handkerchief to her nose, but it did no good. The stench of whiskey and sweat and sour breath nearly choked her. Four hours wedged like a tinned kipper on a wagon seat between Floyd Canter and his hungover friend Ezekiel was more than she could bear.

"Can't we go any faster?"

The mule team clomped along the rocky road at a pace twice as slow as she could have walked it.

"Get up thar, mules!" Floyd cracked his whip in the air and snapped the jerk-line. The team picked up its pace. "Lucky for you we was making this trip today, Miz Crockett."

"Aye, lucky me. How much farther."

"Just 'round that bend up there." Floyd nodded off in the distance at what looked to be a crossroads.

The sun had already begun to dip in the western sky. Late afternoon, if Kate had to guess. "I hope we're not too late."

Mr. Mustart had conveyed the news that Dan Dunnett's wagon had gone off the road somewhere west of the small tent city the miners called Spanish Camp. Looters were thought to be the cause.

That morning Floyd Canter and his friend had been charged with running a mule team back that way for a couple of teamsters who'd taken sick on the trail. Something about bad water. They must have been desperate, in Kate's estimation, to entrust the task to these two. She held her breath as she cast them each a sideways glance.

Mustart had tried to stop her from going, had begged her to wait until Will could be fetched from the claim. But she wasn't certain Will was even at the claim, or if he was, if he'd come. She hadn't had any choice but to go with Floyd and Ezekiel. Vickery was out of town that day, as were the Chengs, and Mustart wouldn't leave his business, even for an afternoon.

Kate pursed her lips, her eyes fixed on the road ahead. Gold had been paid in advance for those goods. And if Will Crockett never returned, she'd need the profits they'd bring more than ever. If business didn't pick up in Tinderbox, she'd just have to do as Mr. Landerfelt had, and go south.

They rounded the bend and Kate frowned. Thirty or so canvas tents of various sizes lined both sides of the deeply rutted road. It was hardly what she'd call a city. "This is it?"

"Yep. Spanish Camp." Floyd maneuvered the mule team into a trampled clearing off to the side, and the wagon jerked to a halt.

Men crisscrossed the road hauling mining equipment and leading pack animals, ducking into tents and crouching around campfires to talk. It was a busy place. One man waved to them, and Floyd Canter waved back.

Kate peered up the road to where it disappeared again

into the trees. "Mr. Dunnett's wagon should be some-where up ahead."

"So them teamsters said." Floyd hopped down from the wagon and held out a grimy hand to her.

Kate ignored it and jumped, managing to land on her feet. "And you'll help me? To find Mr. Dunnett, and get the load back to Tinderbox?"

"Course we will. As soon as Ezekiel and me wet our whistles."

Ezekiel was already making a beeline for one of the tents. Floyd tossed the jerk-line to the man who'd waved—he'd apparently been expecting them—and fol-lowed in his friend's wake.

Kate eyed the tent. It was monstrously huge and finer than any of the others. A sign was posted outside of it, but she had no idea what it said. She'd seen dozens of saloons and gaming hells set up in tents just like this one in Sacramento City. San Francisco, too. Mr. Cheng ran a similar establishment in the Chinese camp at Tinderbox, though Kate had never been inside it.

"How long, do you suppose," she said to the man un-hitching the mule team, "till they're likely to come back out?"

The man grinned at her. "Depends on which whistles they're aiming to wet, ma'am."

Kate started to ask him what he meant, but the words died on her lips as the tent flaps were thrown back and two scantily clad women emerged, beckoning Floyd and Ezekiel inside.

The women were young—her age, if she had to venture a guess. One was clad in nothing but a shift. The other wore men's trousers held up with suspenders, a corset and little else. Both had rouged lips and provocative smiles.

"You mean it's a—" Her eyes widened. "Those women, they're…"

"Line gals," the man said. "You know. Prostitutes."

Kate opened her mouth to speak, but no words came out. Not that she was a stranger to such women. Each night in Liffey Quay droves of them walked the streets, desperate to make enough to feed themselves and their children the following day.

Aye, that was the difference, she realized. That tense union of hope and desperation fueling such transactions was there all right, but in the eyes of the miners, not the women.

"You're not from around here, are you?" the man said.

"No." She couldn't take her eyes off them.

"They line their tents up along the road. That's why we call 'em line gals."

"Makes sense."

"Don't worry, ma'am. If you ask me, them two'll be out in no time." He shook his head as the women laughed and pulled Ezekiel and Floyd into the tent with them.

Two hours later Kate was still waiting.

It was beginning to get dark. The tree stump she'd been sitting on was bloody uncomfortable. She was tired and cold and growing angrier by the minute. Men had come and gone from the tent, but there was no sign of her escorts.

What could be taking them so long? A man approached her, as had many since she'd arrived. Her father's single-barrel flintlock rifle lay loaded across her lap. She leveled it at him and he backed off, grinning, his hands in the air.

Perhaps this hadn't been such a good idea, after all.

She wondered if Mei Li had made it to the mining claim, if Will was there, and if he was, if he'd ride out to help her. She glanced at the darkening sky and knew she had to make a decision.

Rising stiffly, Kate redoubled her grip on the rifle. Just as she was about to cross the road, the tent flap opened and a woman stepped out. There was just enough light to make out her features. She was older than the other two and dressed in a fancy gown. The woman waved her over, which Kate thought odd. Cautiously she approached.

"Come on in and take a load off, honey."

Surely the woman didn't mean for her to come inside the tent? "I'm fine out here, thank you kindly."

The woman looked her up and down as if she were appraising her market value. Kate tipped her chin at her.

"Floyd Canter says you're Will Crockett's wife."

"Aye. Sort of."

"Sort of?" The woman laughed. "Well, you ain't what I would have expected, that's for sure."

"No, I suppose I'm not." She remembered what Mr. Vickery had told her about Will's first wife.

"Well, come on in." The woman waved her closer. Kate caught a whiff of her overpowering floral perfume. "Had I known who you was, I woulda come out to fetch you a whole lot sooner."

Kate shook her head. "No, I…I can't. I have business up the road."

"Tonight?"

"Aye." She peeked inside the tent, but a potbellied stove blocked her view. "Mr. Canter…is he still in there?"

"Who, Floyd? He's in there all right. Passed out cold, along with that friend of his."

"What?" Kate brushed past the woman and ducked inside the tent.

Sure enough, Floyd and Ezekiel were laid out like

corpses on the hard-packed dirt floor in a corner of the huge tent. Kate snaked around tables of soused miners who had prostitutes draped over them like icing dripping off tea cakes.

"Get up!" She kicked at Floyd's limp body. His mouth opened and he hiccuped. Kate swore.

"What did I tell you. Dead drunk." The woman who'd asked her inside stood shaking her head at them, her hands fisted on her more than ample hips.

Kate gripped her father's rifle so tight her knuckles went white.

"Hope you wasn't counting on them for anything important."

"Not anymore, I'm not." Kate turned on her heel and made her way to the opening of the tent, noticing for the first time the handful of curtained stalls running all along the wall. One of the drapes was open. Inside she spied a narrow bed and a washstand. "Jesus, Mary and Joseph," she breathed, and crossed herself as she stepped outside.

The woman followed. "If you don't mind my saying, it seems mighty strange to me that any wife of Will Crockett's would be out and about with men the likes of them two."

Kate ignored her.

"You'd best stay with us till tomorrow. By then, them two varmints should be up and around."

"Mrs....?"

"Beecham. Rose Beecham." The name explained the woman's dizzying trademark scent. Rose arched a neatly plucked brow at her. "And it's Miss."

"Miss Beecham, then. I appreciate your hospitality, but everything I own in the world is up that road." She nodded toward the dark woods. "I can't wait on Mr. Canter and his friend. I'm going."

"But—"

"I'm going," she said, and marched toward the trees, cocking her father's rifle on the way.

Will galloped into Tinderbox and jerked the mare to a halt in front of the store. Locked up tight. He peered through the window and saw that Mei Li hadn't been kidding. The counter was swept clean, the shelves empty. Not a tin pan was left.

He swore, and was still swearing as he charged through the back door into the cabin. An open powder horn, scattered garments and hardtack crumbs on the table told him that Kate had come and gone in a hurry.

At the bed, he ran his hand over the rumpled blankets and the soft dip in the pillow where her head had lain.

Two minutes later he hauled the blacksmith out into the street by the scruff of his neck. "Which way did she go?"

"S-south. Then w-west. You know. The usual way." Mustart trembled in his grip.

"Yeah, you ought to be shaking." Will released him and started to pace. "Just like that, you let her ride out of town with two drunks."

"I tried to stop her. Honest, I did. When I sent Floyd out after her with the news, I figured she'd go on to the claim to fetch you back. I had no idea she'd—"

"Save it." He glanced at the sun in the blue sky overhead, and judged the time at three. Four, maybe. "When did they ride out?"

"Before noon."

"Then they're already there." He whistled for his horse and the mare clopped down the street toward him.

"Maybe not. Them mules moved outta here slow as molasses in winter."

Will grabbed Mustart by his wool vest and jerked him close. "You'd better pray nothing's happened to her."

"I swear, Will, I—I did everything I could to stop her. But you know how she is when she gets an idea in her head."

He did know, and bit back another curse. Glancing back up the street, his gaze lit on Landerfelt's Mercantile. The shades were drawn across the storefront window.

"He's not back yet," Mustart said. "Tomorrow maybe. Speaking of which…" He nodded at the bay mare.

"I'm keeping her—for now."

Mustart didn't argue.

Will mounted, ready to ride out after Kate, then turned in the saddle as the rumble of livery and a thunder of hoofbeats sounded from up the street near the Chinese camp.

"Well I'll be damned," Mustart said. "Looks like Dunnett. But what's he doing coming from that direction?"

Will took off like a shot, his gaze narrowed on the seat of Dunnett's wagon. Kate wasn't with him. He reined the mare up short in front of the draft team, forcing Dunnett to stop in the middle of Main Street.

"Where is she?"

"Who?" Dunnett's brows rose in question.

"Kate, you idiot. Didn't you see her?"

Dunnett shook his head. "Didn't see no one. That was the whole point of taking that Injun trail 'round north of the road."

"What?"

"Them Packett boys tipped me off. Their wagon did a cartwheel off the road into a ditch just outside Spanish Camp. Busted a wheel."

"The Packetts? Mustart said it was *your* wagon

that—'' Will glanced at the neatly packed load and realized Mustart had heard wrong.

''Then they was looted. Some gang outta Coloma. Lock, stock and barrel—everything gone. Landerfelt's gonna raise Cain.''

''The Packetts are still out there?'' Will's gut tightened.

''Can't rightly say. They was tryin' to fix that wagon wheel when I last saw 'em.''

''And Kate's on her way—'' He didn't finish the thought.

Will's heels dug into the mare's sides as he reined her around to the south. Clods of dried mud flew up, pelting Mustart, as he galloped back down the street and out of town.

Three hours later Will had to stop himself from beating Floyd Canter senseless outside Rose Beecham's tent in Spanish Camp. Not that Floyd had any sense to begin with.

''That's for letting her out of your sight.'' Will hauled him to his feet and pushed him toward the tent. Floyd stumbled inside, a shaking hand cradling his bloodied nose.

''Tell that mangy partner of yours that as soon he wakes up he'll be getting some of the same.''

Floyd glanced back at him and hiccuped.

Will swore.

''You think mighty highly of her, don'tcha?'' Rose Beecham stood just inside the circle of light pouring from the tent.

''What?'' He hadn't noticed her until now.

''Never seen you get this worked up before—over a woman, I mean.''

He ignored Rose's comment as he mounted up and

slipped his borrowed rifle from its saddle holster. "How long ago did she take off?"

"'Bout an hour. She couldn't a got far."

He hoped to Christ she hadn't. "Seen any sign of the Packett boys?"

"Not hide nor hair." Rose glanced inside at the handful of miners drinking with the girls. "Wish they'd come on in. We could use the business."

"If Kate shows up, keep her till I get back. I don't care if you have to hog-tie her to do it."

Rose batted her false lashes at him and smiled. "Why wait? I've got a couple o' gals right here who'd be obliging, Will, if that's the kinda thing you like."

"Just keep her," he said, and kicked the mare into action.

Kate trudged steadily up the steep, winding road in the dark, the sounds of cicadas keeping time with her pace. A sliver of moon peeked over the ridge top, its ghostly light filtering through the trees. She cursed herself for leaving her cloak behind in Spanish Camp. The night air was cold as the devil.

She'd been walking about an hour, and had seen no signs of Dan Dunnett or his wagon. No signs of anyone, in fact, which she thought odd. The occasional whoosh of a bat overhead and the scurrying sounds of small animals were the only evidence she wasn't entirely alone.

At the top of the heavily forested rise the road took a sharp turn, cutting across the ridgeline. When she rounded the bend she stopped dead, redoubling her grip on the rifle.

"Good Lord."

A wash of pearly moonlight reflected off the debris peppering the road. Kate stepped gingerly around odd bits of metal and wood, empty flour sacks, and yards of twisted homespun snaking across her path.

She blinked a couple of times, adjusting her eyes to the moonlight. Then she saw it. Just ahead—the dim outline of a wagon wheel, poking out of the trees on the downward slope of the ridge.

"Mr. Dunnett?" She approached cautiously. "Are you here?"

The sound of hoofbeats somewhere in the distance broke her concentration. Closing her eyes, she listened, but it was gone. Perhaps it had been her imagination.

A branch snapped behind her.

Kate's eyes flew open and she whirled, leveling her rifle at the sound. "Jesus, Mary and Joseph!" The saucerlike eyes of a raccoon stared back at her from the edge of the trees.

She stood there for a moment, gripping the rifle, and let her heartbeat return to normal. It wasn't like her to be this jumpy. As the raccoon waddled toward the empty flour sack, Kate turned her back on it.

Peering ahead, she saw that the wagon—what was left of it—had overturned, and was perched precariously at the edge of a steep drop-off. A thick stand of trees had kept it from plummeting over the side all together.

Narrowing her gaze, she studied the wreck. Smashed barrels and more open sacks littered the steep hillside around it. Her nose wrinkled as she caught a whiff of whiskey on the air.

Something wasn't right.

She couldn't put her finger on it, but something seemed strange about the wagon. "Mr. Dunnett?" She inched closer. "Is anyone here?"

Then it struck her. The wheels. They weren't plain like those on Dunnett's wagon. They were...

Yellow.

Why, this wasn't Dan Dunnett's wagon at all. It was—

A deep, guttural sound spooked her nearly out of her skin. Kate lurched back and lost her footing. A thick pine saved her at the last minute from tumbling down the slope.

"Who's there? Show yourself!"

Someone was on the far side of the wagon. She heard scuffling amidst the rocks and pine needles littering the forested hillside, then the sound of splintering wood. She tried to get up, but her boot was wedged fast between two trees.

Hoofbeats sounded behind her. She'd been right! Someone was coming. She gripped the rifle, twisted her foot and pulled with all her might. She was free, but instantly started to slide down the slope. Her hand shot out and caught an edge of the wagon.

Eldridge Landerfelt's wagon.

As she righted herself, every instinct told her that on the other side she'd find Jed and Leon Packett. The hoofbeats were louder now. No telling who the rider was. Better to act than not, her father always said.

She cocked the rifle and stepped purposefully around the wagon. "If you value your life, you'll not move a—"

A bone-shaking roar split the air. Kate screamed and nearly dropped her weapon.

"Kate!" Hoofbeats thundered toward her. "Where are you?"

"Will!" Thank God!

She inched backward down the slope, her gaze riveted to the enormous shape lumbering toward her in the moonlight. She'd heard of them, of course, but had never seen one.

"I—I'm here," she breathed, not managing more than a whisper.

The grizzly bore down on her.

Kate fired.

Sharp pain streaked like lightning across her ribs. Her last conscious thought as she tumbled backward and the rifle slipped from her hands was that Will had, indeed, been where he'd said he'd be. At the mining claim.

And when she'd needed him most, he'd come.

Chapter Thirteen

He hadn't known the kind of fear that made a man's mouth go dry, that caused his breath to seize up in his chest—until that moment.

Will jerked the mare's reins and leaped from her back, borrowed rifle in hand, while the horse was still moving. Rounding the far side of the wagon, he skidded to a stop just before the drop-off.

Thank Christ Matt had changed the antique flintlock over to percussion fire. Will cocked the hammer. Aimed.

"What the—?"

Kate rolled dangerously close to his line of fire, grappling not with the Packetts, as he'd expected, but with a bear! A grizzly.

Will flung the rifle aside and yanked his buck knife from its sheath. A second later he tackled the bear, driving nine inches of tempered steel into its back. It went over easy, already dead, he realized, and thudded as it hit the ground.

"Kate!" He scrambled to his knees, fighting the slope, and reached for her.

"W-Will?"

"I'm here. It's all right." He pulled her to her knees,

brushed the pine needles from her hair, turned her face into the moonlight to get a better look at her. "Are you hurt?"

"I...I thought you weren't coming." She gripped him tight, her head lolling back, her eyes closing. "That you didn't—" her knees gave out beneath her and he took up her weight in his arms "—care."

"Oh, Kate." His gut twisted in knots till his insides burned.

"Kiss me," she breathed, and opened her eyes. Moonlight reflected from their vitreous depths. "L-like you did before. In the rain."

On the hillside, near the elderberries. He remembered. He'd thought about it a hundred times, maybe a thousand, since that afternoon.

With a ferocity born of fear and desire, and shame for his inability to protect her—feelings so violent he feared he might ignite—Will crushed Kate to his chest and kissed her.

She opened her mouth to receive his greedy tongue, but when he deepened the kiss and his hold on her, she pushed at his chest and began to whimper.

Instantly he pulled back. "You *are* hurt." Holding her at arm's length, his eyes raked over her body. Then he saw the blood. Trickling black in the moonlight from a set of parallel slashes across her side. "Christ."

"If I die, I...I want you to know..."

He swept her into his arms as she lost consciousness. Whispering the only prayer he could remember, Will scrambled up to the road, carrying her. He laid her out and tore away the shredded part of her dress where the bear had mauled her.

Probing gently with his fingers, he realized the slashes

went clear through her corset and shift to her soft skin beneath. His fingers came away bloody.

"Kate!" He grabbed her shoulders and shook her, but she didn't respond. "Stay with me. Do you hear?"

He gripped her tighter and closed his eyes against the blast of memories exploding in his mind. A vision of his first wife, writhing on her deathbed despite all that had been done to save her, seared the backs of his eyelids.

"No," he said, shaking his head.

He opened his eyes and stared at Kate's gentle face, gone ghostly white in the moonlight. This was different. She was different. And he, God help him, felt differently about her than he had about any other woman in his life.

A second later he scrambled back down the rocky slope, gathered up his weapons, and the rifle Kate had used to kill the bear. She was strong, brave, a fighter. She couldn't die. He wouldn't let her.

On his way back up the hill he nearly tripped over the damnable thing that was responsible for the bear's presence: an open bag of sugar wedged under Landerfelt's overturned wagon.

He scanned the area one more time as he sheathed his knife and jammed the rifles together into the mare's saddle holster. There was no sign of the Packetts, or of any of the looters Mustart had told him about.

But one of the wagon's wheels was missing. The Packetts had probably taken it and Landerfelt's draft team south to Coloma, where there was a wheelwright who could repair it.

Kate was still unconscious. Will lifted her into his arms and, after a couple of tries, mounted the mare and settled her limp body across his lap, her head tucked under his chin.

Spanish Camp was the closest settlement, but there was

no one there who knew any more about medicine than he did. He remembered a Miwok camp to the south, not much farther than Spanish Camp was east.

Doc Mendenhall frequented the place. Swapped herbs and tinctures with the medicine woman there. Doc had left Tinderbox, heading in that direction, just after Liam Dennington died. If they were lucky, damned lucky, maybe he'd still be there. And if not, the medicine woman could help.

There was no time to think about it. It was full on dark now, and the temperature was dropping fast. He whispered a hasty apology to his exhausted horse, and spurred her into action once more.

She had wondered what it would be like to awaken to the sound of his voice, the feel of his hands on her skin. Mmm, what a lovely dream.

"You're going to be just fine." Will's voice was a whisper, comforting and low and soft.

Kate felt his fingers caress her cheek. She rolled toward him, a soft moan escaping her lips. "Aye," she breathed. "Fine."

Her eyelids fluttered open. Will's face came into focus above her. His jaw was tense, his brow furrowed with concern. His eyes had gone that warm shade of chestnut she loved and saw all too rarely, reflecting the fire she heard crackling somewhere at the edge of her awareness.

Her hand reached out blindly, of its own accord, and connected with Will's face, tracing the angry line of his scar, grazing a three-day stubble of dark beard growth.

"How did you…get it?" She'd wondered about it since the very first time she'd seen him. "The…scar."

"My wife did it. It doesn't matter now." His hand closed over hers and gently squeezed.

''W-wait...'' This was no dream. She blinked her eyes a few times and sucked in a breath. ''What on earth—?''

''Easy, Kate.''

All at once she remembered. The overturned wagon. Hoofbeats in the distance. The bear. ''Sweet Jesus!''

She bolted upright as her vision, and her mind, finally cleared. Her ribs burned, and her head— ''Ow!'' Her hand flew to the spot that throbbed like a sledgehammer breaking rock.

''It's all right. You hit your head. Something fierce, by the look of it.'' Will grasped her shoulders—her bare shoulders, she realized with a start—and eased her back down.

''Where am I?'' She clutched at the soft furs covering her naked body, her gaze darting from Will's face to the unfamiliar surroundings.

''A Miwok camp.''

''Oh.'' They were in a sort of tent, made not of canvas but of deerskin. A teepee, she guessed. She'd seen them on her journey to Tinderbox, but only from the outside. A small fire blazed in the center, smoke curling out a hole in the roof.

''Where are my clothes? W-what's happened?''

''Rest now.'' He pulled another fur over her. ''Everything's going to be all right.''

''But the bear. What—?''

''It's dead.''

She closed her eyes and exhaled, crossing herself as she offered up a silent prayer.

''How do you feel?''

She blinked her eyes open again and met his gaze. ''Grand. Just a bit tired.''

''You're lying.''

She forced a smile as she slipped her hand under the

furs and gingerly felt her ribs. They were bandaged, one side tender as the devil.

"Doc says it'll be a few days before those scratches are healed up. They're not as deep as I'd thought. Most of the blood was the bear's. We cleaned them out and—"

"*You* cleaned them?"

"Well, Doc did. I helped."

"Oh." Their gazes locked, and heat flushed her face. "Thank you."

He shrugged, as if he were uncomfortable, then turned away to stoke the fire.

Kate heard footsteps outside. The flap covering the teepee's entrance was thrown back and a man she'd never seen before—a white man—ducked inside.

"You're awake. Good." The man knelt beside her and smiled. He had an easy manner about him, and a soft, encouraging voice. Right away he made Kate feel comfortable.

"I told her she has to take it easy," Will said.

"For a few days." The man placed his hand on her forehead, as if he were checking for fever. "That's quite a goose egg on your noggin. Must have been a hard fall."

"N-noggin?"

"Your head," Will said.

"Oh." She laughed, then winced, her ribs on fire.

"Doc Mendenhall, ma'am. Pleased to make your acquaintance."

"My thanks, Doctor, for all you've done."

"Wasn't much, really. Just cleaned you up a bit. Will here did the smart thing by getting you out of the night air."

"Aye. I don't know what would have happened had he

not come.'' She looked at him, but he wouldn't meet her gaze.

''You'd best get some rest now, Mrs. Crockett.'' The doctor turned to leave.

''Wait.'' She struggled to sit up a bit, pulling the furs with her. ''You're the same doctor who tended my father, are you not?''

''That's right. My condolences, ma'am.''

''Thank you.'' She knew, now, what it must have been like for her father here in this wild place, ill and alone, with no one to look after him save strangers and what few friends he'd made. She reminded herself that in a fortnight, she, too, would be alone again. ''I know you did everything you could for my father, and for that I'm grateful.''

Mendenhall frowned. ''Funny thing, him dying like that.''

''What do you mean?''

''He means he was getting better,'' Will said. ''Then he died, all of a sudden. Just like that.''

''Did he…suffer much?''

''No, it was over merciful quick.'' Mendenhall shook his head. ''The only time I ever saw anyone go quicker 'round here that wasn't shot, was from strychnine. Drank it by mistake in a glass of milk meant to poison a pesky varmint. Died right before my eyes.''

''Oh.'' Kate's head throbbed. She eased herself back down. ''Thank you for telling me.''

''G'night, Mrs. Crockett.'' The doctor opened the teepee's flap to leave, and a Miwok face peered in at them.

A woman. The same woman who'd come to Tinderbox a week ago with her husband and babe. She entered the teepee as Mendenhall left, and knelt beside Kate.

Will said something to her in her own language. The woman spoke back.

"What does she want?"

"Just making sure the doc did a good job," Will said.

Without warning, the woman pulled the furs back, exposing Kate's breasts and torso to view. Will's view. She snatched at the furs, trying to cover herself, but the Miwok woman was strong, too strong, and Kate was spent.

Will's gaze fixed on hers as she lay there, rigid, holding her breath. Then he politely looked away.

None of this was lost on the Miwok woman. She frowned, looking back and forth between the two of them as if they were the strangest people she'd ever seen. As she prodded Kate's bandaged ribs, she spoke.

"W-what's she saying?"

Will kept his gaze on the fire. "She said that she thought we were married."

"Oh."

He said something to the woman, and she answered back, shaking her head. Will fidgeted by the fire, as if his clothes were suddenly too tight or the close quarters of the teepee over warm. "I...I told her we were."

"She said something else. What was it?"

He turned to look at her then, his gaze roving boldly over her bared body. Kate lay there, her nipples hardening in the cool air, and let him look.

"That white people made no sense."

"Aye, perhaps we don't."

He looked back at the fire, and Kate breathed. The Miwok woman finished her examination and covered her again with the soft furs. Before she left the teepee, she paused and spoke.

"She offers her thanks to you for that day in town," Will said. "For standing up to Landerfelt."

"Tell her she's very welcome, and that I hope her babe fares well."

Will translated. The woman nodded but did not smile. A moment later she was gone.

"It's been a long day," Will said. "Let's get some rest."

He stoked the fire a final time, then laid out his buckskin jacket on the hard-packed dirt floor opposite from where she lay on a lush pile of blankets and furs. Kate knew that ground would be wicked cold, fire or no fire.

"You're welcome to sleep here." She edged closer to the fire and patted the expanse of available fur beside her.

For a long time Will didn't move, then, as if he'd finally come to terms with something in his own mind, he lay down beside her and covered himself with his jacket. Kate pulled one of the furs off the thick pile cloaking her and offered it to him.

"Thanks," he said.

"Not at all."

They lay there, side by side in silence, watching the firelight dance on the stretched deerskin walls of the teepee.

After a while, Will said, "What you said, out on the road…"

She remembered her words with a shock. "I…I thought I was dying."

"So did I."

The fire crackled, providing a momentary respite from the awkward silence.

He turned on his side to look at her, and she was forced to meet his gaze. "You said that you wanted me to know something. What was it?"

"I…don't remember. I was frightened. I'd hit my head and was probably delirious."

He seemed to accept her answer.

"Why'd you do it, Kate? Why did you cut that deal with Landerfelt?"

She'd known he would ask her and had decided that afternoon she'd tell him the truth. "I thought that maybe you weren't coming back. That I was on my own again."

"You really thought I'd just leave you there alone to fend for yourself."

"I didn't know what you'd do."

"I said I'd come back, and I did."

"Aye, you did. And I'm grateful to you."

"You shouldn't be. We had a bargain. I gave my word." He fidgeted beside her, and she could tell by his eyes that he was annoyed. "You didn't trust me."

"I didn't know what to think. You were so angry the day you left." He couldn't argue with her there, now could he?

"What were you doing coming up to the claim anyway?"

"Mei Li was hell-bent on it."

"Hell-bent?"

"Aye." She realized she was picking up his vernacular. "I couldn't let her go alone, now could I? It was just by way of being a good Christian act, is all."

"And was it a good Christian act to ride off with the town drunk?"

"What choice did I have? Mr. Dunnett's wagon—"

"Rolled into town yesterday, unscathed, right before I left."

Kate shot up and instantly winced with pain. Will pushed her back down.

"Mustart heard it wrong. It wasn't Dunnett's wagon that was ambushed, it was—"

"Landerfelt's. Aye, I recognized it once I saw it. I

thought it was the Packetts making all that racket beside it. It was dark and I couldn't see until—'' Her gaze flew to his. "Will, I was so scared."

He looked at her, silent, for what seemed an eternity. God forgive her, but she would have sold her soul to the devil if he'd only take her in his arms and hold her, kiss her as he had mere hours ago on the road in the moonlight.

"You did just fine," he said evenly.

"You saved my life."

"No, I didn't. I was too late, Kate."

"You weren't. If you hadn't come—"

"*You* killed the bear. Not me."

"But I might not have. And if you hadn't come…"

She'd been foolish to venture out on her own. She knew that now. Will had been right all along. The streets of Dublin were one thing. She was at home there, familiar with the dangers lying in wait for lone women. But here, on the frontier, she didn't know what to expect. The incident with the bear had proved that.

"I was too late, Kate. Too late." He turned away, and she stopped herself from reaching for him.

In all her life she'd never relied on any man for anything. Her father had meant well, God rest his soul, but her mother, when she was alive, had been right not to count on him. Kate had always looked out for herself and her brothers. It was hard to believe that someone would want to look out for her, that a man like Will Crockett would go out of his way to protect her.

"I know I'm not your responsibility. That you have your own life, your own plans, and that my petty troubles don't concern you."

"They do concern me. You're my wife."

"Not truly, I'm not."

"Doesn't matter. I'm responsible for you. It's my fault you were hurt." He rolled over again to face her. "You could have been killed, Kate. That would have been my fault, too."

"Why? You told me to stay put, and I didn't. I chose to go on a wild-goose chase after that wagon."

"All the same. If you'd died…"

All at once, the reason for his self-reproach was clear to her. "You think it was your fault."

"It was."

"No, I don't mean that. I'm talking about Sherrilyn— your wife."

"What?"

"She died of cholera—that's what Mr. Vickery said. But you blame yourself."

"What the hell are you talking about?" Will threw off his jacket and sat up.

"That's why you've been so…overprotective. Your first wife died on the frontier, and so naturally—"

"I told you once, and I'm telling you again, it's none of your business." His eyes were live coals, and she felt suddenly vulnerable under the furs without a stitch on.

In his eyes she read bitterness and pain, and a guilt she imagined was a hundredfold greater than that which she bore like a weight and reflected on each time she thought of her brothers.

"It was cholera, Will. Claiming another life."

"Two lives," he said, his voice barely a whisper.

"What do you mean, two?"

All the light went out of his eyes then. He lay back down and rolled away from her, as far as he could get. The fire crackled, spitting ash and sparks that whirled like a dervish upward toward the hole in the teepee's roof.

"Two lives," he said again. "She was pregnant."

Chapter Fourteen

A crow's insistent squawk jarred her from a fitful sleep. Kate squinted against the flat light blasting through the hole in the teepee's roof. It had to be well past dawn.

Last night's fire was reduced to ash, the furs beside her cold. She didn't have to look to know that Will was no longer beside her. Blindly she ran a hand over the place where he'd slept.

Or hadn't slept. She'd lain awake last night long after their conversation had ended, and could tell from Will's breathing that he'd been awake, too.

Even now, in the cold light of morning, the raw twist of emotion wrought from this news of his unborn child was still with her. She understood him now. Her own feelings were irrelevant. They had no place in her plans, or his.

The flap of the teepee opened and the Miwok woman who'd examined her wounds last night entered, carrying her clothes and a crude wooden bowl of something steaming. It smelled like a meat broth. Kate sat up to greet her. Her head still throbbed, and the soft flesh where the bear had mauled her burned.

The woman knelt and thrust the bowl at her. The last

thing Kate had eaten had been some hardtack on the road yesterday afternoon. She realized she was starved. In less than a minute she downed the broth.

"Good," she said. "Thank you."

The woman nodded, then said something to her that she couldn't understand. Kate shrugged. Handing her the garments, the woman pulled back the furs and gestured for her to dress.

"Oh, aye." As she struggled into her shift, Kate noticed it had been mended. As had the slashes in her corset and dress. She pointed at the neat stitching and smiled. "Thank you."

The woman nodded again, and helped her to finish dressing—not an easy task given how stiff Kate was, and the fact that her head was still spinning. Obeying panto-mimed instructions, she left the laces of her corset loose enough so the garment didn't press against her wound.

"All ready," she said, once she'd slipped into her dark woolen stockings and boots.

They stepped outside and Kate squinted against the light. The sky was white and dreary, the air biting cold. No surprise, given it was mid-November.

The Miwok village was a bustle of activity. Another woman approached, carrying a babe wrapped in beaded buckskin and fur. Kate recognized the infant. The woman who'd helped her smiled—the first smile Kate had seen from her—and held out her arms to accept the child.

"So lovely," Kate said.

The woman thrust the infant toward her.

"Oh, no, I..." The baby grinned her at her, and her heart swelled. "All right. I'd love to hold him." She wasn't certain the child *was* a him, but when the mother adjusted his tiny garments, his gender was confirmed.

Kate cradled the child in her arms as the women chattered away in their tongue, flashing her an occasional smile. The babe was a wee strong thing, about the same age as Michael and Hetty's would be now, she guessed. It had been a long time since she'd held an infant. He was warm and sweet, and reminded her of the twins, Patrick and Frank, when they were his size.

Out of habit Kate paced a tight circle as she rocked him. A lullaby her father had sung to her when she was a toddler and that she, in turn, had sung to her brothers when they were small, came to mind. She began to sing it, and the women laughed with delight.

She turned again, the babe in her arms, the final notes of the lullaby on her lips. Then she saw him.

Still as a statue, Will stood not ten paces from her, staring at her and the babe, his face a bittersweet fusion of warring emotions Kate could only guess at. The bay mare stood saddled and ready at his side.

"Come on," he said. "We're leaving."

Her heart went out to him, but she dared not acknowledge his pain. He wasn't a man who shared his emotions, or who wanted comfort. At least he didn't seem to want it from her.

She handed the baby back to his mother and thanked the woman again for her kindness. The woman grasped her arm for a moment, long enough to say something to her that Kate couldn't understand. Then she and the other woman slipped away into the bustle of the village.

"She says not to worry."

Doc Mendenhall came up behind her. Will joined them, busying himself with the horse as the doctor examined the sizable bump on Kate's head and pressed gently on her wound.

"Another couple of days and you won't know it happened. Except for the scars, of course.'' He nodded at her ribs, which were heavily bandaged under her clothes.

"Scars?" She hadn't thought of that. The bear had raked clean through her dress, her corset, everything. She was lucky to be alive. "It doesn't matter. No one will ever see them."

Will looked up from what he was doing, and their eyes locked. She felt as naked, now, under his grim scrutiny as she had last night when she'd allowed him to look at her breasts. Heat spread from her center, flushing her face.

Struggling to fix her mind on something else, anything else, she pulled her gaze away and focused on the doctor. "What did the woman mean? That I shouldn't worry?"

Doc Mendenhall grinned. "Really want to know?"

"Of course. Tell me."

"Come on," Will said, and took her arm less than gently. "Time to leave." He steered her toward the horse, while the doctor stood there grinning like the cat who ate the canary.

"Tell me," she repeated, as Will recinched the mare's saddle.

The Miwok man whom Kate had met in Tinderbox— the woman's husband and baby's father—called out to them, interrupting the doctor's reply. He approached, and he and Will shook hands, exchanging words in Miwok. The man handed him an overstuffed cloth sack, then nodded at Kate.

"Meat," Will said, answering her unasked question. He hung the sack from the saddle horn.

To Kate's surprise, the Miwok man approached her, reached into a beaded pouch hanging from his breech-cloth, and held something out to her. It looked rather like a necklace, though not like any necklace she'd ever seen.

She looked to Will, unsure of what to do, and he nodded. The Miwok nodded, too. Kate opened her palm and he draped the odd-looking necklace over it. Fashioned from a long strip of leather, it was adorned with seashells and feathers and—

"Sweet Jesus!"

"Well I'll be damned," the doctor said.

Kate grasped the enormous bear claw that hung from the necklace and rubbed it between her fingers.

"It was her kill," Will said, flashing her and the necklace a quick glance as he mounted the mare.

The Miwok nodded to her again and gestured with his hands.

"Oh. Yes, of course." Carefully Kate slipped the necklace over her head.

The Miwok smiled.

"My thanks," Kate said to him.

He said something to Will, and Will responded with the same words. A farewell, she suspected. The Miwok nodded to her again, then disappeared between the teepees.

"That…meat." Kate nodded at the cloth bag suspended from the saddle horn.

"Bear," Will said.

She realized with a start that the meat broth she'd all but sucked down that morning had been neither venison nor hare, nor any game recognizable to her.

"Ready now?" Will offered her his hand, and Doc Mendenhall boosted her up.

She winced as she settled onto the mare's back and wrapped her hands gingerly around Will's waist.

"We'll go slow," he said, glancing back at her. It was the first kind look he'd offered her since last night.

As they started for the trees, Doc Mendenhall raised a hand in farewell. "The woman," he said.

Oh, right. Kate had almost forgotten.

"Says you've got a fine, strappin' husband there, Mrs. Crockett. And not to worry. You'll be havin' your own baby in no time." The doctor grinned at Will. "No time at all."

Kate felt the taut muscles of Will's abdomen turn to stone beneath her touch. The ride back to Tinderbox was uneventful, and he uttered no more than a handful of words to her the whole long way.

It didn't surprise Will to see Matt waiting for them when they rode into town that afternoon. Dunnett's wagon, still loaded, sat in the street in front of the store.

Matt lounged in a comfortable-looking depression fashioned from a pile of grain sacks, his hat pulled low over his eyes, his hands laced together across his chest.

"Is he asleep?" Kate asked, and finally loosened her grip on Will's waist.

For the last four hours, as they'd slowly made their way from the Miwok camp back to town, she'd held on to him, so tight she seemed almost afraid to let him go.

"Probably," he said, shaking off the confusion of feelings that had muddled his thinking the past twenty-four hours.

He reined the mare to a halt beside the wagon and eased Matt's rifle—the one he'd borrowed from him yesterday—out of the saddle holster and poked him with it.

Matt jumped like a polecat, hands and feet flailing. As he scrambled for his pistol he somehow managed to knock his own hat off.

"Whoa, boy. Easy."

Matt squinted against the sun, his eyes focusing on them at last. "You're back!" He scrambled down off the wagon, and Will handed him the rifle. "What the hell happened out there?"

"Grizz decided to help himself to some of Landerfelt's sugar."

"So I heard." Matt helped Kate off the mare, his gaze riveted to the Miwok necklace. "Lordy." He fingered the enormous bear claw and let out a long, low whistle. "I seen where it happened, but didn't know it was so big."

"You were there?" Kate said.

"Tried to catch y'all up. By the time I got there, the Injuns had already hauled the carcass away. They told me what had happened."

Will dismounted, stiff from all the riding, unstrapped the game bag and handed it to his friend. "Here, take some of this. For the loan of the rifle."

Matt opened the bag, peered inside and grinned. The odor of fresh meat cut the air. Kate's face blanched. She reached out to steady herself, and Will caught her arm.

Her fortitude amazed him. She hadn't complained once on the long ride back to town. He knew she had to be hurting. He'd seen where the bear had mauled her. While it was only a flesh wound it had to sting like hell as she'd bumped along on the mare's back.

"Go on inside," he said. "Get some rest. Matt and I will unload the wagon."

"I'll help." Kate started around the storefront toward the back door. "Just give me a few minutes to clean up a bit."

"I said we'll do it."

She stopped, and turned to look at him.

That night at Vickery's when she'd been dressed to the nines, Will thought he'd never seen a more beautiful woman in his life. He was wrong.

She was more beautiful now than he ever remembered

her being, standing there in her mud-caked boots and ragged dress, her hair mussed and her freckled cheeks ruddy from the exertion of a long, hard ride.

He was treading on dangerous ground.

It had to stop. Now.

"Go inside," he repeated. "We don't need help."

"But if three of us work toge—"

"Damn it, woman, don't you understand?" He closed the distance between them and watched her eyes widen in trepidation as he approached. "We made a deal and I'm sticking to my part. But we won't get out of here with you laid up hurt. I've got a ship to make. So do you. If we ever get enough damned money together to get the hell out of here, that is."

The more he said, the angrier he got—at himself, not her—and the tighter her lips thinned into a hard line.

"We can't leave until you're fit to travel. Understand?" He glared at her, battling the insane urge to grab her and kiss her, to tell her things he shouldn't be telling any woman, least of all one who'd made him question the tenets that had shaped his life since he'd left Philadelphia and come West.

"I...I didn't look at it that way," she said quietly, her expression a bit stunned. "You're right, of course, and I'm sorry. I won't be any further trouble to you, I promise."

She turned away, her eyes downcast, and it took every ounce of resolve he had not to reach for her. He ground his teeth as he stripped the mare of saddle and livery and guided her into Kate's wake, slapping her on the rump.

"Not takin' Daisy, there, back to Mustart's, is ya?" Matt leaned against the wagon and cocked a brow at him.

"No. What of it?"

"Just wonderin' is all. About that, and other things."

Matt flashed a glance at the place where Kate had disappeared around the corner of the building.

"Yeah, well stop wondering. It's not your business."

"Whatever ya say, partner."

"And stop *partnering* me. Help me get the damned tarp off this load."

Matt set his rifle up against the storefront and helped him with the tarp. "Good thing ya got the shipment."

"Why?" Will flashed a look up the street, then down again. "Place is a ghost town."

"Not for long, I'm thinkin'."

"What do you mean?"

They tossed the tarp onto the ground and proceeded to unload the wagon. Kate unlocked the front door from the inside, ducked her head out briefly, then disappeared back inside.

"Dunnett says some old boys up Bear River way mighta struck a mother lode."

"Where is Dunnett, anyway?"

Matt grinned. "Up the Chinese camp. Drinkin' and gamblin' on credit the money ya owes him for the load."

"Yeah, well he'll have to wait on it."

"Not long, I reckon." Matt nodded down the street where a half-dozen prospectors, fresh from Sacramento City by the look of them, just turned into town. "Rumor travels fast in these parts. A strike at Bear River means business for Tinderbox. Lots of it."

"Let's hope you're right." As they continued to unload the wagon, Will glanced across the street to Landerfelt's Mercantile and Mining Supply, still shut up tight as a drum.

Matt read his mind. "Never came back. Probably down in the south somewhere, spendin' your money."

Money from the goods he'd swindled out of Kate. Will swore as he tossed another barrel onto the ground.

"Still chapped about that, I reckon."

Will didn't respond.

"Hey, at least ya got your horse back. For a while, anyway."

"That's not all I intend to get back." He pictured Eldridge Landerfelt's face on one of the flour sacks loaded in the wagon, then punched it.

"Same old Will Crockett." Matt grinned and tipped his hat back on his forehead. "I woulda thought that wife a yours mighta softened ya up a little."

Will shot him a look that would freeze water.

"My mistake."

Kate unraveled the bandage wrapped tightly around her ribs and gently tested her wounds. "Not bad. Not bad at all." She tossed the bandage into the fire blazing in the potbellied stove and quickly dressed.

It had been only four days since her run-in with the bear, but today she felt right as rain. And a good thing, too. The store had been amazingly busy since their return from the Miwok village. Just the rumor of a strike at Bear River was enough to divert part of the steady stream of would-be prospectors pouring out of Sacramento City heading south.

Though the Packett boys had returned to Tinderbox, Eldridge Landerfelt had all but vanished, along with Mr. Vickery's wagon, a rented oxen team, and what had remained of their combined inventories before Dan Dunnett delivered the new goods.

Will was still angry at her for cutting the deal with Landerfelt to begin with. But with the merchant gone, and the Mercantile and Mining Supply closed, Crockett's Grocery and Dry Goods was the only game in town. Kate opened the door leading into the store and peeked inside.

Will stood behind the counter weighing gold dust a transient miner had put down in exchange for supplies. He looked completely out of place dressed in his usual buckskin and fur. Knowing now the things she did about his past, she marveled that he'd stayed with her as long as he had.

Will Crockett was no merchant. And the last thing he wanted or needed was a wife, or any kind of responsibility weighing him down. He'd all but said it the day they'd returned from the Miwok village. His cool demeanor and seeming indifference to her these past few days confirmed it.

"Kate," Will said, as she entered the store. The miner tipped his hat to her on his way out. "Here's another hundredweight for your bag."

She reached into the pocket of her old dress and pulled out the leather pouch that had been her father's. Running her thumb over the smooth, burnished surface, she smiled, remembering him.

"How much?" Will nodded at the pouch.

"Nearly six hundred dollars."

"Another week and we're heading west to Frisco, no matter how much we have."

"I understand." She wondered what he meant to do if they didn't have enough for both his passage and hers.

She'd given up hope altogether of raising enough to pay back the money she'd borrowed from her mother's sister. She'd have to work it off in the laundry in Clancy Street, along with whatever Michael and Sean could make. The twins would have to be put to work as well. She'd hoped to keep them in school, but could see no way clear to that foolish dream. Not now.

Glancing around the packed shelves of the store, she was grateful for Dan Dunnett's last-minute decision on the levee in Sacramento City to put up enough of his own money to bring back a full load of goods. This time he'd bought only mining supplies and food. If business continued at the brisk pace of recent days, they had a chance.

"I heard Jed Packett's voice earlier." Kate pocketed the leather pouch and smoothed her skirt. "What did he want?"

"Wanted me take Daisy back to the livery."

"Oh." Technically the mare was still Landerfelt's property, but since he hadn't returned as promised, she supposed Will saw no reason to return the mare. "What did you tell him?"

Will shot her a cool look. "I said if Landerfelt wants her back, he can come and get her."

As if she had to ask.

"You don't like him, do you?"

"No. Do you?"

"Of course not. He's a snake and a swindler, the worst kind of man. But it's different with you. You more than dislike him. It's almost an…obsession."

"The hell it is." Will skirted the counter and stopped just short of forcing her to step back to accommodate him. "You don't know what you're talking about."

She looked up at him and for all the world wondered what other terrible secrets he was keeping from her. Secrets she could see storming around in those dark eyes of his. "Maybe I don't. It's just that…"

"What?"

"Sometimes it's better to talk about things. To share them with someone who…" Her pulse began to race as a wave of emotion welled inside her.

"Cares?" His expression softened. He stepped closer,

so close that the tips of her breasts grazed his chest, so close that his lips hovered just over hers. "Do you, Kate? Do you care?"

Her head spun and her heart raced. She didn't know how to respond to so bald a question from the only man she'd ever met for whom she truly did care. A man who didn't want her, who couldn't wait to put her aboard a ship and send her away.

The words were on her lips.

If she said them, would he take her into his arms and kiss her as he had that afternoon on the ridge, and again just days ago in the road?

Or would he rebuke her?

Fear and doubt and desire clashed inside her along with the certain knowledge that no matter what she answered, the fact remained that she had to go home to Ireland. She had to go back.

The bell over the storefront door tinkled to life, shattering the moment. Dan Dunnett burst across the threshold, an open bottle of Cheng's finest brandy in his hand.

Will spun on his heel to face him. "What is it? What's happened?"

"It's gold!"

"Gold?" So the rumors were true, then. Kate could hardly believe it.

"Yes, ma'am. A ton of it." Dan raised the bottle in a solitary toast. "At Bear River—right up the road."

Chapter Fifteen

Five hundred dollars in two days! Eleven hundred all told. It was more money than Kate had ever seen in her life.

When she'd borrowed the funds for her journey to America, Aunt Olivia hadn't actually given her the coin. Instead, her mother's sister had paid in advance for her passage. Some distant cousin in the shipping business had made all the arrangements ahead. Kate had seen none of the coin, save for a meager amount of pocket change meant for the journey overland.

Just for good measure, Kate counted the golden eagles again, then swept them into the bulging leather pouch along with the gold nuggets and dust and odd foreign coins she and Will had accepted in payment for the goods they'd sold in the two days since the strike was confirmed at Bear River.

"It's enough," Will said. "Just."

Kate pocketed the bag. It was heavy as sin, and weighed her down as she walked. "You'll make your ship, then. You should be happy."

He didn't look happy. Not by a long shot.

"It was those men, wasn't it? Yesterday. Bidding up

the prices, fighting over the last shovel we had." She
looked at the empty shelves, felt the weight of the money
bag in her pocket, and thanked God they'd done it.

Will stared out the window at the busy street. "If a
man's fool enough to pay that kind of money for a garden
tool, it's no skin off my back."

No, it was something else that was bothering him. She
could see it in the set of his jaw, in the restless way he
paced back and forth, as if he were an animal in a cage.

"You...want to leave, don't you?"

"Hell, yes. I should have done it weeks ago."

He wouldn't look at her, and she was glad of it, for if
he had he would have seen the hurt his words caused her.
She shook off the ridiculous melancholy that had colored
his mood and now hers, and busied herself sweeping up.

"When shall we leave?"

"Tomorrow."

She paused, her broom in midstroke. "As soon as
that?"

"I thought you wanted to get out of here." He flashed
her a cool look.

It had been like that between them these past few days.
He'd kept his distance, and she hers. They'd been so busy,
she really hadn't had time to think about what was going
to happen once they'd made enough money to get on with
their lives.

"I do want to leave. I mean I have to. My brothers..."
She had never told him about the debt. There was no point
in it. It wasn't his problem. It was hers.

"A man down at Mustart's said a clipper's leaving out
of Frisco in another week bound for Dublin. About the
same time that steamer I plan to be on leaves for Sitka."

"It will all work out then, won't it?" She shot him a
tentative glance, but he wasn't looking at her.

His gaze was fixed on a buckboard pulled by two fine horses, rattling up the street, surrounded by dozens of men whistling and catcalling.

Kate strode to the front door, frowning, broom in hand, and pulled it open. Will followed. Her eyes widened as she recognized the garishly dressed woman holding the reins.

"Looky who's here, Will." Matt Robinson stood in the street, grinning from ear to ear as the buckboard rattled to a stop.

Kate gripped the broom, heat rising to her face, as Rose Beecham and her line girls tossed seductive smiles into the crowd.

"Howdy, Will," a pretty young blonde called out. Dressed in bright red silk, she waved to him from the buckboard. Kate recognized her from the afternoon she'd spent waiting for Floyd Canter and his friend to *wet their whistles*.

"Oh, yoo-hoo, Will!" Another girl waved to him. Then another.

Will moved past Kate into the street.

"And where do you suppose you're going?" She took a step after him, then thought better of it.

"To speak to a friend of mine. Do you mind?"

Rose Beecham flashed her a smile. The woman had been kind to her in Spanish Camp. All the same, Kate caught herself scowling back.

"You…know those women?"

"Yeah."

"Not as well as some of 'em would like, eh, Will?" Matt's grin broadened, then his face contorted in pain. "Ow!"

Mei Li stood behind him, gripping what looked to Kate

like a railroad spike, her face bloodred, her eyes blacker than midnight.

"Mei Li, I thought you was—"

"You come now. I make tea."

"Tea? But we wasn't supposed to get together till tonight. At the party, remember?"

Mei Li flashed angry eyes at the line girls who sat giggling like a gaggle of primped-up geese playing at peacocks. After thirty seconds of arguing, Mei Li waving the railroad spike and uttering some choice Chinese phrases, Matt acquiesced and followed her up the street toward her shanty.

"What party?" Kate said, as Matt's words sunk in.

"To celebrate the gold strike. Down in the clearing. Tonight." Will nodded along the street to the place where they'd so hastily married just three weeks ago.

"It'll be a wild time, Miz Crockett." Rose Beecham smiled at her from her perch on the buckboard. "You oughtta come. Your husband'll be there. Won'tcha, Will?"

"I'll be there," Will said.

"Wild time, indeed." Kate spun on her heel and started for the front door.

"Some of the fine men of Tinderbox are settin' up our tents there now. Come see us, Miz Crockett. I might could loan you somethin' prettylike to wear."

Whirling toward the buckboard, Kate gripped the broom so hard she half expected it to snap in two. "I'll do no such shameless thing."

The line girls cackled with laughter. Will just stood there, staring at her. If she didn't know him better and the foul mood he'd been in for days now, she could swear that was a smile she saw threatening to erupt on his lips.

She'd give him something to smile about. Wild time, indeed! "I'll be inside," she said. "Packing."

Will leaned against a naked oak at the edge of the clearing and gazed, unfocused, at the bonfire blazing in the center. Men danced around it to the lively strains of Mustart's fiddle, mostly with each other. Except for Rose and her girls, Will could count the women present on one hand.

Kate wasn't one of them.

For the tenth time in as many minutes, he peered up the dark street toward the store. The soft lamplight flickering from inside earlier that evening was now extinguished.

Kate had spent the afternoon packing what little she intended to take home with her to Ireland. She'd hardly spoken to him the rest of the day, and when the sun went down and it was time to join the festivities, he purposely hadn't asked her to accompany him.

It was better this way. He'd started to distance himself from her days ago, and now, at last, she seemed to be doing the same. It was all for the best. She had a life to go back to, and he had one to get on with.

Nonetheless, he found himself drawing the painted miniature out of his pocket and gazing at her image. The image of a woman who in one breath fought off a grizzly and in the next sang a lullaby to a sleeping child.

He ground his teeth and closed his fist over the image. "She ain't comin'."

He knew who'd spoken without having to look up. Rose Beecham's cloying perfume was unmistakable. He shook off his confused emotions and smiled at her.

"Here, this'll warm you up." Rose offered him a shot

of what looked like Cheng's homemade brandy. "Take it."

"No. You go ahead."

"Suit yourself." She slugged it back and set the empty glass on a stump. "Fifteen dollars a shot, but the Chinaman cut me a deal."

Tents had been staked around the clearing's perimeter, housing makeshift gaming hells, saloons and places where hungry miners could buy an outrageously priced meal. The air was thick with the smell of roasted meat and whiskey, and perfume wafting from the tents where Rose's girls drove hard bargains with reckless men.

The blonde who'd waved at Will that afternoon from the buckboard, crooked her finger at him, beckoning him inside.

Rose cackled. "Go on, Will. It's on the house. After seein' you and your wife together, well, it don't take a mastermind to figure out you ain't gettin' what a man needs from a gal. Not from her anyway."

He thought about it as the blonde batted her lashes at him. Maybe that was exactly what he needed. It had been a long time. Too long. And sleeping on a hard floor not ten feet from a woman who addled his brain so fierce he didn't know what to think anymore only made it worse.

"Mr. Crockett got exactly what he bargained for."

Will spun toward the familiar Irish lilt, his stomach tightening. Kate stood behind them, just inside the cover of the trees. The light from the blaze danced in her eyes and set her auburn hair afire.

"I can see that," Rose said, looking her up and down. "Guess I'll be movin' along, then."

Kate didn't spare her a glance. "Aye, you do that, Miss Beecham."

When they were alone, Will offered her his hand. "You came after all."

"Only to satisfy my curiosity." She ignored his proffered hand and pulled her cloak tighter about her.

"And...have you?"

Her face was luminous, her lips ripe as Michigan cherries. She glanced at the revelers, unimpressed. "For the most part."

He wondered what had really made her change her mind and come out. He half hoped it was because he was here and she wanted to be with him.

"But there are still some things you're wondering about, aren't there?"

Her gaze returned to his. It was tentative now, the tiniest bit of vulnerability shining in her eyes, much like the first day he'd met her.

"Like...what, supposin'?"

"I don't know. Like maybe how it is that we've lived as man and wife for nearly a month and never once—"

"Come on, darlin', dance with me!" A big, burly miner grabbed Kate's hand and pulled her into the crowd.

Will shot forward, but two men pulled him back. One of them was Matt.

"Let her dance with the man. He's harmless. Besides—" Matt glanced at the boisterous crowd "—ain't more than a few decent women here."

He supposed Matt was right. Still, he didn't like Kate being manhandled like that. He watched as she paused in the middle of the dance and fanned her blazing cheeks. Mei Li shot into the crowd and snatched the cloak from her shoulders, then returned to her father's saloon tent.

"God almighty, Will, she sure is pretty."

Will couldn't take his eyes off her. She wore a dress he'd never seen before. Made of blue calico, it had a prim lace collar and buttoned to the neck. But the way it molded to her body, he felt himself harden just looking at her.

She danced with a half-dozen other men—Vickery, Dunnett, even Father Flanagan—before Will saw Jed Packett weaving his way through the crowd toward her. His brother Leon stood directly across from Will and Matt, staring at them.

"Now don't up and do somethin' stupid, partner. This here's supposed to be a party, not a—"

Will didn't wait for Matt to finish. He shucked his buckskin jacket and reached Kate a second after Jed Packett tapped the miner with whom she was dancing on the shoulder.

"Cuttin' in," Jed said, and smiled at Kate with a mouthful of bad teeth.

The miner politely stepped back to allow Jed his turn.

"I don't think so, Packett." Will stepped in front of him.

"It's all right," Kate said. "I don't mind."

"I do." Will grabbed her hand and jerked her into his arms. The music changed to a waltz and he swept her away, nearly off her feet.

Jed Packett glared at him, spat a wad of tobacco onto the ground where they'd been standing, then disappeared into the crowd.

"You didn't have to do that," Kate said. "It wouldn't have hurt for me to dance with him."

"I didn't want you dancing with him."

"Why not? What does it matter? We're leaving tomorrow, aren't we?"

"Yes." He pulled her tighter against him as he guided her around the bonfire in time to the music. She felt warm against his body. And good. So very good.

"You know how to do this," she said, and looked down at his feet. "Waltz, I mean. Did you learn it in Philadelphia?"

He didn't answer.

"I'm not very good at it. We only did step dances back home."

"You're all right." He flashed a glance at the tight-fitting bodice of her calico dress. "Where'd you get it? The dress?"

"I traded for it with that woman over there." She nodded at the wife of one of the miners working the gold strike at Bear River. "We've no more need of my father's cook pots, now do we? Now that we're leaving."

"No, I guess not."

Will looked at her, and what he read in her eyes told him she wasn't thinking about cook pots and calico at all. Still waltzing, he guided her smoothly between two tents into a close stand of pine, just beyond the bonfire's circle of light.

The moon shone in her eyes as she met his gaze. He pulled her close, until her breasts were crushed against his chest. His heart was beating nearly out of control. So was hers.

"What are you doing?" she breathed, her lips inches from his.

"I don't know." He swallowed hard. Every truth he'd based his life on these five years past eluded him as his mouth descended on hers.

She kissed him back with an explosion of passion and innocence, need and desire, that was headier than any drug he could imagine. His hands moved over her compliant body, molding it to his own as if they were made to fit together. In wild abandon their tongues mated. When he felt her hands on his buttocks, he knew there was no going back. He held her fast and pressed his hardness against her. The breath rushed from her lips as she felt every inch of him.

"You do want me, then?" she breathed. "Say that you do."

He kissed her hard, letting loose a visceral groan from deep inside him. "I want you more than anything."

She opened her eyes and looked into his. "We'll find a way, then. A way for me to stay with you. A way for us to—"

His body turned to cold stone in her arms. He knew she felt the change in him. She swallowed her words, her brows furrowing in confusion.

He shook off the hunger threatening to tear him apart, to make him do things he knew he'd regret later. Gently but firmly he pushed her away from him. "My ship leaves in a week. You can't come with me, Kate."

"But you said—"

"No." He shook his head. "You misunderstood. I want you, but—" He didn't want to hurt her, but it was too late for that, now. "Just for the one night."

The lie was like a knife to his gut.

She took a step back, her lips parted, her expression one not of surprise but of raw pain, the kind he knew she'd tried to hide from him in the past. She wasn't hiding now.

"I told you before," he forced himself to go on. "I don't want a wife. Or a family."

It took every ounce of his determination to turn away from her. He slipped between the tents into the crowd, the revelers whirling around him in a stink of whiskey and sweat, a haze of color and heat causing his vision to blur and his head to throb.

Christ, he was in love with her.

And had been all this time. He'd known it but didn't want to see it, didn't want to believe it. It wasn't going to happen. Not now. Not ever.

The blonde who'd flirted with him earlier stood just outside her tent chatting with a prospective customer. Without a second thought, Will marched up to her, grabbed her roughly by the arm and pulled her inside.

Kate forced herself to remain in the cover of the trees a full minute after Will had gone. She wavered a bit on her feet, eyes closed, breathing in and out, fighting to get a grip on her emotions.

What had she been thinking? The things she'd said to him. The words spilling out of her like that. She fisted her hands at her sides and cursed her own foolishness. Did she really think he'd want her for his wife?

For one shining moment she had thought exactly that. *I want you more than anything.*

"Kate Dennington, you're a bigger fool than you know."

Aye, and as if she could just stay here with him. Abandon her brothers, forget about the debt, just as easy as you please. Even if he wanted her, she couldn't stay.

Collecting herself, she tipped her chin high and walked with purpose back to the party. She'd pay her respects to Mrs. Vickery, to Mei Li and Mr. Cheng, and then she'd go. In a few short hours she'd be gone from this place forever. Would that she'd never seen Tinderbox or had ever heard the name Will Crockett.

Men begged her to dance with them as she pushed her way through the crowd. She ignored them and kept moving. Mei Li waved to her from outside her father's saloon tent. Kate strode toward her. When Mei Li read the hardness in her expression, she frowned.

"Hey, little lady." A man grabbed her from behind.

"Let me go!" Kate wrestled out of his grasp. She whirled on him and came face-to-face with Jed Packett.

"I can't dance with you now, I'm sorry." She started to turn away, and he grabbed her arm.

"It ain't a dance I want. In fact, I don't want nothin' from ya."

"Then what?" She flashed her eyes at his less than gentle grip on her.

"It's your husband, Miz Crockett."

"What about him?"

Jed nodded toward a tent she didn't recognize. "I think you'd best see for yourself."

"Let go of me! I'm not interested in—" Before she realized his intent, Packett steered her toward the tent, jerked open the flap and pushed her inside.

Kate skidded to a stop in the soft dirt, her heart racing. There was no lantern in the tent, just soft light filtering through the heavy canvas walls from the bonfire outside.

A man sat on a makeshift bed with one of Rose Beecham's whores on his lap. He was kissing her, his hands groping her scantily clad body. When the tart came up for air, Kate got a clear glimpse of the man's face.

She stood there, openmouthed, gawking at him like a ninny, blinking her eyes in the dim light as if she were just now awakening from a bad dream.

"Kate, you don't understand." Will pushed the blonde off his lap and she landed on her silk-clad rump in the dirt.

"I understand plenty." Before he could say more, she backed out of the tent, right into Jed Packett's waiting arms.

"Got an eyeful, didn't ya?" Before she could stop him, he groped her. "Whatcha got here, missy?" He'd felt the heavy money bag secreted in the pocket of her skirt.

Breaking free, Kate whirled on him. He grinned at her, his foul breath causing her nearly to retch. Without another thought, she slugged him, square on the nose with her fist.

And then she fled. Weaving between the tents, pushing her way through the throng of men, fighting the rage of tears stinging her eyes.

At last she broke free of the crowd and burst onto Main Street. The cold air away from the bonfire shocked her to her senses. She raced toward the store, her lungs burning, her breath frosting the air.

The money bag in her pocket weighed her down and beat against her thigh as she ran. Bloody thing!

Somewhere at the edge of her awareness she heard Will calling her name, the thud of his boots on the hard-packed dirt close behind her.

She skidded around the corner of the storefront, fumbling in her pocket for the latch key. A second later she burst through the back door into the cabin and slammed it shut behind her.

Will's footfalls sounded on the back porch. Kate threw the bolt and backed quickly away from the door.

"Open up Kate. Let me in."

"No."

The door to the potbellied stove was cracked just enough to cast a soft, flickering light across the floor. She raced to the bed, pulled the damnable money bag from her pocket and slapped it into a drawer in the night table, then hunted under the furs for her father's revolver. "Blast!" It wasn't there.

"We have to talk, Kate."

"Go away!" The rifle was a better idea, anyway. She snatched it from its place against the wall and leveled it at the back door.

"What I said in the trees, what you saw..."

"I said go away!"

"So help me God, Kate, if you don't open this door, I'll—"

"Go on, then, you bleedin' bastard, break it down!"

Never in her life did she think he'd actually do it.

The crash of the blow caused her thudding heart to stop. In shock, she jumped back as splintered wood and shards of metal flew across the room. The door crashed wide.

Will stepped across the threshold, his fists balled at his sides, jaw hard, his broad chest heaving with each breath. All that, she could have dealt with. But it was his eyes that struck fear in her. They were black as the devil's own heart, as murderous as she'd ever seen them.

She cocked the rifle, glared back at him and waited.

Chapter Sixteen

She didn't wait long.

Will crossed the room in two strides and snatched the rifle from her hands. He'd known she wouldn't use it. In a second he disarmed it and flung it aside. In the flickering glow of firelight she read his intent.

A heartbeat later he grabbed her.

"G-go back to your blond tart."

"No," he said, and kissed her hard. All the breath went out of her as his tongue invaded her mouth and his arms tightened around her.

She broke free of the kiss and whispered, "Stop it."

"Why?" He backed her to the bed, one hand gripping her waist, the other slipping the pins from her hair. "You're my wife, aren't you?" Her hair tumbled free in his hand and he raked it through with less than gentle fingers.

Not yet she wasn't. There was still time. She could have the marriage annulled. Aye, Father Flanagan had wed them proper, but without consummation, in the eyes of the Church...

She realized she was shaking, that her heart was thudding, her breath coming in short gasps. And it wasn't from the race up the street. "W-we haven't yet—"

"Why haven't we, Kate?" He kissed her again, and this time she kissed him back, her arms snaking around him, her body molding to his as if all along it knew they were meant to be lovers.

"God knows," she breathed against his lips.

He bore her back on the fur-covered bed, and she felt the solid weight of him settle on top of her. A whirlwind of unrelated thoughts tore through her mind as his hands worked to strip her of her clothes.

Short work was made of the buttons of her new dress. One skittered across the floor as Will tugged her bodice down around her shoulders. He didn't ask her consent, but neither did she try to stop him. In a haze of passion, she closed her eyes as he laved her neck with his tongue, tasting his way lower, groping at her breasts, grinding his hips into hers.

He was hungry, desperate. And so was she. She read it in his eyes, gone fire and chestnut in the span of a moment. Felt it in the frenzy of his kisses, the quivering of his hands as they freed her breasts from the corset.

He stripped her to the waist and paused to look at her in the firelight. The angry red slashes healing to scars where the bear had mauled her didn't escape his attention.

"You're beautiful," he said. Then, without warning, he dipped his head and teased her erect nipple with his tongue.

She gasped as he began to suckle. The whole world slipped out from under her and seemed to spin. She closed her eyes and reveled in the pleasure of it.

Her hands, of their own accord, slid downward across the rough flannel of his shirt. She grasped it and tugged it free from his buckskin trousers. His back was hot as a fire iron. Slowly she ran her hands across his smooth skin, feeling his hard muscles working underneath.

They kissed and fondled, and he suckled some more—this time cupping her other breast, pointing it toward his hungry mouth. All the while he rolled his hips with purpose against her body, which now ached in places she'd only begun to discover since the first time he kissed her.

The feel of his erection pressing into her, his beard stubble burning her skin, his powerful hands and hot mouth, the musky scent of him—all fed an overwhelming desire blazing up inside her that conquered rational thought.

"We shouldn't," he whispered against her lips. "Tomorrow we're—"

"I don't care." And God help her, she didn't. She kissed him hard and groped his muscular backside.

He didn't need any more encouragement than that.

A moment later he was stripped of his shirt and suspenders. She wrestled with her own clothes bunched at her waist and tangled between her legs as he rolled off her to dispense with his boots and trousers.

When he returned to her she was ready for him. More than ready. Her dress lay in a heap on the floor, along with her corset and shift. As he pulled off her boots and stockings, his gaze traveled the length of her pantalet-clad legs upward to where the garment split, his eyes fixing on the fire-bright tuft of hair shielding her sex.

She read the hesitation in his eyes, but she would have none of it.

"*Ní fuaireamar,*" she whispered, and pulled him down on top of her.

In a tangle of limbs, they resumed their lovemaking. In seconds he'd relieved her of the rest of what little she wore. Their bare skin connected, and she opened her legs to him, his powerful thighs forcing them wide.

Their gazes locked in the firelight, his eyes slits. His heart beat strong against her breast, as her own raced out of control. Truly there was no going back.

He was pure heat and power. She melted into him, burning like the molten gold she'd seen assayers shape into ingots. The velvet tip of his manhood pressed into her, and she gasped.

"Kate," he breathed.

"Don't stop."

He covered her mouth with his and kissed her with a possessiveness that fueled her own feral desire. Wrapping her legs around his hips, she closed her eyes. *"Ní fuairea-mar,"* she whispered again.

He groaned and drove himself inside her.

The shock of it sent the breath rushing from her. She nearly came off the bed. Gently but firmly, he pressed her back down with his body, whispering soothing words, peppering her face with small, violent kisses.

His breathing grew labored, his brow damp with tiny beads of perspiration that reflected the light of the fire. "Wait," he breathed as she moved with him inside her.

"For what?"

Shifting his weight onto one powerful arm, he slipped a hand between their bodies to the place where she burned for his touch. "For this," he said, and willed her hold his gaze as his fingers began to work some unknown magic.

She bucked in response, and he drove into her again, his jaw tight, every muscle taut, his dark eyes searching her face for signs of fear and pain. She felt none of those things. Only pleasure beyond bearing as his fingers moved faster, his thrusts pushed deeper.

All at once she felt the centering, a union of heat and

tension so powerful she grew suddenly afraid. She pushed against him and cried out, but he would not relent.

"Close your eyes," he said, and kissed her with trembling lips.

She obeyed and her world became him, and him alone. His scent possessed her, his power infused her as he drove her to the edge of a madness from which she feared she'd find no release.

And then it happened.

Her breath caught in her throat. Her eyes opened to find his fixed intently on her face, his expression a tight fusion of emotions she could not fathom.

Raw waves of pleasure radiated from her as her hips moved of their own accord beneath him. "Will," she breathed.

He thrust harder, faster, and as fulfillment spread from her center he focused on his own mounting need. He shifted his weight to both hands and drove deeper. A moment later he cried her name.

Bathed in firelight, his face was the most beautiful thing she'd ever seen in all her life. Closing her eyes, she drew him down close, her legs ringing his waist, her arms wrapped tight about him.

"*Ní fuaireamar,*" he whispered, repeating her words. "What does it mean?"

Her eyes guarded the truth as her lips spun a lie.

The fire in the stove had gone out, and the cabin was cold as a tomb. Will slid from the warmth of the bed, grabbed a handful of kindling and a log from the wood box, and started it up again.

It was late, well past midnight if he had to guess. He snatched back the drape from the window, and moonlight spilled into the room, illuminating the peaceful countenance of the woman sleeping naked beneath the furs a few steps from where he stood.

He paused for a moment to look at her before slipping into his buckskin trousers and boots. Her breathing was slow and steady, her face luminous in the pearly light.

Easing onto the bed, taking care not to wake her, he brushed a kiss across her forehead, stroking the silken softness of her hair, which spilled across the pillow in seductive disarray.

Why had he done it?

He closed his eyes and silently cursed himself.

He'd been out of his head, desperate for her. Angry at himself for wanting her, for running after her like that, but unable to live with her thinking he wanted anything to do with the whore she'd caught him with.

She stirred in her sleep, and he quieted her with whispered words.

He hadn't been with many women. His first wife and a handful of others. Whores mostly—Sherrilyn included. He reminded himself that she'd been bought and paid for just like the others, but with his father's money.

Kate was nothing like those women. And he was nothing like himself—the man he thought he was—when he was with her. Nothing in his experience with any of them had prepared him for the raw emotion he'd felt making love to Kate. Or the way he felt now, looking down at her in the moonlight.

He inched closer and heard the rustle of paper in his trouser pocket. Frowning, he slipped a hand inside and retrieved a forgotten San Francisco letter sheet Mustart had given him at the party before Kate had arrived.

Not bothering to reread it, he crumpled it in his fist and pitched it toward the open door of the stove, where a bright little fire now blazed. He missed, and it skipped across the floor. He cursed under his breath.

He needed to think, and he couldn't do it here beside her. The temptation to take her into his arms and make love to her all over again was too strong.

Slipping his suspenders over his shoulders, he rose and moved toward what was left of the door. Kate didn't stir. He eased outside and closed it behind him.

The frigid air was bracing. Just what he needed. He sucked in a breath and settled onto the porch. A million stars blinked back at him as he studied the night sky, a question on his mind.

What if he simply didn't go?

Or what if he did, and he asked her to go with him?

All that he'd read in her eyes when they'd made love, and afterward, when he held her in his arms until she drifted off to sleep, told him that she would.

If he asked.

Kate padded to the stove, gooseflesh rising on her bare skin. Lord, it was cold! She knelt and retrieved the crumpled paper Will had meant to toss into the fire.

With Mei Li's help, her reading had improved greatly. Still, after smoothing out the letter sheet, she could make out only some of the words staring back at her in the soft firelight. One word in particular, printed below the drawing of a ship.

Sitka.

In her head she counted off the number of days between now and what could only be the sailing date printed next to the word. A week from today—or tomorrow rather. Not long.

Quiet as a church mouse, she crept to the window and peeked out at Will sitting there on the porch, staring up at the sky as if he were having a sobering chat with the stars.

He was sorry they'd made love. She'd felt it in his touch when he sat beside her on the bed moments ago, certain she was asleep. But why was he sorry? That was the question burning in her mind, twisting her insides into knots as she watched him.

Was it simply because he was an honorable man and had never meant to take advantage of their situation? Oh, he'd wanted her, that was clear. And she him.

Her body burned where the stubble of his beard had raked her skin. She felt her lips, swollen from his kisses, and ached again for his touch.

Just for the one night.

His words played over and over in her mind. Regardless, a man like Will Crockett didn't seduce virgins for sport. She knew him well enough to know that what had happened between them had not been intended.

Countless times he'd made it plain to her that he didn't want a wife, and she understood his reasons. Sherrilyn had meant the world to him, and he grieved her still. Her and the lost babe.

Besides, had he wanted for love, why on earth would he choose a poor Irish immigrant, plain of face and with not a penny to her name, as a replacement?

Love was what she longed to see reflected in his eyes as he gazed skyward and ran a hand through his tousled hair. But all she saw was remorse. She knew him, knew he felt responsible for her. And now that they'd…

She closed her eyes and recalled their heated coupling.

Oh, Kate, you selfish fool! After what had happened between them he would never leave her. Whether he wanted her or not, he'd stay with her. And that she could not bear.

It was her fault—all of it. Aye, he'd come after her, had battered in the door to get to her, but she'd allowed it. She'd wanted it, burned for it. One word from her and he would have stopped. On his own he'd considered it. Twice. But she hadn't wanted him to stop.

Not then, not now, not ever.

A sound pricked her ears. She opened her eyes and— Lord, he was coming back!

Like a shot she raced for the bed. The letter sheet slipped from her hand, but there was no time to retrieve it. As the door swung open on rusted hinges, she dived under the furs and went still as a stone.

The rustling of clothes sharpened her ears, and a few moments later Will slid naked into bed beside her. The night was wicked cold and his body warm, and it took all of her will to stop herself from reaching for him.

He lay there on his back, and she on hers, as the seconds ticked away in her racing mind, the space between their bodies almost painful. A dozen times she started to speak, and each time held her tongue.

What was there to say? There was only one thing to do now, and she intended to do it.

Dawn came at long last, and with it a fog so thick Kate could hardly see as she made her way to Father Flanagan's small tent on the hillside just above the Vickerys' cottage.

The town was quiet as death. Last night's revelry likely had gone on into the wee hours of the morning. Squinting into the mist, she walked down Main Street, avoiding the broken bottles and other trash littering the way. The party evidently had been quite a success.

As she passed the livery she shook her head. Floyd Canter lay facedown in the dirt, an empty whiskey bottle in hand. "Saints preserve us." The gate was open on the corral beside Mustart's shed. Luckily the horses and pair of oxen housed there seemed in no mood to make an escape.

Kate continued on, turning up the hillside just before reaching the clearing. She was in no mood to view the aftermath of last night's festivities.

The trees dripped with moisture. Wet branches cracked under her boots as she made the steep climb. The smell of burnt wood from last night's bonfire was thick on the air.

After Will had come back to bed last night she hadn't slept at all. He hadn't either, from what she could tell. While it was still dark he'd dressed and gone out, her father's rifle in hand.

That was not unusual. He often hunted at first light, and she knew he meant to leave the Chengs with game in payment for all their help, in addition to a cut of their profits for Mei Li's hard work.

Profits.

Kate stopped dead on the wooded hillside and felt for the leather pouch housing their coins and gold. It wasn't there! Her mind raced to recall what had—

Ah, she remembered now. She'd taken it out of her calico dress and had put it away in the night table as usual. Her thoughts had been so full of Will that morning, she'd forgotten to retrieve it. No matter. After her visit to the priest, she'd hurry back. And then they'd be on their way.

As she passed the Vickerys' cottage, she noticed their wagon was perched askew on the hillside. She must remember to say goodbye to the lawyer and his wife before she and Will left town.

Breathing hard, she finally reached her destination. "Father Flanagan, are you up?" she called out as she approached his tent. No answer. She called his name again, and this time heard him stirring inside the tent.

"Sunday already, is it?" His voice was thick with sleep, and a hangover, if she had to guess.

"No Father, it's Friday. But might I have a word with you all the same."

"Is that you, Kate? Mrs. Crockett, I mean." The tent flap slapped open and the portly priest peered out at her, squinting. He was dressed in nothing but his long johns, which were stained with what smelled distinctly like whiskey. "What the devil are you doin' up so early? I don't hear confessions before nine you know."

"I know, Father, but I can't wait that long. And while I've got some confessing to do, it's not absolution I've come for, but advice."

"Advice, is it? Well, why didn't you say so?" He snapped the tent flap shut again, and she waited while he dressed. A few minutes later he emerged from the tent, and once he found his balance, led her to a couple of stumps near the dead campfire where he obviously did his cooking. "Now, what might I advise you on?"

She took a seat on one the stumps and struggled with how to begin. He was young, not that much older than herself, she suspected. Had he been a more experienced priest she might have felt more comfortable with what she was about to tell him.

"Go on, lass. Spit it out."

"All right." She drew a breath. "It's like this, Father."

Father Flanagan sat on the stump across from her and listened to the whole long tale. How she came to Tinderbox and met Will, how she shamelessly asked him to marry her so she could keep the store. She related the terms of their bargain, what they each hoped to gain, and how they hadn't really been living as man and wife.

Until last night.

The priest's green eyes grew wider and rounder with each new revelation. She told him about Will's first wife, how she and their unborn babe had died of cholera. The hardest part was telling him about Will's guilt over her untimely death, and his wish to never marry again. She finished by describing the magnitude of the obligation he surely felt after what had happened between them last night.

"So you see, Father, I must have the annulment. His ship leaves in a week, and I would not have him miss it for the world."

Father Flanagan sucked in a breath and slowly exhaled. "You haven't told me everything, Kate."

"But I have." She'd left nothing out, nothing of importance.

"Aye, you've explained the mess you're in, and how you intend to skittle across the pond back to Ireland and send your husband on his merry way north."

She nodded, wondering what else she possibly could tell him.

"But you haven't said how you feel about this man, or how he feels about you."

"Oh." She blinked her eyes a few times before answering. "Does that…matter?"

Father Flanagan snorted. "That's the only thing that does, you silly girl. I'm a priest, but I'm not stupid. I was there last night, and saw with my own eyes how it is between you."

"At the party, you mean."

"Aye, at the party. Where else?"

She met his annoyed gaze and struggled for the right words. "I…I don't know how I feel."

"Aye, you do. It's plain as the nose on your face, Kate."

"But he doesn't want me, Father. And I won't be a ball and chain around his heart." Father Flanagan started to bluster, but she cut him off. "Besides, I've got to go home. My brothers are counting on me. We've the debt to pay and—"

"Was does your husband say about it?"

"The debt?" She shook her head. "I haven't told him. Aye, and thank God for it. That's exactly the kind of thing that would keep him with me against his will."

Father Flanagan rose from the stump and, to her shock, plucked her straight off hers. They stood head to head, and he squeezed his face up in exasperation. "Go home, Kate. Tell your husband you love him, and tell him about the debt."

"I'll do no such thing."

He turned her so she was pointing down the hill, and gave her a little push. "And say a dozen rosaries—on your knees, mind you—for your sins." He made the sign of the cross, and blessed her.

"Aye, well, I'll surely do that, Father. That and more. But about the annulment. Is it possible, do you think, to—"

"Go home, Kate." He shook his head and moved on wobbly legs back to his tent.

As she lifted her skirts and started back down the hill, she let out a string of Chinese swearwords she'd learned from Mei Li. Fine. She'd just have to convince Will that she didn't care about the annulment. That it didn't matter that she was…that they had…oh, blast!

She'd see him on that ship if it was the last thing she did. On the rest of her walk back to town, Kate crafted a few grand lies she could use if he resisted.

When she turned into Main Street it was still quiet as death. The fog had begun to lift, which would make the first part of their journey back to Sacramento City go easier. Floyd Canter was still lying in the street, snoring. Mustart's corral was still open. Kate kept moving.

A minute later she stepped onto the cabin's back porch. Daisy was back in her pen along with her father's gelding, which meant Will had returned from hunting. Both horses should be saddled and ready, but they were not. As she'd suspected, he didn't intend to leave. Not after what had happened between them.

Will met her at the door.

"It's time," she said, and brushed past him. "Everything's packed."

"Kate, there's something I want to—"

"If we hurry, we can make Sacramento City by tomorrow." She strode to the night table and jerked open the drawer.

"We need to talk, Kate."

Her mouth dropped open. She whirled on him. "Where is it? Have you got it?"

"Have I got what?"

"Sweet Jesus, the money bag!"

"What?" Will's brows collided in a frown. "You mean you—" He stepped around her and jerked the drawer completely out of its track. A second's worth of inspection proved what Kate already knew was the terrible truth.

"But you always have it on you."

"Not this morning. I—it slipped my mind."

He grabbed her by the shoulders. "Think, Kate. When was the last time you saw it."

"Last night, when I ran back here from the party. I put it there, in the night table, right before you—" she glanced at the battered door "—before we…"

"It's all right. It doesn't matter. We can—"

"It *does* matter." Oh, God, not this. Not now. "I have to go home, Will. I *want* to go home. Can't you see that?"

He looked at her, and for the briefest moment she thought she read something she never expected to see in his eyes. Then it was gone, and his face turned to stone.

"All right," he said. "We'll get the money back."

"How?"

"I've got a pretty good idea who stole it."

So did she. She recalled Jed Packett's hands on her at the party last night.

Will slid his pistol out of his belt and checked the firing device. "Stay here." He strode to the door and shot her a hard look. "And this time, I mean it."

Chapter Seventeen

Stealing was a hanging offense.

But only if the thief lived to see the local vigilance committee carry out the sentence. Kate had come to learn that more often than not the wronged party took matters into their own hands.

Fearing for Will's safety, Kate waited in the cabin as he had bid her, sitting on the edge of the bare, straw-stuffed mattress, tapping the toes of her boots nervously on the floor.

Early that morning before her visit to Father Flanagan's, she'd made a bedroll of the furs and blankets that had covered the bed, and stashed it in the corner with the few things she and Will would need for their respective journeys.

Only the pillows were left. She grasped the one Will had slept on and pressed it to her chest. It smelled of him. His scent was on her, as well. She closed her eyes for a moment and recalled their passionate lovemaking.

Never in her life had she fathomed the intensity of emotion and sensation that had fused inside her at the moment of her release at his hands. It had been nearly too much to bear.

Now what she could not bear was the thought of their parting. Never to see each other again.

She cursed herself and cast the pillow aside. She must be strong now. For Will and for her brothers. Father Flanagan was dead wrong. It didn't matter what she felt or what she wanted. She had obligations, and Will Crockett had dreams of a life that didn't include her.

Drawing a measured breath, Kate rose and looked for something to occupy the time while she waited for Will to return. She'd been enough trouble to him already, and promised herself she'd do as he asked her and stay put while he retrieved their money from Jed Packett. The ruffian couldn't have gotten far. He must have slipped into the cabin while Will was out hunting and she was paying her visit to the priest.

One last time, she paced the perimeter of the store and living area, inspecting every shelf and corner, making sure they weren't leaving anything important behind. Will had deeded the building and the land to Matt Robinson. Matt hadn't really wanted it, but Will had Mr. Vickery draw up the papers all the same.

Crouching down, Kate peered into the cubbyhole under the counter where her father had kept his battered old money box, the one she and Will had ceased to use weeks ago. The package of letters she'd discovered her second day in Tinderbox was hidden behind it. She'd almost forgotten them. Smiling, she pulled the parcel from its hiding place and carefully unwrapped it.

Her father had kept all of Michael's letters to him. She turned the pages, running a hand over the fluid script, her smile turning to a laugh as she recognized some of the pictures Patrick and Frank had drawn in the margins.

Michael had written to their father regularly. Mei Li had taught her to read the months of the year, and Kate recognized the words as she leafed through the individual missives. The first was dated April 1848, more than a year and a half ago, when her father had first come to America.

There were many letters after that, nearly one each month, though some months were missing. It was startling that so many of Michael's letters had arrived at all. They'd been hand-carried by friends of friends, and sometimes by strangers or seamen. So many were emigrating to California from Ireland, Michael had always found someone willing to carry a letter.

She leafed through to the end of the stack, then frowned. The last letter was unopened. She broke the seal and unfolded the crisp paper. Lord! It was dated the twenty-first of June 1849, nearly two months after she herself had left Ireland! But…how on earth could it have arrived before she had?

Kate stared hard at the date on the letter, and then it dawned on her. ''Of course!'' She'd come by steamer to New York, then by another ship to Panama, over land, and by yet another vessel to San Francisco. The journey had taken six long months. It was cheaper, but far slower, than the clippers that left out of Dublin and Limerick and sailed straight for San Francisco without pause.

She quickly scanned the words, but could make out very few of them, save for names and the date at the top of the page. ''Blast!'' Stepping to the window, she looked out on Main Street. The fog had thinned, but there was nothing to see. The street was quiet.

She had no idea when Will would return. It might be hours. He'd said to stay put, but what he really meant was that she shouldn't go after him. Fine. She wouldn't. But that didn't mean she couldn't pay a visit to Mei Li.

She raced to the back room, grabbed her cloak and was out the door like a shot. Mei Li could read her the letter.

Oh, how she missed her brothers! She was dying to know how they fared, whether Hetty had had a boy or a girl, if Frank and Patrick were still in school.

She rounded the corner of the building, turned into the street and stopped. "That's odd." Narrowing her eyes, she peered down the street, her gaze fixed on the front door of Landerfelt's Mercantile and Mining Supply.

It was open.

The Packetts weren't allowed inside while Eldridge Landerfelt was away. That's what Mr. Vickery had told her. Then why would—?

An image of the Vickerys' wagon, covered in mud and parked askew on the hillside next to their cottage, flashed in her mind. Kate started down the street, remembering, too, the pair of oxen she'd seen that morning munching grass in the open corral at the livery.

Hired oxen. And a borrowed wagon.

Eldridge Landerfelt was back!

She stuffed the unread letter into the deep pocket of her calico dress and walked toward the open door of the mercantile. Will had told her to stay back, but she couldn't stop herself. The Packetts were one thing, Eldridge Landerfelt another all together.

"Is anyone there?" She pushed the door wide and peered inside. The front room of the store was empty, the shelves as bare as the day Landerfelt rolled out of town with all his inventory, and theirs.

Tentatively Kate stepped across the threshold. "Will? Is anyone—?"

"I told you to stay put." Will charged through the door leading from the back room, his face twisted in anger.

"What's happened? Is Landerfelt—"

"He was here, but he's gone." Will checked his Colt,

just as he had a half hour ago. "And I'm going after him."

"Whoa, partner! Hang on." Matt poked his head into the store from the back room. Kate hadn't even realized he was there. "I think you'll want to see this, Will."

"What now?" He left her at the door and stormed into the back room with Matt. Kate followed.

She'd never seen the small room Eldridge Landerfelt used for storage. The building had a second story and his living quarters were upstairs. She'd never been up there, either, and was glad of it.

She entered the dusty storage room and saw Matt holding a small vial. It was fashioned of brown glass, the kind you'd see on an apothecary's shelf or in a doctor's bag. She remembered that Doc Mendenhall had a collection of them in his valise the night he treated her in the Miwok camp.

"What is it?" Will plucked the open vial from Matt's hand and sniffed at it. "Christ."

"That's what I thought, too. Found it over there behind some old tins."

"What's wrong," Kate said. "What is it?"

"Strychnine." Will looked past her, eyes unfocused, and she could see he was grinding his teeth.

"I don't understand. What...does it do?"

"That stuff'll kill a man, ain't used proper." Matt handed Will the stopper to seal it up again. "Works quick, too."

"Yeah," Will said. *"Just like that."*

Kate frowned, remembering what Doc Mendenhall had told her about her father's last days. How he'd nearly recovered from his long illness, and then died all of a sudden for no good cause, as if... "You don't think—?"

"I don't think," Will said. "I know." He jammed the

stopper back into the vial and stuffed it in his pocket. "Come on—" he grabbed her by the arm and pulled her toward the door "—we're going."

Will waited while Kate hugged Mei Li goodbye in the street in front of the store. The Chinese girl had tears in her eyes. Kate kissed Matt on the cheek, then he boosted her into the saddle atop Dennington's black gelding. The few belongings they had kept for the journey were divided equally between Will's mount and hers.

Kate had sold nearly everything left in the cabin and store two days ago. All that they'd made had been tucked away in the leather pouch Landerfelt had stolen from them that morning. Over a thousand dollars. Money enough to put Kate on a ship and buy him his passage north.

He still didn't know what he was going to do on that count.

One thing he did know. Come hell or high water, he'd get that money back, and settle the score on the matter of Liam Dennington's murder. Only there was no time to go after Landerfelt on his own and then come back for Kate. He'd have to take her with him now.

The *Orion* sailed for Sitka in eight days. And the letter sheet he'd read mentioned two or three clippers making return trips to Ireland at about that same time. His plan all along had been to see Kate safely aboard one of those ships, and pay the captain extra to look out for her.

That's what was best, for him and for her. He knew that. Besides, each time he looked at her she looked away. It was as if what they'd shared last night had never happened. It shouldn't have happened, damn it.

"Let's go," he said, and kicked the mare into action.

Matt and Mei Li waved to them as they trotted down the street toward the road leading south out of town. Mustart was hauling a barely conscious Floyd Canter to his feet in front of the livery when they passed.

"Goin' for an early ride, eh?" he called out.

Few knew they were leaving town for good. Vickery, Matt, the Chengs. It was better that way. Will didn't like goodbyes. "Something like that," he called back.

Kate urged her mount in line with his. "I haven't thanked him proper, or the Vickerys."

"Doesn't matter. You won't see them again."

"No. I won't."

His gut tightened as she pursed her lips and trotted on ahead. Maybe he was wrong about her. Maybe she wouldn't have come with him or stayed married to him if he'd asked. He knew she'd gone to see the priest that morning. She'd mentioned it when they were saddling the horses.

As they passed the clearing, a few slow-moving miners, hungover from last night's drinking, mulled amidst the makeshift saloons and gaming hells ringing the still smoldering bonfire. Rose Beecham's line of tents stood quietly among the others. Will swore under his breath, remembering his fool-headed behavior of last night.

"I'd like to stop up ahead for a moment, if you don't mind," Kate said, jarring him back to the present.

"Where?" He picked up the mare's pace to keep up with her.

"At my father's grave."

He hadn't expected that. Maybe because she hadn't talked all that much about Liam Dennington.

"Sure," he said. "We can spare a few minutes."

Landerfelt would be miles ahead of them by now, anyway. It didn't matter. Will knew just where to catch up with him. Along the levee in Sacramento City, where the riverboats and barges from San Francisco arrived. If he knew Landerfelt, the bastard would be spending their hard-earned money buying up God knows what to sell somewhere else for ten times what he paid for it.

The more Will thought about it, the angrier he got. On impulse, as Kate dismounted, he said, ''You hate him, don't you?''

''Who?'' She looked up at him and frowned. ''My father?''

''Yeah. For leaving you all to come here. For getting you into this mess in the first place.''

She looked at him as if were out of his mind. ''He did what he thought was best for us, that's all.'' Dismissing him with her eyes, she handed him the gelding's reins and started for the hill.

Will called after her. ''He wasn't around much for you and the boys after your mother died, was he?''

Kate stopped dead, then turned and looked him in the eye. ''Perhaps he wasn't, Mr. Crockett. But he was a man, not God. He made mistakes, as we all do.''

''And…you don't hold those mistakes against him?''

Her expression softened then. ''No, of course not. He was my father, and I forgave him.''

Will shook his head, baffled by her easy acceptance of all the wrongs that had been heaped on her. ''You forgave him, as simple as that.''

''Aye,'' she said. ''As simple as that.''

She turned and climbed the few steps up the hill to the stake in the ground marking the spot where Will had buried Liam Dennington a month ago. He started to dismount to go with her, then thought better of it. Instead, he waited and watched as she spread her cloak on the ground and knelt, bowed her head and made the sign of the cross.

She seemed so small, kneeling there in her old ragged dress. She'd changed into it for the journey, and had wanted to sell the blue calico back to the miner's wife she'd gotten it from, but Will wouldn't let her. He'd made her keep it, along with the evening gown Vickery's wife had given her.

Will watched as Kate pressed her hands together, her lips mouthing prayers he'd heard her whisper at night in the next room after she thought he'd gone to sleep.

He was reminded of the first day he met her, that first dark night when he'd surprised her at her father's graveside in the rain. He'd thought her unfeeling then. Hard and calculating. A woman much like Sherrilyn had been. He'd been as wrong as a man could be on that count.

No. He was the hard one.

When Kate finished her prayers and returned to the gelding, Will could see she'd been crying. His gut tightened with a feeling he didn't recognize. A feeling that had started when he first met her, and had grown stronger over the past weeks. A feeling that, last night, was so overpowering as they'd made love, he knew he wasn't the same man afterward.

He started to get off his horse to help her onto hers, but she waved him off. "I don't need you," she said, avoiding his eyes, and remounted on her own.

As they rode out of town in silence, he wondered how much more he could possibly hate himself had Kate been the one to die, pregnant, in some wilderness, loathing him for his negligence and pride.

The thought of it was so incomprehensible to him, he knew now he'd never ask her to stay. He didn't deserve her. He didn't deserve anyone.

He'd put her on a ship if it was the last thing he did.

They rode all morning and half the afternoon with only a couple of brief stops. The day was cold, the sky overcast. Out of the south a howling wind blew dead oak leaves across the narrow trail Will had chosen for them out of Horseshoe Bar.

Kate closed her eyes for a moment, breathed winter on the air, and listened to the rhythmic crackling of the leaves under their mounts' hooves.

If the weather held and if they forwent a full night's sleep in favor of short rests, they'd make Sacramento City sometime in the middle of the night.

"You hungry?" Will said.

Her stomach had been growling for an hour, in fact. The only thing either of them had eaten all day were a couple of biscuits Mei Li had brought them before they'd left town.

"I could use a bit of something, if we can spare the time."

"There's an old cabin just ahead. We can stop there."

It had been like that all day. They'd talked of nothing more significant than the weather or what route they would take each time they happened on a crossroads.

From the moment they'd left Tinderbox, Will had been distant and coolly polite, as if he were a stranger charged with her care, but who cared nothing for her. It reminded her of the way he'd treated her when they'd first met.

So much had happened since then.

Absently she traced a finger along her lips, recalling his mouth on hers. She watched him from behind as he rode ahead of her, stiff in the saddle. He acted as if nothing had changed between them. Perhaps nothing had.

A couple of times that afternoon he'd dismounted to study the muddle of hoofprints other travelers who'd preceded them had left on the route. He did so now and frowned.

"What do you see?"

"I'm not sure." He remounted and pulled her father's rifle from the saddle holster. She heard the distinctive click as he cocked it. "Wait here. I'll check things out up ahead and whistle for you if it's clear."

"And if it's not?"

He met her gaze, and for the barest instant she thought she saw a hint of the intimacy they'd shared last night shining in his eyes. Then it was gone.

"If you hear shots, turn that nag around and ride like hell for Horseshoe Bar. Can you do that?"

She nodded.

"Good." And then he was gone.

Kate waited for what seemed an eternity. They'd seen no one since they'd left the main road nearly an hour ago in favor of the narrow trail. It was a shortcut, Will had told her, suitable for horses but not wagons, which explained why she hadn't come this way on her journey from Sacramento City to Tinderbox.

As the seconds ticked by she battled a strong urge to disobey Will's order, and calmed her nerves by studying the thick stands of trees and uneven ground of the closed in landscape surrounding her.

She nudged the gelding forward a few steps and examined the ground where Will had dismounted. Wood shavings, a burnt match and some broken hardtack littered the spot, almost as if someone had emptied their pockets here. And recently. That's why Will had gone on alone.

A low whistle cut the air. Kate breathed relief, letting go her trepidation, and snapped the gelding's reins. Rounding the bend in the trail, she came upon a small clearing and was relieved to see Will waiting for her beside a ramshackle cabin that had clearly seen better days.

"It's abandoned," she said as she dismounted, noting

the missing door and caved-in roof, the rusted animal traps hanging from a nearby tree.

"Trapper I knew built the place when there was still plenty of beaver, and a market for it." Will grabbed their water bag and started for the creek running alongside the dilapidated structure.

"I'll just be a minute," she said, and turned toward the trees.

"Wait for me, I'll go with you."

"I'd…like some time alone, if that's all right. Not long," she added, and watched him grind his teeth as he considered her request.

"All right, but don't go far, and take the pistol."

She rummaged around in the gelding's saddlebag and found the percussion cap pepperbox she'd almost blown Will's head off with the night he returned to Tinderbox to watch over her, three weeks ago.

The ground was rocky underfoot as she started down a gentle slope choked with gnarled oaks, pine and madrone. The trees would afford her the minute of privacy she'd been desperate for but hadn't wanted to make a fuss over.

Just below her she heard the rushing of another stream, this one much bigger than the creek beside the cabin where Will had gone for water. When she was finished she made her way toward it, the sound of the water so deafening that, by the time she reached it, she could no longer hear her own footsteps or the chirping of the birds overhead.

It was a minute well spent. The icy water felt grand on her face. She washed away the road dust, then reached for the pistol she'd laid on the ground beside her.

Her hand froze in midair as a familiar-looking snake-skin boot came out of nowhere and crushed the weapon into the dirt.

"Afternoon, Kate."

Her heart stopped. Looking up, she met Eldridge Landerfelt's cool blue gaze.

"Nice day," he drawled, "ain't it?"

Chapter Eighteen

He didn't like this place. He never had.

Will frowned as he filled their water bag at the small creek gurgling beside the abandoned trapper's cabin. Something about what he'd seen back there on the trail bothered him, but he couldn't put his finger on just what.

He looked past the horses to where Kate had disappeared into the trees. Another minute and he'd go after her. He'd driven her hard that day, and she hadn't complained once. All the same, the sooner they were out of here the better.

Even the water tasted lousy. He swished it around in his mouth and spat it out. On the ground, not two paces from where he stood, something caught his eye.

Narrowing his gaze, Will knelt and plucked a couple of curled wood shavings from the trampled meadow grass in front of the cabin. Pine. Just like the scattered pile he'd seen a few yards back on the trail.

Breathing in the green scent of wood pitch, he tried to remember where and when he'd seen fresh shavings like this before, and why it bothered him.

Then he saw something he'd missed on his first inspection of the area while Kate waited for him to whistle that all was clear. Something that made his heart seize up in his chest.

A cigar butt—still warm, he realized when he snatched it from the tall grass. And not made from not just any tobacco. His nose wrinkled at the stench.

Landerfelt.

Kate's scream pierced the air.

In less than a second Will's Colt was in his hand. He raced down the hill, dodging trees and stumps, his gaze sweeping the thick forest for some sign of her.

Damn it! Why had he let her go off alone?

Rushing water filled his ears, drowning out all other sounds as he skidded to a stop in a carpet of dead leaves just short of the raging stream at the bottom of the hill. Kate's revolver lay at his feet.

Will swallowed hard. "Kate!"

"I—I'm here."

He whirled toward the shaky, hollow sound of her voice in time to see Eldridge Landerfelt step out from behind a tree, jerking Kate along with him. One arm snaked around her waist, Landerfelt held her at gunpoint, using her body as a shield. "Afternoon, Will," he drawled.

"Let her go, you spineless bastard."

The pearl handle of Landerfelt's pistol quivered almost imperceptibly in his hand as he grazed the barrel along Kate's throat and smiled. "Oh, no, I don't think so. Not just yet."

Will trained his Colt between the merchant's icy eyes as Landerfelt moved cautiously along the uneven stream bank, dragging Kate along with him.

"Sh-shoot him," Kate said.

"Now darlin', why would your husband want to do that? We're all friends here."

Will's finger slid along the cool metal of the trigger.

He was conscious of his heart beating wildly in his chest and the thin sheen of perspiration filming his hands. "I said let her go."

"As soon as I've relieved y'all of somethin' I'll be needin'."

"You already got the money. What else do you want?"

"Th-the money's gone, Will." Anguish shone in Kate's eyes, as Landerfelt slid the pistol's barrel to her temple. "He gave it to—"

"Zundel," Will said, finishing her sentence.

A split second after he'd plucked Landerfelt's cigar butt from the grass, it dawned on him what the pine shavings were, and where he'd seen them before. In Tinderbox, nearly two weeks ago, the day Brett Zundel served notice to Eldridge Landerfelt that his debts in Hangtown had finally caught up with him.

Will had never seen Zundel when he didn't have a buck knife in hand, whittling away at fist-sized blocks of pine—scrap wood from his lumber mill that he always seemed to have in his pockets.

"She's right." Landerfelt cocked the pistol's hammer. "All that nice money's gone."

"I don't care about the money."

"Well, I did." Landerfelt's smile twisted into a scowl. "Zundel took my horse, too. That's why I'm relievin' you of yours—or mine, rather." He meant the mare. "And that old nag of Dennington's, too."

Will fought to keep his gaze fixed on Landerfelt's eyes. One look at Kate and he knew he was likely to do something stupid. Somehow he had to get her away from him so he could get off a clean shot. She was just too close, and at this range the Colt's accuracy too unreliable. He couldn't risk it. He wouldn't risk it.

"My…father," Kate said, turning her forehead into the

handgun's barrel in order to look Landerfelt in the eye. "He didn't just die. You…you killed him."

Landerfelt's scowl deepened. "Prove it."

Will slowly slid a hand to his coat pocket, his gaze willing Landerfelt's to follow. The merchant's eyes widened and his gun hand shook as Will retrieved the vial of strychnine they'd found in his storeroom. Casually he tossed it onto the ground at Landerfelt's feet.

"That proves nothin'."

Will inched closer. One small step. Two. If he could just get her—

Without warning, Landerfelt jerked Kate tight against his body, lifting her nearly off her feet.

"Will!"

"Don't!" he cried, and pulled his gaze from Landerfelt's to couple with hers, where he read not fear but cool-headed intent. Will smiled at her, and that's when Eldridge Landerfelt made his mistake.

"Drop the gun, Crockett!" Landerfelt cried, and swung the pistol toward him.

Kate wrenched herself free, and in that split second Will saw his chance and took it.

They both fired. Kate screamed.

In a flash of smoke and heat, Will watched as Eldridge Landerfelt staggered backward, his gun hand flailing, the other grasping at his chest where blood was already spreading across the gray paisley silk of his vest.

Landerfelt's eyes widened in shock. A second later he pitched backward into the raging water. Will watched, his heart racing, as the merchant's body was carried downstream and out of sight.

"Are…are you all right?" Kate's voice brought him back to the moment.

"Yeah," he said, and checked himself for signs of

blood. He'd thought Landerfelt's shot had missed him clean, but he was too numb to feel anything, so he looked to make sure.

Kate moved toward him, uncertainty in her blue eyes. "I'm fine. What about you?"

She nodded as the color returned to her face.

A visceral urge to pull her into his arms and kiss her, to tell her he wanted her with him always nearly broke his resolve. But he held on, just barely, forcing himself to look away and casually holster his gun.

"Let's get the hell out of here," he said.

Her eyes dulled. She retrieved her pistol from where it lay in the dirt. "What do we do now? About the money, your…ship?"

He studied her, his face hardening to the cool look he'd begun to perfect the day he left Philadelphia. There was only one thing left for them, now. Only one way out. "I know a place we can get more."

Kate frowned, and he knew she didn't understand. She didn't need to. He turned his back on her and started up the hill, mentally counting off the hours it would take them to reach San Francisco.

Chapter Nineteen

Once, a heady draft of sea air had conjured up for him dreams of freedom and adventure. New beginnings. But now, as Will steered Kate along the crowded wharf in San Francisco, the brackish stench of the bay evoked only a hollow premonition of closure.

An end to things.

The incident with Landerfelt three days ago had shaken them both more than Will wanted to admit, and only served to reinforce his decision.

In Sacramento City they'd sold the horses, and after a two-day riverboat trip marked only by the increasing coolness between them, he and Kate had arrived in San Francisco. Just moments ago he'd secured for them a tiny room in a boardinghouse just off Clay Street.

All that was left to do now was to find Kate a clipper home, and to come up with the money to pay for it.

"Do you mind if I duck into that shop for a moment?"

Will followed Kate's gaze to a squalid little building perched at the end of the wharf where, outside, fishmongers slapped carp and crabs onto trays for their customers' inspection.

"See the dried herring in the window? It's cheap, and something we can take back to our room to eat later."

He'd noticed a subtle change in her behavior over the past week. It had started right after her run-in with the bear, and had grown in the last few days. She asked his permission to do things, and seemed always to be thinking of ways to make their journey easier. It was almost as if she were his charge and feared causing him too much trouble. It wasn't like her, and he wondered what had provoked it.

"Go ahead," he said, and gave her a few coins, then watched as she followed an apron-clad merchant into the fish shop. From the moment they'd sold the horses, she'd insisted he carry what money they had and dole it out to her as need arose.

While he waited for her to come out again, Will scanned the ships at anchor in the shallow bay. Coastal steamers, clippers, more brigs and barges than he could count, and riverboats like the one they'd taken out of Sacramento City.

Shading his eyes against the water's glare, Will read the names off their hulls, his gaze narrowing as he recognized the steamer depicted in the letter sheet Mustart had given him.

Orion, sailing for Sitka in two days' time.

He stared at the fit-looking ship and ground his teeth. It was what he wanted, wasn't it? Why he'd married Kate in the first place. To get enough money to get the hell out of here, to start a new life somewhere else.

Why, then, wasn't he more enthused?

He sucked in the salt air and let his gaze drift along the line of ships. A clipper, newly arrived, stood fifty yards out unloading passengers into rowboats that brought them ashore. He watched as immigrants took their first steps on the rocky beach, their eyes shining with equal parts of hope and fear.

One family, in particular, caught his eye as they tromped past him in their ragged clothes, mouths agape. The young man and his doe-eyed wife paused for a moment, waiting for three freckle-faced boys—one a gangly youth, and a younger set of twins—to catch up with them. They were all talking at once, in rich Irish brogues that caused the edges of Will's mouth to curl in a smile. He watched them as they moved down the wharf and disappeared into the crowd.

"I've got it. We can go now."

Kate's voice snapped him back to the moment. He turned to see her standing there holding a string of dried herring aloft for his inspection. Her cheeks were flushed from the icy air, her eyes bright and trained expectantly on him. Hell, she was beautiful.

He hardened his heart and let his short-lived smile fade. "That clipper out there," he said, nodding toward the ship offshore. "It's from Ireland."

"Is it?" She gazed at it, her soft brow creasing, her bright eyes growing dull.

"Most likely it'll be headed back, and soon. Tomorrow morning I'll see about getting you a place on it, or one like it."

"But what about the—?"

"I told you I'd take care of it."

She pulled him off to the side, behind a pallet of waiting cargo, where they could talk without being jostled by the crowd. Her hand felt good on his arm—warm, strong. It was the first time she'd touched him in days.

"How, Will? You'll never be able to raise that kind of money in so short a time. Besides," she said, "it's not your problem, it's mine."

"It *is* my problem. You're my wife, aren't you?"

She didn't answer.

"Come on. I'm taking you back to the room. I've got something to do this afternoon, and you'll only slow me down." He grabbed her hand and pulled her toward one of the muddy streets dead-ending into the harbor.

Pushing through the rowdy throng of immigrants and street merchants, Will pulled her along behind him as he marched down Clay Street toward the boardinghouse where he'd already paid three nights' lodging in advance.

At the corner, Kate jerked unexpectedly out of his grasp. He turned and caught the fire in her eyes. It was a look he hadn't seen from her in days. He'd forgotten how much he missed it.

She pursed her lips and drew herself up as if she could match his height, though she still had to look up at him to meet his gaze.

For a moment she didn't say anything, then the fire inside her cooled, the color fled her cheeks, and she seemed to grow smaller before his eyes. "I...wanted to ask you something."

"Well?" he said. "Ask it."

"You loved her very much, didn't you?"

"Who?"

"Sherrilyn. Your...wife."

It was the last thing in the world he expected her to say, and he had every intention of ignoring the question. He stood there, teeth gnashing, then heard his whispered words as if someone else were speaking. "I thought I did—once."

Her eyes widened with shock, confusion, maybe both. He knew she tried to hide it, but it was too late.

"That was before," he said.

"Before...what?"

"You really want to know?"

She nodded.

Fine. He'd tell her then. "Before I found out her true reason for marrying me."

"*True* reason?"

"Money. Social standing. I'm a rich man's son. I thought you'd figured that out by now."

"I did suspect it."

"Sherrilyn knew it. Oh, she was very good at making me believe she wanted me—before the wedding, that is. Afterward, once she and my father both got what they wanted, her *affections* for me changed."

"I—I had no idea, Will. I'm so sorry."

He snorted. "Save your pity. Besides, it's history now." He turned into the crowd, then paused when he felt Kate's hand grip his forearm.

"I don't understand. What had your father to do with it? Surely he—"

"He arranged it all. Our first meeting, chance encounters in the park, parties and weekends. No expense was spared. He needed the union between us to cinch a business deal with Sherrilyn's father, another up-and-comer he feared would one day cross him when he grew rich enough."

Will stopped himself, just short of telling her the rest. They stood there in the crowd, Kate looking up at him intently, hanging on every word, and him looking away just as intently.

"There's more," she said, as if reading his mind. "Tell me."

When he finally met her gaze, he could see that she'd already guessed the rest. "That's right," he said. "The child she carried...I can't say if it was mine or not."

Kate said nothing, merely nodded, as if it all made perfect sense. He wished to God it didn't.

"I didn't stay in Philadelphia long enough after that to ever find out who the man was. Or men. Sherrilyn had several lovers, it seemed."

"Yet, when you went west you took her with you."

"I had to," he said. "She was my wife."

"Your...*obligation.*"

"That's right."

Kate looked away, her pale lips tight, her expression as hard as he'd ever seen it. Very like the moment he first saw her in Dennington's Dry Goods when she first learned her father was dead. Her eyes darted to shop signs, faces in the crowd, everywhere but at him.

"Come on," he said. "I've got business to do. Let's get you back to the room."

A few minutes later he left her sitting on the narrow bed in the boardinghouse. As he turned to leave she said, "That's why you hated me so much in the beginning."

"What are you talking about?"

"I reminded you of her, didn't I? Because of the money. Our bargain."

He didn't deny it. He couldn't. Though he knew now Kate was nothing like his first mercenary bride.

"Landerfelt, too. His greed and deceit. You were obsessed with defeating him simply because he reminded you of your father."

Will's lips thinned in a hard line. He stood there in the open doorway of their tiny room, looking down at her, gripping the doorknob so fiercely he thought he might pull it clean off.

"Tell me, Will. Where are you getting the money?"

* * *

Kate sat there on the shabby bed after Will left and watched the light fade in the room as the late autumn sun dipped into the sea.

All of it made sense to her now.

He made sense.

At first she'd thought he'd married her only for the money. He had, in part. He'd needed it for his passage to Sitka. Later she thought he'd done it for her. Well, if not for her, at least as a favor to her father, whom she was certain he'd befriended. Now she realized his motivation was likely something else altogether. He couldn't stand to see Eldridge Landerfelt win.

Perhaps he'd married her for all those reasons. Taken together they were compelling, but knowing what she now knew about his history, she marveled that he'd done it at all.

No wonder he hated himself. And her.

She glanced at the open bedroll laid out on the floor where Will intended to sleep—alone. His fur hat lay beside it, forgotten in his rush to leave her, to take care of the business he'd alluded to in the street.

She knew what he intended, and the thought of it made her stomach twist into knots so tight she could hardly breathe. A second later she was out the door, fumbling to lock it behind her and to button her cloak all at the same time.

It only took her ten minutes to find the right bank.

She remembered what Mrs. Vickery had told them at dinner that night about the wealthy Philadelphia businessman newly arrived in San Francisco, in Montgomery Street.

Kate gazed upward at the finely crafted sign. *Crockett* was the only word she recognized. That, and the quality of the masonry compared to the slapped-together construction of the buildings surrounding it, told her she'd found the right place.

What now, Kate?

She stood there in the street as sunset colors washed across the blur of faces pushing past her in the crowd, weighing all that Will had told her, and what he hadn't.

Unsure of what to do next, she stepped off the muddy street onto the wooden planking edging the bank and peered into the barred window. Will wasn't there.

Three clerks in fine attire serviced customers who waited patiently in line to complete their transactions. Kate stepped closer, narrowing her gaze. Behind the clerks were desks, and behind those another room.

Her heart beat erratically as she crept around the side of the building, moving slowly toward the window she hoped would afford her a view of the bank's back room.

Lamplight spilled from the window, splashing across the creaky planking. She inched closer, holding her breath. And then she saw them.

Will stood rigid in front of a huge mahogany desk, alternately fisting his hands at his sides and relaxing them. Behind the desk in an overstuffed leather chair sat a man who looked remarkably like him save for his graying hair. The same dark eyes and square jaw, the same heavy build underneath his fine clothes. Kate knew at once he was Will's father.

There were characteristics, however, that the elder Crockett did not share with his son—the bitterness reflected in Will's eyes and the stone-cold hardness of his expression as his father rose and turned to the safe behind him.

Kate felt a sting of tears as Will's father pushed a canvas bag across the desk toward his son. Coolly Will counted out seven hundred dollars in twenty-dollar coins, rare double eagles so shiny they must have been newly minted in the East.

With a shock she realized the sum wasn't nearly enough for them both. Her passage to Ireland alone would cost better than six hundred dollars.

His father said something, then pushed the canvas bag still stuffed with coins toward his son. Shaking his head, Will slipped the golden eagles he'd counted out into the leather pouch that had been her father's, then pocketed it.

She knew what it cost him to beg the money. His pride, his convictions, all that he was. The least she could do for him, the only thing she could do, was to take it and go home.

Set him free.

He didn't want her. It was as simple as that.

Coldwell Crockett briefly turned his back on his son to close the safe, and for one startling moment Kate read the pain in Will's face.

She swiped at her eyes and watched as the banker held out a manicured hand to him. After a long moment Will took it, shaking it briefly before muttering something Kate suspected was his promise to repay every cent.

The last thing she saw, before her tears blinded her and she had the presence of mind to race back to the boarding-house before Will's return, was the anguish in Coldwell Crockett's eyes as his son turned away from him, stone-faced, and quit the room.

"No lamp?" Will said, as he entered the tiny, dark room of the boardinghouse where he'd left Kate nearly two hours ago. The sun had long since set.

"No." Kate pulled her feet under her on the narrow bed to allow him more space. "Not even a candle."

"Thirty dollars doesn't buy what it used to here." He

shucked his jacket and retrieved the money pouch from his shirt pocket. Matter-of-factly he set it on the table flanking the bed, along with the passenger ticket he'd bought for her trip home.

Kate stared at the ticket.

"She sails tomorrow on the evening tide. I've spoken to the captain. You can board in the morning. Everything's arranged."

To his surprise she didn't ask him how he'd come by the ticket or the coin. She said nothing, in fact.

He should have felt calm, in control of his emotions, now that he'd finally done what he'd had to do. But he didn't. "Did you eat?" He poked at the string of dried herring draped across the table, shimmering in the occasional flickering light shining in from the street through the undraped window.

"I'm not hungry."

He wasn't, either. "We'd better get some rest, then." Will pulled off his boots and stretched out on the thin bedroll he'd placed on the floor beside the bed where Kate would sleep.

When he heard the rustling of her clothes he politely rolled onto his side, away from her, to afford her some privacy to undress. It had been three nights since she'd slept in a bed. The last time he'd slept with her, sheltering her body with his, drifting off, sated from their lovemaking, the scent of her drugging him to sleep.

He drifted now, remembering her kisses, the softness of her skin, the passion in her eyes when she'd cried his name. Hours later he thought he was dreaming when he rolled over and caught her looking down at him, her face bathed in moonlight, nestled just above him on a pillow at the edge of the bed.

No, he wasn't dreaming.

The floor underneath him was hard and cold, the look in her eyes warm, almost pleading. Without a word she opened the covers to him.

It was all the encouragement he needed.

Chapter Twenty

He knew it was wrong, that he shouldn't take advantage of her vulnerability.

She'd weathered more in the past week than most women would in a lifetime. As he slid into the narrow bed beside her, Will told himself she needed comfort, not sex.

But there was more than a need for comfort in the way she kissed him, the way her arms snaked around his waist, pulling him close, the way her legs tangled with his in the cool sheets.

She sighed as he cautiously kissed her back, his tongue mating with hers, slowly this time, deliberately, not at all like their first frantic coupling.

She was warm and yielding and soft, and he was far past wanting. He looked at her in the moonlight and knew if he made love to her now he'd never be able to put her on that ship tomorrow.

"Kate," he whispered against her lips.

"No more words," she breathed. "Not tonight." She closed her eyes and kissed him with a raw tenderness that was his undoing.

He willed himself to stop, but he couldn't. He told himself it didn't matter, that in the morning he would be the same man he always was, and she the same woman, and that he was right to send her home where she belonged.

A minute's work on both their parts and he was freed of all his clothes. He moved under her, naked, and pulled her gently on top of him, her loose hair silking across his skin. Through the fine-weight cotton of her shift her taut nipples grazed his chest and caused the breath to rush from his lungs.

When her legs spread around him and he felt her heat, he knew he was lost. She wrestled with the ties of her shift. No pantalets tonight, he realized with a heady shock, as the pearly light of a full November moon spilt across her body.

She was so lovely he could barely breathe.

Desperate to crush the torrent of untried emotion welling inside him, he fought to stay focused on the physical: working his hands down her narrow back, circling her waist, molding the curves of her buttocks and hips.

At last she settled atop him, naked. The slick velvet between her legs grazed his manhood, and he cried out.

"Aye," she breathed, and rolled her hips against him in a fluid motion that seemed not of this world.

His hands moved to her breasts, shaping and cradling, delivering each in turn to his greedy mouth. When he began to suckle she gasped, her hips grinding into him hard, her nails piercing his shoulders so deeply he was sure she drew blood.

He encouraged her, while deep inside himself he battled an overpowering yearning to tell her what he felt, what he longed for and feared.

He thrust upward again and unexpectedly slid inside her. They both cried out as he filled her, her eyes widening with the shock. She was small and tight, and he feared—as he had their first time together—that he would hurt her.

''Slow,'' he whispered, but she ignored his instruction. Rising up, she rode him, her hands braced against his biceps, her thighs gripping his hips.

They moved together, and he knew from the sweet tension building in her face, from the tightening of her sheath around him, that already she was as close to the edge as he.

He didn't want it to be as good as it was between them. He pretended that it wasn't. It was dangerous to need her, impossible to want her as much as he knew he did.

All the same, when she at last reached her peak he let himself go with her, giving in to feelings he knew he could not fight.

When it was light enough to see, Kate rose and quietly dressed, careful not to wake him. Will hadn't slept more than a few hours a night in days, not since the last time they'd lain together. She knew, because neither had she.

She gathered up her few things and stuffed them into her satchel: her old dress, so tattered now it wasn't much more than a rag, Mrs. Vickery's evening gown, which she planned to sell before she sailed, her father's pistol and a few keepsakes Mei Li had given her to remind her of her time in Tinderbox.

Not that she'd need reminders.

The image of the man sleeping naked in the bed not a foot from where she stood—one muscled arm thrown casually over his head, dark hair framing features she knew by heart—was permanently etched in her mind.

She stood there for a moment watching his chest rise and fall with each steady breath, and knew she'd always remember with perfect clarity what his hands felt like on her body, the dizzying rush of heat and want and fear she felt when he kissed her.

Last night they'd made love slowly, wordlessly, with an aching tenderness between them that seemed almost a living, breathing thing to her. For a moment she'd thought his feelings for her had changed.

And in that moment perhaps they had.

But she knew when he woke he'd be the same man he was yesterday and the day before that. The same man who, after each intimate encounter with her, would distance himself abruptly, as if to disavow the ungovernable want his body betrayed but his heart did not share.

She knew she couldn't bear it were he to wake and look at her with that familiar edge of bitter remorse glittering in his eyes.

It was time for her to go.

The ticket Will had procured for her journey home stared coldly at her from the night table. She took it and stuffed it into the pocket of her calico dress. She ignored the bag of coins.

After one last look at the man who for a turbulent month had been her husband, she turned toward the door, her cloak and satchel in hand.

Will's buckskin jacket lay in a heap blocking her exit. She picked it up, then stifled a gasp as something *thunked* to the floor. Kate went still as a statue, her eyes darting to Will. From the bed he let out a deep, contented moan and turned restlessly in his sleep. When his breathing slowed again, she knelt to retrieve the object.

Whatever it was had rolled under the bed. She reached for it blindly along the green floorboards, and after a few seconds her hand closed over something small and hard with surprisingly sharp edges.

Dawn's light bleeding through the window shone on

the keepsake when she opened her palm. Her breath caught. Staring up at her was her own image painted on an oval sliver of ivory encased in fine silver filigree. The memento had belonged to her father, and she'd wondered what had happened to it when she didn't find it among his things.

She wondered why Will had it, and why he'd kept it from her. Why he kept it at all. She told herself it didn't matter, and set it on the table beside the money pouch.

Cold, damp air hit her like a sobering force when she stepped into the street. It was early and still quiet, though merchants were already up and about preparing for another day of commerce.

The walk back to the wharf took her less than five minutes. Gulls cawed overhead, circling fishmongers out on the pier cleaning the morning's catch. The salt air smelled surprisingly good to her, reminding her a bit of home.

Her gaze slid along the line of ships anchored in the bay and listing in the light breeze. A steamer caught her eye, one she'd seen Will glance at yesterday when he thought she wasn't looking. The name stood out in bold white letters. *Orion.* She remembered it from the discarded letter sheet Will had meant her not to see.

After a moment she moved on toward the building Will had pointed out to her yesterday at the end of the long street where shipping agents and importers gathered to do their business.

Through big double doors men were already coming and going, leather-bound journals and stacks of paperwork in hand. One of them tipped his hat to her as she entered.

"May I help you, ma'am?" a bespectacled agent said to her when she reached the front of the line.

"I've a ticket for Dublin." She fished around in her dress pocket for it and frowned. "What on earth...?"

"Something wrong?"

"Um...no. Here it is." She pulled the handwritten ticket from her pocket along with a wrinkled parchment. Suddenly it dawned on her what it was—the last letter Michael had sent her father from home.

She remembered stuffing the letter into the deep pocket of her calico dress the morning she and Will had left Tinderbox, but she'd changed into her old dress for the journey, and hadn't worn this one since. In the blur of the past few days she'd simply forgotten it until now.

"Ma'am?"

"Oh, sorry." She pushed the ticket across the counter to him. "My...husband bought it for me yesterday, and said that this morning I might..." She stared at Michael's unread letter and promptly forgot what she was going to say.

"Mrs. Crockett, isn't it?" The shipping agent inspected the spidery script on the front of the ticket.

"Oh, aye," she said, snapping back to the moment.

"I remember your husband. Sold him the ticket myself."

She looked at the letter again, and for some odd reason all the hairs on her nape prickled.

"Crockett," the agent said again, flashing her a look of approval over his spectacles. "Just like the banker."

At their brief reunion yesterday afternoon, Kate had seen the pain edging both Will's face and his father's when they'd thought neither of them was looking at the other. "Aye, you might say that."

"Now, if you'd like to board early—"

"Actually..." She unfolded the crumpled letter onto the counter and spun it around so the agent could see it.

"Before I do…could you…would you mind very much?" She nodded at the unintelligible scribble.

"Want me to read it to you?"

There was no one else waiting in line behind her. "If you would, I'd be most grateful."

The agent gripped the letter between inky fingers and started to read it aloud. Less than a minute into Michael's chatty dialogue, Kate's heart stopped.

"Wait! Read that part again."

The agent's eyes narrowed on the words. "Says they're sailing 'round about August twelfth."

Nearly four months ago! Kate gripped the counter, sure she would faint dead away. "You mean my…my brothers are coming *here?* When?"

Pointing out the double doors, the agent squinted toward the high drafting clipper anchored fifty yards offshore. Kate's gaze followed, her eyes stretching so wide they hurt.

"There she is right there—the *Marta Marie.*" He glanced again at the letter. "Yep, that's the one."

"You mean…?"

"That's right, ma'am. Your brothers are already here."

Chapter Twenty-One

He knew before he even opened his eyes that she was gone.

Will sat on the narrow bed in the squalid boardinghouse room staring blankly at the painted miniature on the table. Kate's guileless blue eyes stared back at him. Her ticket was gone, the money bag left untouched. He should have realized she'd refuse the coin.

Gray light shone through the window but gave off no warmth. For a long time he just sat there, not bothering to dress, watching the play of light on the floor, thinking he'd been wrong after all.

He *was* a changed man.

Kate had changed him.

He didn't know how long he sat there sifting over the tiniest details of their month together. Remembering her stalwart pride and her matter-of-fact acceptance of the harsh realities she'd faced—not only here, but in Ireland.

She simply dealt with what life heaped on her, and moved on. For Kate, it was as uncomplicated as that. She wasn't bitter, didn't hate. When there was blame to be laid, she almost invariably forgave, and when she couldn't, she at least sought understanding.

He thought, too, about the brief meeting last night with his father and how, after five years, Coldwell Crockett wasn't quite the same man Will remembered.

Perhaps it was because his father was alone now. Will's mother had died a year or so after he'd taken Sherrilyn west. Will had found out by accident, from an acquaintance he'd run into at Sutter's Fort.

There had just been Will and his mother—no other family. Meaning all his father had had to keep him warm these past years was his money. Once, that would have been enough.

But for a fleeting moment last night, as they'd stood together in his office talking, Will suspected it was not. And that the realization, when it had finally come, had hit his father hard.

He closed his eyes, pushing all of it from his mind, and to his frustration breathed in the lingering scent of Kate on the bedsheets. The everyday clamor of people in the wakening street below the room called him back to the present.

He'd need to get a job of some kind, he supposed. Something to fill his time until spring, a way to make up the cash to repay the loan. His father had wanted to make him a gift of the money, had wanted him to take more. Will had refused. He'd pay back every cent if it was the last thing he did.

But a job could wait until tomorrow. For now, he rose and dressed, and a few minutes later found himself wandering down Clay Street toward the wharf.

The Dublin-bound clipper sat in the bay taking on provisions. Will wavered as to whether or not to hire a dinghy to carry him out there, just to make sure Kate had gotten safely aboard. A second later he dismissed the idea.

Hell, she was a grown woman and had been perfectly

capable of traveling all the way here without his help, or anyone's. She'd likely have no trouble finding her way without an escort a mere fifty yards from where he now stood. Besides, he'd paid both the shipping clerk and the captain extra to see that no harm came to her until she was dropped safely back on Irish soil.

He stood there a moment longer and watched as stevedores loaded barrels into the hold, and realized that by tonight there'd be an ocean between them.

It was better this way. For him and for her.

He couldn't give her what she wanted, what she deserved. He wasn't cut out for it, didn't have it in him. He simply had nothing to give. Moreover, she had to go back. She wanted to go back—she'd said so all along. That's what had driven her to marry him in the first place.

He watched the clipper a second more, then turned into the first saloon he saw—a clapboard building that looked as if it had been constructed overnight and would collapse in the first stiff wind.

The bar was little more than a row of barrels with planks laid across them. Hogsheads served as stools for the amazingly diverse collection of men lined up along the bar. Will heard foreign languages he didn't recognize as he walked through a haze of smoke that made his eyes burn. There were no women, and the only drink served was whiskey.

This was the place.

He pulled a barrel up to an empty spot at the middle of the bar and nodded to the man selling drinks. Didn't matter that it was barely breakfast time.

The short, balding Irishman waddled over with a tin cup and a full bottle, took one long look at him and said, "Want me to leave it?"

"Yeah," Will said, and slapped his money pouch on the bar.

It didn't take Kate very long to find her brothers.

The shipping clerk had pointed her in the direction of a rooming house catering especially to the Irish. The first thing she saw when she stepped inside the downstairs parlor was a wrestling match on the proprietor's Turkish carpet—the combatants her twin brothers, Patrick and Frank, who'd grown considerably since she'd last seen them.

They were all there—and all safe, thank God. Michael and Hetty and their new babe who'd been born just before they sailed. Sean, who was now taller than Kate, and had a mouth on him that she longed to wash out with soap. And, of course, the twins.

She burst into tears the moment she saw them, and then spent nearly the whole of the morning with them gathered around her, recounting much of what had happened in the seven months since she'd left home.

In the early afternoon Hetty took the twins out to purchase some things for supper. Up in the sleeping room Michael had rented for them for the night, Kate had a frank conversation with her brother as she rocked his baby in her arms.

"I still can't believe you're really here."

"And I can't believe Da's dead," Michael said, his eyes glassing again.

He'd taken the news hard. Sean and the twins seemed much less affected, which made sense, really, since their father hadn't spent much time at home these past years. Only Kate and Michael really remembered him well.

She reached out and stroked her brother's downy cheek, reminding herself he was barely nineteen. The weight of the world—a wife, a babe, carting his entire family five thousand miles to a place he knew nothing about—had hardened his boyish features.

"Tell me again about Mother's sister."

Michael's face lit up again. "Oh, it was grand, Katie. When her husband died and left us all that money, Aunt Olivia was fit to be tied."

"You paid my debt with part of it."

"*Our* debt," he said. "We're a family, aren't we?"

She smiled. "That we are."

Michael went on, elaborating on some of the details he hadn't related in his first frantic telling of the tale. "The tight old biddy would have rather cut off her own arm than give over the rest of the coin. Even hired a solicitor of her own to contest her husband's will."

"Doesn't surprise me." Kate had only met her aunt a few times, and the reception she'd received on all those occasions, particularly the last, had been frigid at best. "So you settled for passage to America for all of you."

"Aye. She paid her cousin—the one in the shipping business—a pittance for our transport compared to what we'd likely get if we'd waited for the court to sort it all out. But at the time it seemed the best move. Had I not done it, we'd no doubt still be waiting to receive a farthing of what her husband had left us."

"It's a smart man you are, Michael Dennington."

"Not so smart as desperate. There was nothing left for us in Dublin. I lost my job a month after you sailed, and we had to take the twins out of school to make ends meet. We were close to starving, Katie."

Her stomach twisted in a knot. "I was wrong to leave you."

"Christ, no. It was the best thing in the end—what drove the idea for us to come in the first place. With you and Da here, well, naturally we thought…'' He shrugged, and a bittersweet smile graced his lips.

''You thought right.'' She handed the baby to him and walked to the small window overlooking the bustling street.

''We've a bit of savings to get us started, too.''

''That's grand, for I haven't a cent of my own.''

Turning away, toying idly with a tendril of hair that had come loose from her twist, Kate wondered where Will was now, and what he was doing—if he'd already put her neatly out of his mind.

''Tell me about him, Katie.''

''Hmm?'' She'd been drifting.

''Your…husband. This…Crockett.''

''Oh, there's not much to tell really.'' She pressed her hands against the cool window glass and watched the parade of faces in the street below, alternately hoping and fearing one of them would be Will's.

''You're a poor liar, Mary Kate.''

She flashed her brother a somber smile. ''Da used to call me that.''

''I know.''

Earlier, when the younger boys had been part of their conversation, Kate had parted with only the sketchiest details of how she'd survived the last month, and what her plan had been. Michael had known instantly she was holding back.

''What you said downstairs—about the marriage being in name only…'' He paused, willing her to his gaze, but she refused to look him in the eye. ''That bit wasn't true, was it, Kate?''

Her lips thinned as she turned back to the window and stared blankly into the street. ''No.''

''Aye, that's what I thought.''

"Is it that obvious?" She shot him a quick glance.

"No, but you do seem changed. More...I don't know...grown-up."

You don't know the half of it, she thought, recalling a dozen precarious situations she'd gotten herself into since the day she'd arrived in Tinderbox.

"Do you love him, Katie?"

Father Flanagan had asked her the same question. She met her brother's steady gaze, not prepared to answer. Her silence, it seemed, was enough.

"Aye, you do."

"That's obvious as well, is it?" She watched as Michael laid his sleeping son on the bed, then joined her at the window.

"Where is he, Kate? Why isn't Crockett here with you?"

She hadn't told him the truth about why she was here in San Francisco. She'd let all of them believe she'd come to meet them, that she'd read the letter and had known exactly when they would arrive.

And now that they were here, she could think of no good reason to tell them that she'd been minutes away from boarding a clipper back to Dublin, and might have missed them all together had she not found the letter in her calico dress.

"Well?"

She knew Michael, and knew, too, he wouldn't let it go until he'd wheedled every last detail out of her. She was the eldest, but he was the eldest son and fiercely protective of her.

"He's gone," she said, having made up her mind to tell him the whole of it. "Well, not gone yet. Not exactly. He'd planned to be on the *Orion* when it sails day after tomorrow."

''What?'' Color flooded into Michael's tight face. ''You mean to tell me he's ruined you and now he's leaving?''

Kate raised her voice in order to be heard over the string of foul words rolling off her brother's tongue. ''Calm down. I told you earlier, it was all arranged at the beginning.''

''Aye, but the dallying between the sheets was not part of the bargain, or am I wrong?''

''No,'' she said quietly, her face heating under her brother's angry scrutiny. ''You're right, it…wasn't part of our…bargain.''

''The bleedin' bastard. When I get my hands on him, I swear to God I'll—''

''It was as much my fault as his.'' She shot Michael a sheepish glance, and he returned it with a scowl. ''Besides, it's better this way—Will leaving, I mean.''

''Why? If you love the man, Kate, how could it possibly be better?''

She turned away from him again and tried to think of an explanation that didn't make her look like the fool she felt.

''Good God, you mean he doesn't want you? The son of a—''

''Stop it,'' she said. ''You don't know him. You don't know what he's been through, what it was like between us and—''

''Aye, well, he'd best be on that ship then, lest I get my hands on him. I swear to God, Kate—''

A blast of footfalls clattered on the floorboards outside the room. Michael stopped in midsentence and they both looked expectantly at the door.

A moment later it burst open and Sean crashed, breathless, across the threshold. "It's bloody marvelous here! You won't believe the things I saw!"

"Didn't I tell you to watch your mouth." Kate thumped the ever-wayward youth affectionately on the back of the head as he collapsed onto the bed with the baby. The wee thing woke and instantly started to wail.

"Oh, now look what you've done, you lummox." Michael flung an annoyed look in Sean's direction, then plucked the baby from the bed.

While Michael was busy checking to see if his son was wet, Kate grabbed the chance she'd been waiting for all morning. "Sean, come here." She crooked her finger at him and moved as far out of Michael's earshot as she could get.

"I know that look, Katie darlin'," Sean said, and grinned. He bounded from the bed and joined her at the window. "You'll be wanting something from me—a favor. Am I right?"

He knew her too well. And she knew him. Sean had none of Michael's scruples—and, at fifteen, little of his elder brother's sense of caution, either—which was why Kate feared to charge him with this particular task. But he was smart as a whip and he loved her, and would do as she asked without question.

Kate fished around in her pocket until her hand closed over what she sought, then slipped it covertly into Sean's waiting hand. "Now, here's what I want you to do…"

Someone had crushed his skull.

Will planted his hands firmly on the bar and pushed himself upward until his face rose a couple of inches from its rough and stinking surface. His head pounded a Miwok drumbeat, and he felt every rhythmic blow down to his toes.

"Coffee?" a familiar voice said somewhere at the edge of his awareness.

Will cracked an eye and, once he was able to focus, saw his flattened money pouch, the painted miniature of Kate beside it, an empty bottle and the short, balding Irishman who'd happily sold it to him. The room was only spinning a little, now.

"Yeah," he rasped, his throat raw from imported whiskey. "Coffee would be…good."

The bartender leaned over until his red, doughy face was an inch from Will's. "Well, laddie, if we had any coffee—and we don't, mind you—but if we did, I'd be happy to sell you a dram for a fair price."

The rough collection of men jammed up to the bar on both sides of Will erupted into laughter that slammed into his already throbbing head like a brick. The stench of whiskey and sweat and tobacco drove his gut to a slow roll.

"Forget it," Will said, and continued to push until he was sitting upright on the hogshead he'd used as stool for the last—hell, he had no idea how long he'd been here.

Squinting toward the door, he saw the endless crush of miners and merchants and immigrants moving like cattle down the street. Cold autumn sunlight streamed into the bar. He guessed it to be afternoon, or thereabouts.

Will drew himself up, blinking his eyes in a poor attempt to clear his head, paying no mind to the long, skinny arm reaching over his shoulder. A second later he snapped to full attention as the white, freckled hand attached to it closed over the painted miniature of Kate resting on the bar.

Before he knew what he was doing, Will had the would-be thief bent backward over the bar in a death grip.

The bartender shot him a hard look. "He's just a lad. Have a care, man."

Will blinked some more, his eyes at last focusing on the young face staring up him and the devilish-looking smile that went along with it.

"Will Crockett, is it?" the boy, who Will guessed at sixteen or so, said matter-of-factly, as if he was in no danger at all of having the life wrung out of him.

"What if I am?"

The youth's blue eyes, which seemed familiar to him in a way he couldn't quite grasp, flicked to Will's stranglehold on his neck.

Hmph, must be the whiskey.

Will shrugged off the odd feeling of recognition, and in response shot a glance to the youth's hand that was still curled around the miniature of Kate.

For a moment it was a battle of wills to see who would relent first. Finally the boy gave in and let the miniature slide from his palm to the bar.

Will let him up.

As if the incident hadn't occurred, the youth said brightly, "Delivery for you, sir."

Will ignored him, pocketing the miniature and the money bag, which was nearly empty. Will swore under his breath.

"I'll just leave it for you, right here, sir." The youth plucked an envelope from his pocket, slapped it onto the bar and slid it neatly under Will's hand. He waited, likely to see if Will was going to open it.

Will didn't. He already knew from the crisp engraving on the front who it was from. *Crockett Bank, Montgomery Street, San Francisco.*

When the youth turned to leave, the bartender called out to him. "Newly arrived?"

"Aye."

"You'll be wantin' a job then."

The youth grinned, and again Will had the strangest feeling he'd seen him somewhere before. The bartender waved him close. "Well, here's what I've got in mind, lad…"

Will fingered the envelope, the conversation between the bartender and the boy sliding to the edge of his awareness. He wondered what was in it, and how the hell his father had found him. Glancing at the open doorway, he half expected to see Coldwell Crockett's grave features staring back at him. All that was there was the blur of the crowd outside.

"Aye, well," the youth went on, "with my da newly dead and all, and with the four of us boys just arrivin'— well, I don't think my sister would think much of the idea."

"Well, the job's here if you want it, lad."

The cacophony of bar talk and laughter and the street sounds outside melted into a dull, throbbing roar in Will's head as he opened the envelope.

His heart stopped. "How in the hell…?" A steamship ticket slipped from the fine, watermarked paper onto the bar.

Orion, departing for Sitka, December first. Tomorrow. His own name, Mr. William Crockett, stared back at him in the space where the shipping agent had neatly penned the passenger's identity.

Will sat there, stunned, just staring at it, his whiskey-fogged mind racing over the details of the conversation he'd had last night with his father. How could he have known? It was…impossible.

Not bothering to acknowledge the bartender's jovial

farewell, Will burst into the street, the steamship ticket in hand, and winced against the assault of blinding sunlight.

By the time he reached his father's bank a half-dozen blocks away, his head was clear and his blood near boiling. Ignoring the smartly dressed clerks behind the counter, Will vaulted over the polished mahogany barrier and stormed into the bank's back room.

His father looked up from his desk, startled by the intrusion. "It's all right," he called to one of the clerks, who'd already slid a late-model pistol out from under the counter and was striding toward Will. "He's my...son."

Will shot a murderous glance at the clerk, his head throbbing, his heart pumping to the beat. He didn't wait for the clerk to back down, but simply dismissed him by slamming the interior door.

"Something's wrong," his father said, rising. "What is it?"

"You know damned well what it is." Will flung the ticket across the desk. "Why'd you do it? And how the hell did you know?"

His first suspicion was that his father had had him followed and watched, had somehow learned about Kate, had wormed out of her God knows what.

His father glanced at the ticket and frowned. "I don't know what you're talking about. But now that you're here—" He came around the desk and stood before him.

Will felt the blood rage hot to his face, his temples throbbing so intensely now he thought his head would explode. "Trying to run my life again, aren't you? Well not this time, *Father*."

"We need to talk, Will. Sit down." He gestured to the same chair Will had ignored last night.

"No."

"All right. Let's get this out standing up, then. I know

you blame me for what happened between you and Sherrilyn.''

Will let out a derisive sound.

"I didn't know, Will. I tried to tell you before you left Philadelphia, but you wouldn't listen. I want you to listen to me now.''

"Why should I?''

Something happened, then, between them that Will wasn't prepared for. His father's dark eyes warmed, his face twisting into a desperate union of pain and defeat. Will had never seen him like this. Not ever.

"Because I'm your father,'' he said gently. "And because, despite what you think of me, what I'm to blame for and what I'm not…I love you, and always have.''

Not once in the whole of Will's life had his father ever made such an open and raw declaration to him. Will remembered him not as a cold man—for that would have called for emotion—but merely a cool one, distant, self-absorbed, focused on power and money, barely cognizant of his wife or his son.

To his own surprise, Will found himself taking the seat his father had offered. And he listened, and he learned. He recalled, too, Kate's unguarded sentiments about her own father.

He did what he thought was best for us, that's all. He was my father, and I forgave him. It's as simple as that.

Was it?

Will ground his teeth, reflecting on the void of years he'd spent drifting after Sherrilyn's death. Running was perhaps a better word for it. Running from the unbearable idea that perhaps he, though wronged, was the one who'd made the biggest and most costly mistake of all.

Rather than face that, he'd clung to his distrust of

women, his hatred of his father and men he'd thought just like him—Landerfelt, for one.

Kate had been right about that, and other things.

He'd allowed that hate to burn unchecked inside him, he'd fueled it at every opportunity, had used it to keep him warm at night. To dull his need for intimacy, for love, for the kind of life he'd always wanted but was convinced after Sherrilyn's death he didn't deserve.

"It was all her doing, then," he said quietly, letting his father's words sink in. "Sherrilyn proposed the match to you, not the other way around."

"Yes, but I was all too ready to agree. I needed the deal with Browning, was desperate for it. So desperate I didn't stop to wonder what her motives might be. I…thought she'd be good for you. You were so restless, Will, so unhappy." His father paused and willed him to his gaze. "I didn't know about the…others. Not until after you'd already left."

He meant Sherrilyn's other lovers.

Will sucked in a breath, his mind still a bit muddled from drink. "I didn't even know she was pregnant until after she'd died."

His father's face went ash-white.

"You didn't know, did you?" Will could tell just by looking at him that he hadn't. Shaking his head, he marveled at his own stupidity. "Of course you didn't."

He paused for a moment and watched some new understanding breach his father's hard-edged features.

"For months after she died I tormented myself with the question of whether or not the child was mine. I guess we'll never know and, in the end, it doesn't really matter, does it? She died, and an innocent child with her.

"I'm to blame. I dragged her West against her will, to

places so remote, so rugged, she didn't have a chance once she took sick.''

''We're all to blame, Will.''

Will rose from the chair and walked to the barred window.

''Don't you think we've paid enough for our sins, you and I?'' His father's voice was soft.

Maybe they had, maybe they hadn't. Maybe it wasn't even possible. Will glanced at the steamship ticket lying on the mahogany desk, and after a long moment he picked it up.

Was this what he really wanted? Or was Sitka just another place to run to? He folded the ticket carefully and slipped it into his pocket. The sharp edges of what he knew to be silver filigree brushed the tips of his fingers.

Slowly he drew the painted miniature from his pocket and let his gaze wash over the proud features and bright blue eyes of the woman who was his wife.

A woman who'd offered him her love in spite of his self-loathing. Who'd unknowingly taught him that freedom begins not on a ship bound for Sitka, or anywhere, but in one's own heart.

''I've seen her,'' his father said, smiling at Kate's painted image. ''Last night, right here, watching you through that very window.''

''You mean…she was here? She saw us? And the money change hands?''

''Yes, I believe she did. Who is she?''

A series of short, low horn blasts drew Will's attention to the street outside. The sun had dipped low in the sky. Dusk came early this time of year. In an hour it would be dark.

''What's that?'' He strained his ears, trying to hear.

''The last call,'' his father said.

"Last call for what?"

"The tide's about to turn."

With a shock it dawned on him. He looked at Kate's image, eyes wide, gripping the miniature so tight it cut his hand. "Christ," he breathed.

"What's the matter?"

"There's no time—I'll explain later." Will ripped the bank's interior door wide, and knocked over a startled clerk as he vaulted over the mahogany counter and shot into the street.

Chapter Twenty-Two

He was too late.

Will splashed into the icy water of the bay, shouting, frantically waving his arms at the dinghy that was already halfway back to shore after having delivered the last load of passengers to the Dublin-bound clipper before she sailed.

He couldn't risk waiting. He swam for it, not bothering to remove his jacket or boots. When he reached the dinghy, two oarsmen pulled him, gasping, into the boat.

"T-take me out there," he wheezed, and spat a mouthful of seawater over the side.

"Sorry, sir, it's too late. She's ready to cast—"

"Do it!" Will shouted, and ripped the Colt from his belt.

"Whatever you say." The oarsmen exchanged wide-eyed looks and rowed as he held the gun on them.

Will holstered the Colt and swung himself onto the rope ladder the second the dinghy scraped up against the clipper's oiled side. The crew had just begun to unfurl the sails when the captain called them off.

"What the devil do you mean by—"

In one fluid motion Will vaulted over the top rail and

a second later twisted the fine navy lapels of the captain's jacket into his fists. "Where is she?"

"Who? Ah, Crockett. I didn't recognize you soaked to the skin like a river rat."

"My wife, where can I find her?" He let go of the captain's jacket and quickly scanned the shocked faces of the passengers crowded onto the deck eyeing his dripping clothes.

"Mrs. Crockett's not aboard. Didn't you—"

"What do you mean she's not on board?" He grabbed the captain by the arm, but this time two crewman stepped between them. "Where the hell is she? I paid you extra to—"

"Yes, all right. You can have your money back. The clerk down on the wharf told me early this afternoon."

"Told you what?" Will's head pounded more with fear now, than the remnants of too much whiskey. Where the hell was she if she wasn't here?

"She exchanged her ticket."

"Exchanged it? For what?"

All at once, in a blinding flash of understanding, his head was clear. Everything was clear.

Will ripped the soggy steamship ticket from his pocket and stared at the bleeding ink. Kate had exchanged her own ticket for the one he held, dripping, in his hand. But why?

She'd wanted to go home as much as he'd wanted to get away. That's why she'd married him in the first place. Her brothers were waiting, she'd said. They were counting on her to come home and—

The words of the blue-eyed boy who'd delivered Will's ticket to the saloon came crashing back on him in a perfect Irish brogue.

What with my da newly dead and with the four of us

boys just arrivin'—well, I don't think my sister would think much of the idea.

Sister!

That's why the boy's eyes had seemed so familiar to him. Will's head whipped around toward the other Irish clipper—the *Marta Marie*—that rocked gently at anchor in the bay.

He'd watched, unknowing, with his own eyes, Kate's whole family come ashore—the young man with his wife and child, twins around about twelve years old and the gangly whippersnapper who'd delivered the ticket to the saloon.

Will ripped the painted miniature from his pocket and stared at those bright blue Dennington eyes. That's how the boy had known him—by the miniature propped beside him on the bar. Sean. That was his name. He remembered all their names, and all the stories Kate had told him about their life together.

Had she known all along they were coming? No, no he didn't think so. If she had, she would have told him. He knew from her changed behavior this past week that she'd rather have cut out her own heart than have been a burden to him.

A hundred unanswered questions whirled unchecked in his head.

''If you're sailing you'll have to pay,'' the captain said, shocking him out of his stupor.

''No, no I—'' Pushing past the crewmen and passengers, Will shot to the stern of the ship, but the dinghy had already pushed off. Closing his fist over the painted miniature, he threw a leg over the top rail and jumped.

The autumn sun hissed into the bay, casting a red-gold shimmer across the icy water. Michael haggled with a merchant, while Kate worked alongside Sean and the twins loading provisions onto the riverboat leaving for Sacramento City on the tide. Hetty and the babe were already aboard.

They'd decided to return to the foothills, to make a go of it together as a family. To live out the dream their father had spun, and perhaps spin some dreams of their own.

For the hundredth time that day Kate wondered what Will was doing, if he was happy to be rid of her, to be free—to get on with the life he seemed so determined to live alone.

She wondered, too, if things might have been different between them if she'd been just a wee bit braver. She'd battled a bear in the dark, for God's sake, but hadn't the courage to tell a man in the light of day that she loved him.

Without warning, Sean dropped his end of a fifty-pound grain sack they'd been hauling from the dock to the boat, and Kate stifled a curse. "Why'd you do that?"

Sean grinned, then flashed his eyes mischievously past her toward shore. "No reason, Katie, darlin'. It's just that...well, if I'm not mistaken, I think your husband's comin' to call."

"What?" She dropped her end of the sack and spun in the direction Sean was now pointing. "Jesus, Mary and Joseph!"

"Aye, that's him all right. A wee bit wet around the edges, though, isn't he?"

Kate watched, openmouthed, as a very wet and very determined looking Will stopped every man in his path and thrust something small into their faces. The miniature, she realized with a shock. Lord, he was looking for her!

"But he don't look nearly as wicked pissed as he did in that saloon."

"Saloon?" She flicked Sean a sideways glance. "You didn't tell me you'd found him in a—" The words died on her lips as Will, not thirty feet from her now, grabbed the next man's shoulder and spun him around.

The man just happened to be Michael.

"Oh, no." Kate held her breath, her stomach fluttering wildly, as Will showed the painted miniature to her brother.

Kate knew what was coming a whole second before Michael raised his fist and Will dodged the blow.

"He's fast," Sean said, admiration in his voice. "Even hungover. He'd make a grand boxer, Katie."

Kate shot her brother an icy look. "Go find the twins. Get aboard and wait for me there."

"What, and miss all the fun?"

"You're too big to spank, Sean Dennington, but I'm not above a good thrashing."

"Oh, all right."

Kate watched, transfixed, as Will and Michael got into it. It took two men to hold her brother back, and all of Will's self-control, she imagined, to keep from decking him. She could hear Michael swearing all the way down the dock where she stood riveted in place, unable to move.

Then Will saw her.

And her heart did a flip-flop in her chest.

Ignoring Michael's curses and the amused men cluttering his path, Will moved toward her, his jaw set, the look in his eyes unreadable.

She didn't know whether to launch herself into his arms or to run. If he'd come merely to see she was safe—to complete, in his own mind, the terms of his obligation to her as her husband, she didn't think she could bear it. In truth, she knew she couldn't.

But if he'd come to…

Oh, Lord, the thought of it started her knees to shake under her skirts. She fisted her hands at her sides and focused on her feet planted squarely on the dock to keep herself from fleeing.

He stopped, mercifully, an arm's length away from her, and pulled a sopping steamship ticket from his pocket. Kate recognized it from that very morning when she'd traded hers in to acquire it.

"You did this," he said evenly. "Why?"

Though he betrayed not a hint of emotion in his hardened features, she knew the time for half-truths and holding back—at least on her part—had come to an end. "Because you…wanted it so very much."

"No," he said, shaking his head. "That's not what I wanted at all. I just didn't know it until today."

Her heart beat faster.

"When did you find out?" He nodded over his shoulder toward Michael who, from what Kate could tell, was being told the whole of it by a very animated Sean. "That your brothers were here."

"There was a letter. I discovered it in my father's things the morning we left Tinderbox. I'd forgotten about it, and I couldn't read it anyway. I found it again when I went to board the clipper. I asked the shipping clerk to read it to me."

His eyes warmed then, his face twisting into a painful expression she dared not interpret. "You could have turned your ticket in, kept the money for you and your brothers. Why didn't you, Kate?"

"Because you were so desperate to get away. Not just

from me, but from your father, this place—all of it. You wanted your freedom. It was as simple as that."

"And you were ready to give it to me, no matter the cost to you."

He stood there, dripping all over the dock, his black hair plastered to his head, rivulets of seawater slicing down the grim, chiseled features of his face.

"Ní fuaireamar," he said, stunning her, repeating the words that had slipped from her mouth when he'd made love to her the very first time. "What does it mean, Kate?"

"You're drunk," she said, smelling the whiskey on his breath.

"I was, but I'm not now. Tell me."

She felt her skin grow hot, then icy, all at the same time. Her heart skittered wildly in her chest. "W-why do you want to know?"

"There are things I need to get straight in my own mind."

"Like…what, supposin'?"

"Like maybe I was the biggest kind of fool—and a coward."

"No," she said, shaking her head. "You were nei-ther." She looked into his eyes and in their warm, lucid depths read many things. "You were just hurting."

She held her breath as he stepped closer. He took her hand gently in his and brushed a kiss across her palm. "You're the one who's been hurting, Kate, and I'm the one who hurt you."

Now she was the coward.

For a long moment she didn't move, didn't breathe, didn't utter a sound, only looked at him, really looked at him, trying to fathom his feelings.

"Kate, what does it mean?"

His hands moved to her hips, and hers flew to his chest where she felt the beating of his heart, strong and sure. He drew her close and their gazes locked.

"Ní fuaireamar," she breathed. "I love you."

A tender, dizzying meld of raw emotion shone in his eyes, and at last she knew why he'd come for her.

"Ní fuaireamar," he repeated, butchering the words, though nothing in her life ever sounded so wonderful. "I love you, too."

He kissed her, crushing her to him, and she gave herself up to his warmth and strength, the surety of his embrace, the power of her own feelings for him surging through her, making her giddy and weightless.

"I always have, Kate," he whispered against her lips. "Since the first day."

She pulled away to look at him. He was soaked to the skin, and now she was, too, though she didn't care.

"I was too afraid to let myself feel it, to feel anything for anyone, besides the hate I felt for myself."

"What changed you, Will?"

He smiled at her tenderly and brushed a kiss across her forehead. "You did. Your love did."

"And your…father?" she asked tentatively.

"I saw him. We talked for a long time."

Kate closed her eyes for a moment and exhaled in relief. "So then…?"

"I honestly don't know. He wasn't much of a father when I was growing up, and I wasn't much of a son when I left. All the same, I'd like to give it another shot if he's willing."

"Something tells me he will be."

"You were there."

Kate nodded, and he smiled.

Distracted by Sean and Michael, who eyed them with

respective amounts of amusement and tolerance as they passed, Kate spied the steamship ticket, now reduced to a wet, inky pulp, on the dock where Will had dropped it when he'd taken her into his arms.

"What about Sitka?" she said.

"It'll still be there next year, if we have a hankering for adventure."

"We?" Kate held her breath and waited to hear the words from him.

Will laughed. "We're already married, aren't we? Be a shame to waste it."

"Aye, it would. Though I did the askin' the first time— and what a shameless thing it was, too."

"No. It was a brave thing, Kate. And I'll tell you now that the idea had crossed my mind before you sprang it on me—and not just because of the money."

"I'd hear the words from you, then, Mr. Crockett. All proper."

She gasped as Will lifted her clean off her feet. Never in their month together had she seen a smile from him quite like the one he gave her now.

"Will you marry me, Mrs. Crockett? That is, will you stay married to me, for as long as we both shall live?"

"Aye, Mr. Crockett." She couldn't contain her joy, and kissed him again. "You've got yourself a bargain."

* * * * *

Silhouette Books invites you to cherish
a captivating keepsake collection by

DIANA PALMER

They're rugged and lean…and the best-looking, sweetest-talking men in the Lone Star State! CALHOUN, JUSTIN and TYLER—the three mesmerizing cowboys who started the legend. Now they're back by popular demand in one classic volume—ready to lasso your heart!

You won't want to miss this treasured collection from international bestselling author Diana Palmer!

LONG, TALL Texans

CALHOUN, JUSTIN & TYLER
(On sale March 2002)

Available at your favorite retail outlet.

Silhouette®
Where love comes alive™

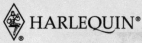

If you enjoyed what you just read,
then we've got an offer you can't resist!

Take 2 bestselling
love stories FREE!
Plus get a FREE surprise gift!

Clip this page and mail it to Harlequin Reader Service®

IN U.S.A.
3010 Walden Ave.
P.O. Box 1867
Buffalo, N.Y. 14240-1867

IN CANADA
P.O. Box 609
Fort Erie, Ontario
L2A 5X3

YES! Please send me 2 free Harlequin Historical® novels and my free surprise gift. After receiving them, if I don't wish to receive anymore, I can return the shipping statement marked cancel. If I don't cancel, I will receive 6 brand-new novels every month, before they're available in stores! In the U.S.A., bill me at the bargain price of $4.05 plus 25¢ shipping and handling per book and applicable sales tax, if any*. In Canada, bill me at the bargain price of $4.46 plus 25¢ shipping and handling per book and applicable taxes**. That's the complete price and a savings of over 10% off the cover prices—what a great deal! I understand that accepting the 2 free books and gift places me under no obligation ever to buy any books. I can always return a shipment and cancel at any time. Even if I never buy another book from Harlequin, the 2 free books and gift are mine to keep forever.

246 HEN DC7M
349 HEN DC7N

Name	(PLEASE PRINT)	
Address	Apt.#	
City	State/Prov.	Zip/Postal Code

* Terms and prices subject to change without notice. Sales tax applicable in N.Y.
** Canadian residents will be charged applicable provincial taxes and GST.
  All orders subject to approval. Offer limited to one per household and not valid to
  current Harlequin Historical® subscribers.
  ® are registered trademarks of Harlequin Enterprises Limited.

HIST01   ©1998 Harlequin Enterprises Limited

When California's most talked about dynasty is
threatened, only family, privilege and the power
of love can protect them!

THE
COLTONS

Coming in January 2002

TAKING ON TWINS

by

Carolyn Zane

With Wyatt Russell's reappearance in Wyoming, Annie
Summers realized the safe life she'd built for herself and
her twins had just been blown apart! She'd loved Wyatt
once before—until he left her to pursue his ambitions.
She couldn't open herself up to that kind of heartbreak
again—could she?

Available at your favorite retail outlet.

Silhouette®
Where love comes alive™